Originally from Essex, Faye ha
London and the Middle East, w
Trained in stage management, sh
theatre and communication, mar
well as training in, performing and directing improv comedy in
both London and Dubai.

In 2015 Faye was awarded an MA in Professional Writing and
set up a copywriting business alongside her own improv theatre
company. In the gaps between client work and performing, she
began penning her first novel, *Tinker, Tailor, Schoolmum, Spy*,
which won the 2020 Comedy Women in Print Prize and secured
her first book deal, with HarperCollins.

Faye lives in London with her husband and teenage son.
When she isn't busy writing, she still treads the boards in
musicals with her local theatre company and is proud to be a
trustee for Home-Start Merton.

Keep in touch with Faye at www.fayebrann.com or by
following her on social media.

instagram.com/writerfaye

facebook.com/fayebrannwriter

KISS, MARRY, MURDER

A JESSICA SINCLAIR MYSTERY

FAYE BRANN

Enjoy! Faye Brann

Published by Bronze Books 2025

Bronze Books
www.bronzebooks.co.uk

E-BOOK ISBN 978-1-0369-1336-6

PAPERBACK ISBN 978-1-0369-1335-9

Book Cover Design by ebooklaunch.com

Enquiries info@bronzebooks.co.uk

For Steve, who I have kissed, married
but not murdered

'Whoever would foster love covers over an offence, but whoever repeats the matter separates close friends.'

Proverbs 17:9

'Most friendship is feigning, most loving is folly.'
As You Like It, William Shakespeare

'JESSICA SINCLAIR MUST DIE'

Jessica Sinclair (average height, cheekbones, fringe) perched on a stool in the tiny studio with its fake brick walls and fancy-looking bank of screens and reluctantly waited for the signal from her director to start the final segment of their weekly live show. The high-top table in front of her held a small tumbler of water and a laptop with a logo reading *I Know Where You Live* bouncing about the screen. The same logo was scrawled in neon lights on the wall behind her. Jessica sighed inwardly. Hosting a mid-morning reality show from a set that looked like a basement comedy club was not where she thought she'd end up.

She'd presented the private investigation show for the past seven years, chasing extra-marital affairs, secret gambling addictions and tax dodgers who didn't want to be found. She'd exposed them on national television, all for the sake of public entertainment. Her audience was a typical mix of retirees, housewives and people in nail salons who couldn't use their phones until the varnish was dry. For most of the time they'd been on air, the show had enjoyed a comfortable level of popularity and a steady stream of people desperate to be on television and get their ultimate revenge on cheating partners. But in the last six months, viewer figures had dropped drastically, and the researchers had been charged with finding increasingly outrageous stories and set-ups to try and tease them back.

A VT played their latest story: a woman who'd been using the back of her electrician husband's van as a kinky sex cave while he was recovering from knee replacement surgery. The segment was titled *'Absorbing the shock'*. Jessica – Jess to her friends – waited for her cue and watched the monitor dispassionately. The capacity for people to be awful to each other had ceased to surprise her a long time ago. She sighed, this time out loud. How many times had she sat here lately, thinking this show might be the last? Jess had been expecting the death rattle to shake for some time now, even if Lucas, her producer, tried to claim otherwise. She wasn't stupid; after seven years, people were fed up with seeing the same old thing, week in, week out. It didn't matter how you dressed it up: cheating is cheating and familiarity breeds contempt. She, of all people, knew that.

'Live in five, four—' the director counted down the remaining seconds and Jess turned to face Camera Two.

The autocue scrolled onwards, and Jess barely noticed the words coming from her mouth. The end of the show was always the same: a witty pun, a serious message and a meaningful goodbye.

'That *electrifying* story brings us to the end of another show,' she said, giving a suggestion of a smirk. Not too much; never too much. She'd learned the hard way it didn't take much for

2

her audience to pen a letter of complaint – and being glib was a sure-fire way to antagonise them.

'Go to Camera One,' came the voice of the director in her ear. She turned on her stool to face her audience head on and continued to read the autocue.

'Before we go, we have a little teaser for you, for a story we plan to bring to you over the coming weeks. We love receiving your emails and messages,' she read, in what she hoped sounded like a vaguely sincere voice.

This wasn't the usual sign off though. She glanced quickly at Lucas (tall, bearded, overconfident) who was standing at the back of the studio. He motioned for her to get on with it and dutifully she turned back to the autocue.

'It's especially heartening to receive thank you letters from those of you who've been inspired by *I Know Where You Live,* to confront the cheaters, liars and fraudsters in your own lives.' The autocue read '[smile]', so she forced one, with one eyebrow raised in what she hoped was a clear communication to Lucas that this was highly irregular. The autocue rolled on, oblivious, and she had no choice but to continue reading.

'But today I received something a little different that I'd like to share with you.'

'Cut to screens,' the director said, and the bank of screens and her laptop buzzed into life, revealing words stamped in ugly, thick black capitals against a glaring white card.

JESSICA SINCLAIR MUST DIE

Jess stared in stunned silence at the laptop in front of her and then at the bank of screens.

Lucas's voice was in her ear. 'Jess. We're still live.'

Was this some kind of sick joke? She looked around the studio, then back at the laptop: the words jumping out at her, menacing and so... so *final*. A cold, clammy feeling crept over her.

'Jessica!'

'Erm... sorry.' Her voice wavered slightly and took her by surprise. She could imagine what she looked like now: a rabbit in the headlights, with a million thoughts racing through her mind... Was it someone on the crew? A fan waiting outside, getting ready to pounce when she left the building? She glanced down to see her hands were shaking; she crossed them together, gripping her own fingers tight to each other to try and control it.

'*Jessica!*'

She forced herself to focus on the autocue and cleared her throat.

'This was delivered to our studio yesterday.'

She imagined her viewers gasping with shock, then leaning into their screens for more; she knew this was the sort of thing that would have them salivating. A fleeting thought crossed her mind, that maybe her killer was too.

'Go to Camera One.'

She stared at the bank of screens again, multiple copies of the note staring back ominously. The thought, that it was meant specifically for her, was sinking in. Someone was out there, watching her with the intent to harm her. Who was it? A disgruntled viewer? Someone who'd been featured on the show? She swallowed, trying to keep the panic at bay.

'Camera One, Jess.' The director sounded annoyed and Jess flicked her head away from the screens and back to her audience, trying to keep her voice steady.

'Now, I know a lot of you will be wondering if I take this sort of thing seriously, and the answer would be yes,' she read from the autocue again, suddenly glad for the security of someone else's words scrolling across a screen. 'In seven years of the show, we've never had anything like this happen,' she continued. 'And so that's why, for the first time on *I Know Where You Live*, I'll... be... I'll be working on a very different kind of case.' The autocue scrolled down and revealed her next line. She stared at it, aghast.

'Mine?' It came out as more of a question than she'd intended. 'I'm sorry, this is all coming as a bit of a shock to me—'

But not to her team, she realised, with a rush of indignation. Lucas had known about this – and, seemingly, so had the rest of them. They all knew that she'd never have agreed to go along with this, unless they gave her no choice.

Another countdown from the director brought her back to the present moment. 'And we're out in ten... nine... eight...'

Eight seconds to stay professional before she ripped Lucas a new one.

'...five... four...'

She smiled, trying and failing not to clench her jaw. 'More next week, but for now, that's all we have time for. Be good, and if you can't be good, be careful. After all, *I know where you live*!'

She smiled again uncomfortably, frozen in place while she waited for the signal from Lucas.

'And we're out,' Lucas said, taking off his cans and running a hand through his poofy blonde hair. 'Nice wor—'

'Was this your idea?' Jess interrupted her producer, stabbing her finger at the screens and tearing off her microphone. She glared up at the galley, watching her director and his editing team disappear quickly out of the back door before she had a chance to yell at them too. She turned back to Lucas. 'Where's the note? I want to see it.'

Lucas crossed to her, waving it as though it were a telegram from the King. 'I know it's not very nice,' he continued, completely unbothered by the anxiety pouring off her, 'but look at it this way: you know you've made it when people threaten to kill you. You should be very proud of this moment. I mean the delivery is a bit 1990...' He frowned, deep in thought. 'We should probably Insta it...'

Jess snatched the note from his hands, stared at it and then at Lucas.

'Did it ever occur to you, Lucas, that the person who wrote it might really intend to kill me?'

'It's why we put it on air,' Lucas replied smoothly. 'Who's going to try and kill you, now they've been on national television? I was only thinking of you, Jess.'

Her eyes narrowed. 'You did it to save the show, not me.'

'Not true, absolutely not true.' He avoided meeting her gaze. 'I mean, sure, it's perfect for the show. Something fresh to capture the audience's imagination. You've spent seven years solving other people's mysteries. Now you can solve your own.' He formed an imaginary banner with his hands. 'Award-winning journalist on the hunt for her own killer. It's t he *ultimate* reality TV. BAFTA nomination stuff. Trust me.'

If his grin got any wider, it could replace the Forth Road Bridge. How could he be so obtuse? Jess eyed her producer suspiciously. It was convenient that the note had arrived just when they were desperate to keep things interesting. Could Lucas be behind it? Was he *actually* capable of stooping so low, simply for the sake of boosted ratings and a PR opportunity?

Lucas read the look on her face and dropped his hands. 'I swear, Jess, it's a genuine threat. Totally bona fide, the real deal.'

Jess growled. 'Somehow that doesn't make me feel any better.'

A squeal came from the corner of the studio. From the second the show finished, the three production assistants (ponytails, crop tops, disarmingly young) had resumed gazing at their surgically attached smartphones and could barely contain their excitement.

'OMG,' said the first assistant, her voice grating in Jess's ears. 'Look at the likes!'

The second scrolled frantically. 'That didn't take long.'

'Lucas, you need to see this,' said the third, shoving her phone in her boss's face. He grabbed the phone and let his eyes dart across the screen in the same maniacal fashion as the rest of them. A smile slowly crept across his face.

'Fantastic.'

'What is so fantastic about any of this?' Jess asked, unsure anyone was listening. 'Hello? Answer me!'

'You're blowing up on the socials,' the first assistant said, in awed tones.

Jess got out her own phone and opened the app. The notifications ran into the hundreds and were still climbing. *No!* Panicked, she slammed her phone on the table. She had to take control of the situation, minimise her exposure. 'Lucas, this is dangerous—'

'Obviously we'll get someone onto managing your accounts,' Lucas said, beckoning over one of the PAs. 'Heather, can you organise that for me?'

Heather sashayed over and took the phone from the table. 'May I? I'll need your logins, then I can manage the accounts remotely for you.'

'It needs to be disabled. I don't want—'

'You can't disable it, Jess! This is PR *gold* for the show,' Lucas said.

Jess looked at them all, incredulous.

'Hashtag *I know where you live* is trending,' reported Heather, breathless with excitement. 'It's really happening!'

'Lucas, I did not ask for this. It's not PR gold, it's a *death threat*.'

'It's both.'

'But you seem to be capable of only taking one of them seriously!' Jess said, exasperated, angry and, she realised now, scared. 'You should never have made me say all that on air.'

'What are you talking about? It's the best thing—'

'Lucas. Someone is out there, getting ready to harm me and probably getting off on all the attention being lavished on them before they visit my house and attack me.'

'Or it could be putting them off doing anything about it,' Lucas countered. 'Contrary to what you might think, most murderers don't want the extra publicity.'

'Oh, so you're an expert on murderers now, are you?'

'All I'm saying is, the chances are that it's a hoax. Almost nothing like this ever ends up in an actual murder.'

Jess unthreaded her lead and removed her mic. She had known, deep down, that all that poking around in people's private lives would come at a cost, but she'd assumed it would be less... violent. Less scary. Less *public*. She thought about the strangers who would stop her on her way home today, to offer their opinion: the people in the supermarket, on the train or in the bar where she sometimes went for a post-show glass of wine, who'd tell her in gruff tones she'd been asking for it, that they were sorry, or that they had a theory and would she like to hear it? And each time they stopped her, she'd be wondering if it was the person who wrote the note, who'd threatened her life... and whether they were planning to stick a knife in her right there and then, or wait until she was tucked up in bed that night.

Jess's heart was pounding. Did they know where she lived as well as where she worked? She shook her head, trying to rid herself of the idea. Even if they did, they clearly wanted to make a statement, they wanted her to take notice. God knows how many of her followers had jumped on the bandwagon, sharing the story. And where they were, more crazies would follow, who would plague her on social media and turn the whole thing on its head, so the witch hunt was about her, not the bastard who'd penned the note. It was always the same on the socials – they'd dig up some footage, say she'd been asking for it and she'd end up public enemy number one.

She was sick and tired of it all: of the situation she'd got herself into, of everyone knowing her face, the fans who wanted selfies and the people stopping her in the street, in the shops, trying to have a quiet bite, in a *pub toilet*, for god's sake. It wasn't what she wanted from her life, not even close, and there wasn't enough money in the world, she suddenly realised, to keep her from walking.

She unclipped her mic pack and tossed it on the high-top. 'I'm out.' she said.

The coven of assistants gasped and Lucas huffed out a short laugh. 'What?'

'You heard me. I quit.'

'You can't leave. You made a promise to the viewers, to solve your own case!'

'No. *You* did.' She picked up the note from the table. 'I know we're losing viewers but the cases we've been filming, they're mean and sordid, even by reality TV standards. It's sensationalism, not journalism, and it's no wonder someone's got upset enough to do this. And I'm not willing to risk my life for it.' She tucked the note in her pocket along with her phone. 'I'm deleting my social media accounts and taking that note to the police. It should be looked into by people who know what they're doing, people who can find out who sent it and protect me if they have to.'

'The police won't be interested. People get these all the time. Richard and Judy have received at least a hundred and seventy-three separate death threats since 1991. I'm sure it's nothing, Jess.'

'If it's nothing, why are you putting it out on the show? And worse, without talking to me about it first.' Furious now, she jabbed a finger at Lucas. 'You put my life in danger for ratings! I hope it was worth it, Lucas, but you can get some other mug to do your sodding show and get murdered in the process.' She grabbed her bag from the table and headed for the door, shaking with fury.

'You'll be in breach of contract if you go.'

'So, sue me!' she said, exploding with rage.

'IF NATALIE FLANNIGAN CAN DO IT, YOU CAN TOO'

Some months on, Jess wished she hadn't been quite so hasty. Lucas had been right: walking off set had been a massive breach of contract and the production company were only too happy to take her to court for it. She'd ended up broke, with no real job prospects open to her: she couldn't go back to television – it was a small world, and no production company would touch her with a bargepole once word got out. Plus, she felt increasingly vulnerable and paranoid: if the death threat had been real, maybe she *should* have stuck it out and investigated it more thoroughly with the resource of a TV show behind her. God knows the police wouldn't.

To fix the more imminent issue of money, she'd decided to go back to her roots, to journalism – but trying to make enough as a freelance print hack was a joke. Just when she was seriously considering giving up altogether and getting a job as a receptionist at the local dentist, her agent Damon (bullish, annoying, bleached hair) called her, sounding excited.

'I've had an idea,' he began. 'But you need to hear me out before you say no.'

'Can't wait.'

He ignored her lack of enthusiasm. 'I was thinking... why not start your own private investigation agency? Do what you did on the show, without the show.'

'I'm not trained, Damon,' she'd said, cross with him for momentarily getting her hopes up. 'God, I thought you'd actually had a proper idea. I can't call myself a private investigator just because I read stuff off an autocue once a week.'

'Of course you can,' Damon said. 'How hard can it be? Anyway, you're uniquely qualified. You're a journalist; you're used to digging out a story and you must have learned something from all those years on the show. Plus, you're still famous enough for it to matter. People will be queuing round the block to hire you.'

'That would make a nice change.' In the past few months, she'd interviewed for a couple of staff reporter positions, where the money was steady at least. But no one wanted to hire her: she was too well-known and too overqualified for local news and, although they didn't say it, not the right demographic for the hip online organisations who depended on social media for their audiences.

'My point exactly,' Damon said. 'It's time to try a different approach.'

Jess closed her eyes in defeat. It was true she needed something to change. Her savings had dwindled quickly and in a desperate bid to avoid media attention and stay out of debt, she'd traded in her Mini Cooper and moved from her smart north London home to a scrappy two bed on the outer edges of Tooting in the south. It wasn't long before she'd have to consider leaving London altogether – and that would mean fewer job opportunities, full stop.

Damon gasped, suddenly, making her jump. 'You could write a book about the whole experience,' he said slowly, as though the thought had *just* occurred to him. 'Write a kiss-and-tell about turning into a real-life investigator.'

'Absolutely not.'

'I already spoke to a publisher,' he confessed, launching into the hard sell. 'They're interested. Of course, they want to see a few sample chapters first, but they're very keen to sign you.'

'I said *no*, Damon.'

'Jess, you've been unemployed for months. You've got bills to pay, and I can't keep on trying to find you work if you're not going to be a little flexible.'

'I didn't ask you to find me work.'

'Oh, I'm sorry,' Damon said, snarkily. 'Did you receive your inheritance from the King, then?'

'Ha ha.'

'I don't understand. I've come up with a viable idea to make you money, and you throw it in my face. I'm your friend. I'm only trying to help.'

Jess rolled her eyes and then softened a little. Maybe there was some merit to what he was suggesting. 'I'm not sure I can write a whole book,' she admitted, ignoring the comment about being friends.

'You're a journalist.'

'*Was* a journalist. Anyway, I never wrote anything longer than two thousand words at a time. A whole book... I don't even know what that looks like.'

'If Natalie Flannigan can do it, you can too.'

'Natalie Flannigan?'

'Does the weather for Channel Four. Wrote *Sevenoaks* – a love story between two emergency service workers from Kent, set against the backdrop of the storm of eighty-seven.'

'Sounds awful.'

'It is. But yours won't be. A celebrity autobiography about your midlife career change, filled with intrigue and lies and naughty sex. A reality show in a book. I'm telling you, people will love it.'

'Why can't I write the book without starting the agency?'

Damon sighed. 'You need to be credible, or no one will buy it. The show gave you notoriety, an audience, a platform. But starting an agency would give you gravitas, as an expert in the field. Combine the two, write this book and you're set for life. You could even branch out into fiction afterwards, write a few murder mysteries. It's not just the royalties; we're talking about the big festivals, TV appearances, interviews... the offers will pour in, I promise.'

'I have to write the book first.'

'Which is why you run the agency, for a stable income in the meantime.'

Jess paused. She knew Damon wasn't doing this out of the goodness of his heart. He was doing it for his cut. But he obviously thought he'd make enough from it for it to be worthwhile pursuing. Which meant she'd make money from it too.

'What if I didn't want to do this for the rest of my life?' she persisted. 'I've had it with the celebrity thing, Damon. In case you didn't notice, it didn't work out too well for me.'

'I know that death threat shook you up; but it's been months, Jess. You're still here. And you still have to make a living while you are.' His voice had a steely edge to it. 'Do you realise how lucky you are, to be in this position? The opportunity won't come around again. Ever. In another year, everyone will have forgotten who you are, the publisher will walk away with their advance and you'll be back to pounding the streets trying to make it as a fifty-two-year-old local news ha ck.'

'Fifty-one,' she corrected, irritated.

Damon paused. 'Give it a go. I'll help you get the agency set up, get a website sorted. You'll get plenty of material to use for the book and get paid at the same time, which will mean you can stop worrying about money and focus on putting pen to paper. The sooner we can send the publisher something, the sooner we'll get paid for it.'

A silence yawned between them as Damon waited for her answer and Jess quickly thought through the legitimacy of his plan. She wasn't in a position to say no, and he knew it.

'I'll give it a go, Damon. But this won't end well, believe me.'

Sinclair: *So, Peter, I understand from your email that you suspect your wife of having an affair. Can you tell me a bit more about what's led you to this conclusion? When did you first suspect there might be something wrong?*

PC: *Is this being recorded? You're not putting this on the internet, are you? I've seen clips of your show, and this isn't that sort of thing at all—*

Sinclair: *Peter, I can assure you this recording is merely for my purposes. Everything is completely confidential.*

PC: *If only!*

Sinclair: *Any future reference to you or your case will be anonymous. The confidentiality agreement we signed guarantees my discretion—*

PC: *In that case it's a shame I didn't ask my neighbour to sign one.*

Sinclair: *Your neighbour knows about the affair?*

PC: *Edith MacDonnell is a busybody and a pain in the arse.*

Sinclair: *Can you elaborate?*

PC: *She stopped me in the street last week. I thought it would be a broken streetlamp, or the dog shit outside her house, or maybe the party at number 29 that went on into the small hours of last Sunday. She's always stopping me about something, usually when I'm coming home from work and dinner's waiting on the table. After a busy day at the office, I don't want to be dealing with* domestic matters. Even Susannah – that's my wife – knows better than to try to talk to me when I get home about things that don't concern me.

Sinclair: But Edith didn't want to talk to you about any of that?

PC: No. Instead, she comes straight up to me and tells me I need to keep an eye on my wife. The audacity! As though my wife would ever... we have a perfectly adequate marriage. Happily married for years. I don't remember how many... Twenty-two? But – I'm almost embarrassed to say it out loud – Edith says my wife has been having a regular gentleman caller while I'm at work.

Sinclair: Do you believe her?

PC: I dismissed it as rubbish, told her she was mistaken and should mind her own bloody business. But then it began playing on my mind, that there might be some truth to it. My wife has rather lost interest in me of late, you see.

Sinclair: You mean, sexually?

PC: Well, not that we... I mean, we've been married over twenty years, we don't... I'm sorry, I'm not very comfortable talking about this with a stranger.

Sinclair: So, you'd like me to have a bit of a dig, and see what I can find? Please be prepared, Peter. The truth might not be easy to accept—

PC: I saw an article about you not too long ago, in the supplements. I read you do this sort of thing and... this is ridiculous... so unnecessary... but if you did see anything, I want photos. I want proof. And the name and address of the bastard who's sleeping with my wife.

'SHE'S THAT WOMAN OFF THE TELLY, INNIT?'

Jess sat in a banged-up, silver Ford Focus on a mansion-lined street in Chelsea, reflecting on her words to Damon all those months ago and pondering how much longer it would be before one of them admitted the whole thing had been an utter disaster. Shuffling in her seat, she flexed her buttocks in alternate bursts to try and relieve the numbness. She'd been there for over an hour, and not for the first time, wondered if she'd end up dying of deep vein thrombosis before dinner. As if in response, her stomach gave an angry growl, and she contemplated nipping to the corner shop for a KitKat. She resisted the temptation. On the wrong side of fifty, she couldn't afford the extra calories. And by the looks of her recent bank statement, she couldn't afford the KitKat.

She glanced at her notes. The street had been relatively quiet since she'd arrived. At eleven-thirty, a cleaning lady had stood on the step of number 45, taking the last drags of a cigarette, and there had been an argument at number 30 that she could hear from the car, about Margaret spending money they didn't have *again*. Apart from that, there'd been very little sign of life, with a few delivery vans stopping to deposit dry cleaning and flowers, but not much else.

It was nearing midday when Jess thought she detected movement from inside number 41; a small flick of the curtain upstairs alerted her to the fact that something might be about to happen, finally. She picked up the camera from the passenger seat and focused in on the front door, ready to take the shot.

A couple (him: five foot eleven, mottled skin, cocksure gait; her: five foot five and half, greasy bleached hair, skinny size ten, both in their mid-thirties, both scruffy) turned into the road, walking their dog, a scrappy thing that stopped to pee on every surface it could find. Jess watched as they approached her car. They didn't belong on this street, and they certainly didn't live here, amongst the gracious, candy-coloured Georgian town houses, that crowded on both sides with Range Rovers lined up along the street like maids-in-waiting.

The couple paused for a few seconds each time the dog did its business, slowly making their way along the road towards her.

'For god's sake, not *now.*' Jess put her camera down on the passenger seat and pretended to intensively search for something in her rucksack, willing herself not to catch their eye. She hoped that the combination of unwashed hair, no makeup and the shitty car would mean they wouldn't give her a second glance, but as they neared the car and the dog inevitably stopped to urinate on it, she could feel the man taking a good look at her. Did the man – or the dog for that matter – have no shame? She was right there... maybe he was the sort of person who sought forgiveness rather than permission. Sure enough, before moving on, he knocked on the window and with great reluctance, Jess opened it.

'Sorry, I didn't see you there. I wouldn't have let the dog take a piss if I'd known you was in the car.'

Jess smiled tightly at the lie. 'That's okay. It's what dogs do, isn't it? No harm done.' She began doing the window back up, but the man put his hand in to stop her.

'Do I know you?'

'No,' Jess replied, in a firm voice that she hoped would put an end to the conversation.

'What school did you go to? I'm Phil, Phil Edwards. I was in Mrs. Parker's class in the fifth year? Nah, that's not it, you're too old.' He peered closer. 'Are *you* Mrs. Parker?'

Jess pulled her chin up sharply and let out an indignant puff of air. 'We've never met. I don't know you; you don't know me. Now, if you'll excuse me—'

Phil leaned in and stabbed his finger in her face. 'You look familiar though. Debs!' He turned to the woman who was scrolling on her phone. 'You know who this is?'

The woman cast a brief eye over Jess. 'She's that woman off the telly, innit?'

'Davina McCall?' He scrutinised her. 'Nah, Davina's way more fit.'

'That other one from *Strictly* then. Claudia Whatsherface.'

'Driving about in this piece of shit?'

'Could you please move your hand?' Jess gave a nervous glance towards number 41. Any minute now, she'd see what she'd been waiting for, and two hours of sitting in a stuffy, uncomfortable car would all be worthwhile. But she had to get rid of this man; he was drawing way too much attention to her.

'Alright, love, don't get yer knickers in a twist.' Phil frowned and his voice took an aggressive tone. He didn't move his hand. Irritated, Jess pushed the button to close the window and he ripped his hand away at the last minute to avoid getting his fingers stuck.

'Bitch, what did you do that for?' He yelled through the glass. 'Who the fuck do you think you—' He looked across at the passenger seat where her long lens camera sat, and the penny dropped. He thumped on her window. 'I know who you are! You're the one off that detective programme. The one who catches people shagging.'

She opened the window a crack again. She'd dealt with people like Phil too many times before and knew that ignoring him would lead to the worst possible outcome. 'Look, Phil,' she said, conspiratorially. 'You seem like a nice man, but I'm sort of in the middle of something here.'

From the corner of her eye she saw the door of number 41 begin to open and a man (six foot three, expensive suit, grey hair) appeared on the steps of the baby pink house. Exactly on schedule. Jess looked on helplessly as Susannah Crawford (redhead, alabaster skin, erect nipples) came to the door in a silk dressing gown. Her window of opportunity was closing fast.

'Jessica, that's your name!' Phil folded his arms, looking pleased with himself. 'You filming a new series then? Where's the cameras? Whose house you watching? Bet there's loads of posh twats boning their secretaries round here.' He laughed. 'Fuck me, Debs. We're on the telly.'

Debs lit a cigarette and absent-mindedly picked at a fingernail.

Jess grabbed her camera and waved it. 'I am on a job, as it happens. In fact, Phil, I could do with your help. If you could stand there and pretend like you're talking to me...' She lifted the camera to take a few photos.

Phil looked in the direction of her shot and clocked the couple stood at number 41. 'I can do better than that. That him you're after? Oi, mate, GOTCHA!' He began marching down the road towards them.

What the fu—

Jess frantically got out of the car, tripping slightly as she ran towards Phil, her camera bouncing heavily off her chest. 'No, wait! *Wait!*' she half called out, half stage whispered. 'What the hell are you doing?'

The grey-haired man glanced down the street at the thug barrelling towards them and then at Jess scuttling after him. His face screwed up in a combination of fear and confusion. Susannah Crawford wrapped her dressing gown tighter. 'David, I think you'd better come back inside—'

'She's got you, good and proper,' Phil yelled at the man called David. 'That's Jessica Sinclair off the telly back there – the one that catches all them people having extra-marital affairs and whatnot. You're nicked, mate.'

'Excuse me?'

'I'm not a police officer. I don't arrest people—' Jess caught up with Phil and grabbed at his arm. He shrugged her off, catching the side of her face with his elbow. Balance lost, she fell heavily onto the pavement, the camera making a dull, expensive thud as it hit the tarmac.

The grey-haired man strode towards them both. 'Who did you say you are?'

'No one.' Jess clambered to her feet. It was time to get out of here. She backed up and in desperation, took a couple of photos, hoping her camera was still working.

David's face contorted into anger. 'What the hell are you doing?'

'David, she's obviously spying on us. Get her camera!' Susannah was pointing at Jess, a desperate look on her face.

'You want that camera you'll have to get through me first, you posh twat,' said Phil, who wasn't letting things go without a fight, despite having nothing to do with anything. 'Don't worry, Jessica. I've got this.'

'I don't *need* you to 'got this', Phil—' Jess hissed.

'David! The camera!'

David turned to Susannah Crawford at the sound of her shrill instruction. 'Alright, Susannah, I'm dealing with it!'

He turned back as Phil threw the first punch. It would have been a good one if it had landed but unfortunately for

Phil, it seemed like David really did want Jess's camera and was somewhat more athletic than his solid middle-aged figure would imply. Dodging Phil's fist and shoving him into a hedge with the kind of expertise years of public-school rugby will give you, he broke into a run, heading straight for Jess. She turned and bolted.

'I don't know who you are, or who you work for, but you need to give me that camera!' he yelled. He was gaining on her quickly and Jess accelerated, panicking. She sprinted back towards the car and dived through the open driver door, but David was too quick for her. Grabbing at the camera strap around her neck, he pulled it sharply upwards, yanking at her hair in the process.

'Get the hell off me!' Jess shrieked and shoved him, hard. As he staggered backwards, she slammed the door and quickly locked herself in, leaving David holding her camera aloft like a trophy. Heart pounding, she put the keys in the ignition, but the seemingly mild-mannered David was like a man possessed. As Jess put the car into gear, he pitched the camera heavily onto the roof.

'How dare you!' He yelled. 'How – dare – you – invade – my – privacy – like – that!'

Wincing at the rhythmic thwack of metal on metal, she didn't waver for long before she decided it was best to make a sharp exit. She put her foot down and accelerated off, leaving David, Susannah Crawford, Phil, Debs, the dog, and a fair few curious neighbours all choking on the fumes of a very old, very desperate Ford Focus.

'DEATH THREATS TEND TO PUT A DAMPENER ON THINGS'

Three or four streets between her and the mess she'd left behind, Jess stopped and parked to assess the situation. Her head hurt where the hairs had been ripped out, she had a huge dent in the roof of the car and she'd lost her good camera, which was going to cost her a fortune to replace. Never mind that without it, she didn't have a lot to offer her client, Peter Crawford, who'd insisted on cold, hard proof of his wife's affair, complete with photographs and identification of the man concerned. After that fiasco, all she had was the name 'David' and a description of a posh middle-aged rugby player with anger issues. It wasn't enough.

Jess struggled to steady her nerves before she restarted her journey home. This wasn't the first time she'd been interrupted on a stake out; each time, it had been because someone had recognised her. The situation was getting desperate; how had it come to this? She used to be a professional journalist, for god's sake. Now she was being chased down the street for the sake of a few hundred quid to pay the gas bill. The hours were long, the work was boring and operating by herself all the time was desperately isolating. Sometimes, when she got to sit in a swanky bar or hotel lobby and pretend to read a book, the buzz of people made her feel less alone, but she always ran the risk of a fan coming over to 'chat'. As a result, most of the time she kept her own company, sorting through dirty sheets on unkempt beds or photographing couples in compromising positions in piss-filled alleyways. A lot of writers claimed to do their best work in coffee shops; she was writing *I Know Where You Live: Becoming a Private Investigator* in her car, fifty words at a time, while she waited for various people to do various terrible things so she could take photos of them to scrape a living.

She pulled up at the garages round the corner from her house and parked the car inside the third one from the end. It had come with her rental, and she'd kept the car out of sight and locked up here since she'd moved in. It wasn't so far to walk when she needed it; plus, she worried less about it getting nicked. These were the things she had to think about these days. She shut the garage door and locked it, tucking the key away in her handbag before walking slowly back to the house. Her hips hurt from the fall earlier, and she was angry that it had been such a waste of time. Where on earth was she going to get money to pay for a new camera now? She also had the unpleasant task of calling Peter Crawford to tell him he needed to find another P.I.; that was, if she hadn't scared David off altogether. Jess sighed. She'd assured Peter she was reliable, and he'd believed her when she said she was the best person for the job. Sinclair Investigations was worth nothing if she couldn't investigate without *I Know Where You Live* fans chasing her down the road for autographs. She would never have thought they would still have been so die hard, now that the show had ended. It was all so difficult; she wondered if she should walk away and admit defeat, finally. And yet... on top of the obvious flattering of her ego, there was something about the excitement and the danger of it all which sparked a little joy in Jess, reminding her of the adrenaline she used to feel as a young reporter getting her first lead. To Jess's surprise (and though *loathe* to tell Damon he was right) she had found that she didn't want to give any of this up. If only she could figure out a way to make it work.

She let herself into the house. Technically a maisonette, it was part of a larger, much grander Victorian terraced building, with a flat below her in the basement, and another one above her in what would have been the attic. A small set of steps led up to her own front door and opened into a hallway, her favourite part of the house. Original tiles covered the floor and an ornate banister wrapped around the base of a staircase that led to the bedrooms upstairs. To the right was a living room that doubled as an office. When she wasn't meeting clients, she worked at a battered, old desk with the morning light streaming through the window; when she was, they sat in the two armchairs by the fire. It wasn't ideal to meet clients here – she'd been nervous about letting strangers into her home after the death threat – but had little choice in the matter if she wanted the business. People didn't want to air their dirty laundry in the public spaces of a local Starbucks.

Straight ahead was a small, barely used kitchen with access to a rather tatty patio garden that enjoyed the afternoon sun in the summer months. Jess dumped her bag down in the hallway and went inside to put the kettle on, desperate for a cuppa and something to eat after a disastrous day. Opening the fridge, she swore, remembering too late that she should have stopped at the supermarket on the way home. Pasta and some grated cheese would have to do.

Irritatingly, the phone rang halfway through her dinner. Out of habit, Jess kept it in the hallway to try and avoid spending her evenings scrolling other people's endless social media postings, but sometimes it was a pain in the arse that she didn't strap it to her like everyone else seemed to.

She walked into the hallway, checked the display and picked up. 'Hi, Damon.'

'You could try to sound pleased to hear from me.'

Jess liked Damon; as much as you can like someone whose primary function is to sell your soul if it means they get a ten per cent cut of it. But after the day she'd had, she wasn't in the mood for the 'chat' she knew was coming.

'Look, Damon, enough is enough. You've been calling me non-stop to find out how the book is going, how the agency is going, how I'm going... you're driving me crazy.'

'How *is* the book going?'

'It isn't,' Jess said, hoping being blunt would make him drop it. But he was either completely oblivious to her spiky tone, or steadfastly ignoring the fact he'd caught her at the wrong time.

'You've got to finish that manuscript, Jess,' he persisted. 'You know you won't see any more money from the publisher until you've turned in the book. I've done what I can to keep your profile up, but I can't do much more in terms of PR until you have a tangible product to sell.'

'Maybe that's a good thing.' She sighed. 'Damon, I know you mean well, but I keep getting recognised and hounded for autographs during stake outs, and it's killing me. It's not like on the show where we had a film unit blocking the end of the street and security on hand. I know you think being a celebrity will help sell the book, but it's not helping to write it. I need to close cases.'

'It's a shame you felt you couldn't carry on with the show, and then we wouldn't be in this predicament.'

'I'm sorry to be such an *inconvenience* to your bottom line, but death threats tend to put a dampener on things,' Jess snapped. She heard Damon's sharp intake of breath and considered apologising but stopped short. Why should she? No one seemed to quite understand what it meant or felt like to have your life threatened. The dull echo of fear still rang deep in her chest and she wasn't sure it would ever truly go away.

Damon's voice was clipped. 'If you're still worried, you should go to the police.'

'They weren't interested beyond making sure they were seen to investigate while I was still making headlines. It's too late now to go back and ask them to do more.'

'But if it's stopping you from—'

Jess cut him off before he could go at her again. 'The letter isn't the problem, Damon. I know how much I need to work. I'm running out of savings, I only had peanuts left from the divorce settlement and what I made from the show, and there's not much left of either after legal fees and nearly a year of unemployment. I've gambled everything on this idea and if it doesn't pick up soon, I'm toast.'

Damon was quiet for a moment.

'Have you thought about hiring someone else to help you?'

She gave a half laugh. 'I can barely pay myself.'

'Yes; but with someone else on board, you would have more time to get the book written.'

'No one in their right mind would want to do this job.' Jess sat heavily on the stairs.

'You do it.'

'It has its moments, I'll admit. But poking into other people's lives, taking a wrecking ball to them; it's not a nice thing to do.'

'You're a journalist, Jess. You've literally trained your whole life for this.'

Jess smarted at the remark. 'Maybe I'm starting to think that people's private lives should stay private.'

'We're not in that sort of business, my dear.' Damon paused. 'I think you should take my advice. If someone else was doing the legwork, and I carried on working the PR angles for you to get the clients in, it'd be a win-win situation.'

Jess breathed out, resigned. 'Maybe.'

'Give it a go. Put out a job ad on the socials or something, see who applies.'

'You do remember what happened last time I was on there, right?'

'There has to be some way to find someone to help. Christ, put something on the notice board at Tesco. Or ask around your friends, they might know of someone who's interested.'

'I don't really have any friends.'

'Oh, for god's sake, Jess, snap out of it.' Damon sounded decidedly testy now, and she recognised the warning signs that her agent was losing patience with her. 'It's been months since you left the show. You have to get on with life and stop wishing you were still the queen of daytime television.'

'I'm not wishing anything of the sort,' Jess persisted, but could hear the distinct whine in her voice. There was more than a grain of truth to what Damon was saying.

'Get someone part time, so you don't commit to a big salary,' he said, in a practical voice. 'Call it a trainee position, or even an internship, if you're really that strapped. I do that all the time and they're queuing around the block to make my tea. Imagine what they will do for you – Jessica Sinclair, TV star.'

Jess rolled her eyes.

'Jess?'

She sighed again, smaller this time so as not to antagonise him. 'I suppose getting someone in could work. And it would shut you up at the same time,' she said, only half meaning it as banter.

'Atta girl,' Damon said. He paused before he spoke again, his voice switching to the tone Jess knew he reserved especially for tiptoeing through emotional landmines. 'And perhaps put a call in to that ex of yours. He's still a copper, right? Could be a useful source to have in your back pocket.'

'I think we both know I'm not going to call Ben,' Jess replied. She didn't want to fall out with her agent, but Damon had suggested the one thing they both knew was not up for discussion.

'I'm just saying, having someone with access—'

'I said, it's not an option.' She looked at her watch. 'It's late, Damon. I need to go.'

'Call him, send an email maybe—'

'Speak soon, Damon.'

She put the phone back down on the hall table and stomped back to the kitchen, Damon's words festering like little poison darts in her mind. She stabbed at the remains of her cold pasta and sunk a large glass of white wine before she finally felt calm again. What was Damon thinking, opening old wounds like that? She had half a mind to tell him she couldn't do it after all, drop the whole idea and take the freelance journo job for the local rag. But she had so little money left in the bank. She was a single – okay, divorced – fifty-one-year-old woman with no steady income and no children. No one to look after her in her old age... no one to look after her now. Freelance work paid a pittance; she certainly couldn't afford to retire, and, thanks to the insane London rental market, was virtually broke. She gave a heavy sigh. Unless she wanted to end up homeless, maybe Damon was right about getting someone in. But she didn't want a total stranger coming on board – and there was no need to go public with a request quite yet. She had a huge set of contacts at her disposal from years of journalism and TV work and even if they weren't interested in what she was offering, they might know someone who was.

She opened her phone and coasted through her online address book, the entries reading like an alphabetical shopping list of ghosts from her past. She pursed her lips, thinking of all the history in those names – all the people she'd loved and some who she'd lost... and one who she missed most of all. She stopped at the familiar name, her heart quickening and hesitated a moment before opening her email and starting to type. She wasn't sure if she would ever get an answer from Marianne Hughes, but it was worth a shot.

'IT'S EASIER WHEN YOU CARRY A GUN'

They'd first met over thirty years ago. Jess was a grunge-loving media studies student, while Marianne (blonde, five foot eight, prominent beauty spot on her left clavicle) was studying law and looked like she belonged on a series of Ally McBeal, not sitting in the library of Leeds University. Gorgeous and gregarious, she lit up the room when she was in it, and while she would have made a brilliant and intimidating litigator, Marianne had her heart set on one thing: becoming an undercover cop. When they graduated, Marianne and Jess moved down to London together as flatmates; despite Jess being a journalist, which in the average copper's eyes only put her a notch above career criminal, she and Marianne remained inseparable. While Jess worked a series of crappy local reporter jobs, Marianne went straight into the Met. Quickly promoted, she moved into CID, and with the determination and tenacity only a trained lawyer could possess, she achieved her ambition aged twenty-eight and began life as an undercover officer.

As a female UCO, and an attractive one at that, Marianne was always in demand. Jess was jealous; not of her friend's looks – she wasn't exactly bad-looking herself, but being the brunette girl-next-door type meant she drew *a lot* less attention, especially (and thankfully) from the pervs and crazies of the world. The ease with which Marianne seemed to achieve success niggled at Jess though. She was finding it a little harder in the world of journalism, where it seemed that as a woman, good-looking or not, you could only ever be at a disadvantage.

'How am I supposed to get respect from anyone who takes any sign of a challenge to their way of doing things, as either I'm playing at politics or about to get my period?' she moaned one night over a bottle of wine with her friend.

Marianne grinned. 'I'm not gonna lie, it's easier when you carry a gun. But it's the way it is. You'll get there eventually. You've got to believe in yourself, Jess. No one else will.'

'Don't you believe in me?'

'Of course I do. I'll always believe in you. But I might not always be around.' Marianne said.

'Where will you be?'

Marianne shrugged. 'Who knows. You can never one hundred per cent depend on another person though, can you?'

Marianne had been right about that, Jess thought bitterly. After two days of impatiently waiting for a message to arrive in her inbox, she finally conceded that it was going to take more than a casual email to fix their relationship after all these years. Although given the circumstances, she could hardly be blamed for taking her time to reach out.

Not that it had been one casual email, she chided herself. Never patient, in the forty-eight hours since she'd first made contact, Jess had sent Marianne a text and three WhatsApp messages, each one more urgent in tone than the one before. They'd been picked up and read; she wondered if Marianne was thinking about how to answer or was simply ignoring her. It was impossible to know, after all this time. By Thursday evening she couldn't bear it any longer. She checked the address was still current and decided to pay her a visit in person.

She crept along the riverside in her car and signalled left into the warren of streets that made up the impossibly pretty enclave of Barnes in southwest London. It was only thirty minutes' drive, but it had been a long time since Jess had been there; and the last time, under admittedly harrowing circumstances. The one-sided street outside Marianne's house was narrow, squeezed in as it was by the allotments that backed onto the train line opposite. Bollards were placed politely at either end; there was no room for cars on Penny Hill Lane, not even for residents to park. Annoyed, Jess had to drive two streets away to find a space. She walked back towards the house, passing a row of identical worker cottages painted in complementary pastels, slowly being neutralised by the oncoming dusk. Chatter and laughter bubbled up and over the rows of houses from back garden barbecues, and the clatter of daily life could be heard through the open windows of each home that she passed. Entering Penny Hill Lane, she saw Marianne's house was exactly as she remembered it: a tiny, terraced two-up two-down brick cottage with a low white fence hemming the path to the front door. It had been such a surprise when Marianne announced she was moving in here. Jess had always assumed she'd go for something modern, a flat on the river that was easy to maintain and where it was easy to stay anonymous. But Marianne hadn't wanted that: the opposite, in fact.

'I want to be part of a community,' she said, 'where people can get to know the real me, not the person I have to be the rest of the time.'

Marianne had got a bargain, buying up an old railway-side cottage near the allotments. The cottage gave off a definite Miss Marple vibe, only slightly spoiled by the sound of trains rushing past. Still, it was a peaceful and rather sweet place to be – the closest you could get to being in the countryside with a southwest London postcode.

There were no lights on at the cottage – but it was June, and only just getting dark, even though it was late. It was still warm, and

Marianne was probably sitting out in the back garden having a ciggie, assuming she hadn't given up.

A plane sailed over her head, well into its descent to Heathrow. The noise was deafening. Jess had never understood why the residents of Barnes were willing to part with as much money as they did to live right under the busy flightpath. Between this and the trains, she wasn't sure how anyone ever slept, or watched TV. Maybe that's why Marianne's windows were firmly closed.

She waited until the plane had passed and then knocked on the door with a short, sharp rap. No answer. She peered through the letterbox to try and make out any signs of life, and then knocked again. Still nothing. Jess shivered; the night was closing in a bit now and had taken a turn as a cool, slight breeze blew along the street, giving her arms goose pimples. She moved across to the living room window and stood on tiptoe to see over the top of the half-height shutters. Jess wasn't a giraffe by any means, but she was tall enough to be able to catch a glimpse of the interior. In the half-light, she saw a shape on the sofa.

'Marianne!' she rapped on the window to get her attention, but the shape on the sofa didn't move. 'I can see you, you know.'

She peered at the lumpy outline of her former friend.

'Maz, come on, let me in. I want to talk.' She waited for the other woman to get off the sofa and invite her in, but still Marianne didn't move. Jess went back to the letterbox and stared through the flap. 'Maz?'

Something wasn't right. She put her fist to the door again. 'Are you okay? Marianne!'

'She's not home,' came a voice from the cottage next door. 'Hasn't been for a couple of days now.'

'Oh, hi... sorry for disturbing you.'

A woman in her late sixties (tiny, sturdy, glinting eyes) stood on her doorstep. 'She's always coming and going. Not seen her since Monday though.'

Jess didn't want to alarm the older lady, but she was pretty sure Marianne was sat on the sofa. But if she hadn't been seen in three days... Jess felt bile rise in her throat.

'I don't suppose you have a key, do you?'

'And why would I be letting a stranger into her house at this time on a Thursday evening?' The woman stared at her. 'Do I know you from somewhere?'

Jess thought back to the last time she'd been here, standing in this very spot screaming obscenities at the top of her lungs. Had this woman been one of the curtain-twitchers that night? She wouldn't remember her from all that time ago, surely?

'You probably know me from the television. I had my own reality show...'

The woman narrowed her eyes and folded her arms.

'I'm—' Jess cast her eyes back to Marianne's window. 'I'm an old friend.'

The older lady's eyes narrowed even further, and she looked Jess up and down. 'What's your name?'

'Jessica Sinclair.' Jess held out her hand – it wasn't taken. She tried a different approach. 'Look, I just need to make sure everything's okay. Do you have a key, or not?'

The woman shrugged and shuffled back inside her house, appearing again a few minutes later. 'Here you go. Mind you give it back.' Out of nowhere, she produced a smart phone and... *click*.

'*That's* so I've got a photo of you, in case you aren't who you say you are.'

Jess didn't have the patience for this. She turned back to Marianne's door and let herself in, calling as she did. 'Maz? It's Jess. Are you there?'

The back door was open and knocked against the frame. She was tempted to go and close it, but she had other priorities. Her heart beat a little faster and she tightened her grip on the key, placing it between her first and second fingers as a glorified knuckle duster. With an impending sense of doom, she gently pushed at the living room door and swung it open.

'Maz?'

She could tell by the stillness. She'd never actually been in the presence of a dead person, but there was a sort of unnatural quietness to the house, and a faint sweet metallic smell, like meat on the turn... Jess found the light switch and turned the dimmer. The brightening bulbs confirmed her worst fears. There, her former friend sat, eyes closed, head slightly up and to the left, cushions placed either side of her to keep her upright. There was no knife to be seen, but several blade-shaped cuts had been made to her clothes and the blood from the wounds had flowed downwards to form a sticky pool on the carpet. Jess staggered back in shock, her hand over her mouth and her eyes filling. There was no getting away from it: Marianne Hughes was dead.

'THAT'S A LOT OF VODKA, MAZ'

'Did you find her?'

It was the woman from next door. Jess quickly turned the lights off and exited the living room, trying to mask the shock in her voice.

'You need to leave, Mrs...'

'It's Rosie. The back door's open. Did you check upstairs?' She put her hand out to the banister to begin climbing but Jess stopped her.

'I don't think you should be in here—' Jess grabbed at the older lady's arm but before Rosie withdrew it, she cocked her head.

'What's that smell? Did she leave the fridge open too?' The woman reversed and bustled by her towards the kitchen. 'Someone should shut that door—'

'DON'T TOUCH ANYTHING!' Jess yelled.

'Excuse me?' Rosie stopped in her tracks, shocked.

'I'm sorry. Sorry.' Jess's mind whirred now, as the reality of the situation began to sink in. 'Rosie, something terrible has happened, I need to call the police. It would be better if you waited at home.'

'Did she die? Is that what the smell is? Was it drugs? Drink? She liked a drink—' The woman stopped, registering Jess's distress for the first time, her expression changing to one of concern. 'Are you alright? You should sit down, have a cup of tea. A cup of tea fixes everything.'

'I'm okay.' Jess's voice wobbled. She didn't feel okay at all but she had to keep it together. 'A bit shaken. When I've called the police, I'll come and wait at yours, if that's alright? Have that cuppa with you.'

Rosie nodded. 'I'll go and put the kettle on.' She left, shaking her head. 'What a waste of a life. Silly girl.'

Rosie safely dispatched, Jess dialled 999 and reported an incident at 31, Penny Hill Lane.

'Are you sure the person is deceased?' The call centre operator sounded doubtful. 'Can you check for a pulse?'

'I – I'm pretty sure.' Jess took a deep breath and went back into the living room, switching the lights back on and taking another look at Marianne. 'She – I think she's been stabbed. There's a lot of blood.'

The operator's voice became more urgent. 'Are you in any immediate danger? Is there any sign of an intruder?'

Jess's heart stopped for a beat. 'I don't think so. I mean, I think it happened a while ag—'

'The police are on their way. Do you have somewhere safe you can wait, away from the victim?'

'I'll wait outside.'

'They won't be long, love. Get yourself away from the immediate area and we'll be there soon.'

Jess ended the call with shaking hands and listened intently for any noise in the house that might indicate an intruder. She quickly determined she wasn't in any immediate danger: she didn't know much about dead bodies, but it seemed as though Marianne had been like this for a while and the killer was likely long gone. It occurred to her, that regardless of what the operator had said, she should record the scene. She was the first person here: she knew the house, she knew Marianne and she might see things a stranger wouldn't notice, that could be important evidence. *'Besides,'* a little voice in her head, that sounded a lot like Damon, whispered, *'It might be an amazing scoop for your book.'* Ashamed, she quickly batted this voice away.

Standing at the door so as not to contaminate the crime scene, Jess hit record. She made a slow sweep of the room, before switching to camera mode and taking a series of photographs of Marianne. She was thankful, as she zoomed in, that her friend's face didn't seem contorted, and that her eyes were mercifully closed. She hoped she hadn't been in too much pain, although the multiple stab wounds suggested it couldn't have been peaceful.

Feeling more than a little sick, Jess backed out of the living room. She remembered she had a pair of latex gloves in her bag from her last P.I. job and put them on, before heading upstairs. Old feelings rose inside as the memories came flooding back. Visions of her ex-husband coming down the stairs wrapped in a bath towel, of the moment when her whole life was turned upside down... The recollection threatened to overwhelm her and, like the bloody images of the scene downstairs, she pushed them away, focusing on what was in front of her. It didn't look like much had changed; there was new wallpaper in the bedroom, but the bathroom was still the same brown suite as it had been sixteen years ago when Marianne moved in. Jess checked the bathroom cabinet. HRT patches, paracetamol and a bottle of diazepam. She took a picture, closed the cabinet and went back into the master bedroom.

The double bed was neatly made, the left side pillow slightly indented and the duvet cover folded open in an inviting sort of way, like they do in adverts. She didn't have her UV light with her, but it didn't look like there'd been much action beyond sleeping. She checked out the bedside table: the left contained a few books, some earplugs, a glass and a lavender pillow spray. The right was completely bare.

She came back into the hallway and was about to check the spare room when she heard a noise downstairs. She froze. Had the 999 operator been right – was there an intruder still in the house? She looked around for a suitable weapon, but could only find Marianne's glass. Panicked, she grabbed it and held it out in front of her as she crept down the stairs.

There weren't many places to hide in this house: working quickly now, Jess checked the small downstairs toilet by nudging the door with her foot and afterwards, peered carefully into the kitchen. Once she was sure no one was there, she moved quickly through the kitchen and outside into the small back garden. Backed by a high brick wall, Jess could see the ridged roof beyond, of what she knew was a scout hut in the neighbouring street. Only a single, high window faced Marianne's cottage, not likely to be useful when it came to witnesses. Next door, on the other side to Rosie, the garden was a ramshackle mess of overgrown plants and weeds that gave an impression of neglect. If the neighbours on the other side were even home, they were unlikely to have sat in their garden to see anything.

She turned her attention back to Marianne's garden. The whole area appeared to be undisturbed, no sign of forced entry or anything to indicate a struggle. If an intruder had been there, he was gone now.

A full ashtray sat by the back door next to a mug of cold, insipid tea abandoned next to it, bits of tree floating in the top. She made sure her flash was on and took another photo. Back in the house, she set the glass down and did a final sweep of the kitchen, finding a few bottles of spirits and a cheap bottle of Chardonnay in the cabinets and very little else. It had been a long time but she knew Marianne well enough to know that the good stuff would be in the freezer. She opened the door and found a full bottle of vodka stacked next to a near-empty one. A quick look revealed another was in the recycling.

'That's a lot of vodka, Maz.'

She picked the glass up, intending to take it back upstairs, but the bang of the back door as the wind took it made her jump. Jess gasped in surprise and the glass slipped from her hand, bouncing onto the ground with a thud and a shatter that seemed to reverberate around the house with horrific intensity.

'*Shit!*' The last thing she'd intended to do was tamper with the crime scene. She was supposed to be helping the police, not finding reasons for them to arrest her. Panicked, she looked around for a dustpan and brush and found one underneath the sink. She quickly swept up the shards and put them in a bin by the sink. Forensics would find the glass, no doubt, but hopefully they'd assume Marianne was the one who'd broken it. Jess hoped she hadn't destroyed a key piece of evidence – although how an empty water glass could factor in Marianne's murder was impossible to say.

She heard a siren. Quickly shoving the dustpan and brush away, she slipped off her gloves and tucked them and her phone into her back pocket, noticing a small cut on her index finger.

'*Shit!*' She sucked on the blood. She must have cut herself on one of the glass shards, which meant her DNA could be lurking somewhere in the bin. There was nothing she could do about it now. She exited the cottage and sat on the step, as though she had been waiting for the police to find the right house since she'd called 999.

A squad car arrived, lights flashing, and parked at the end of the street furthest from the level crossing, where they had easier access to Penny Hill Lane. Two uniformed police got out and as Jess watched, a second car stopped behind the squad car – not uniform – and a shiver ran through her. It hadn't occurred to her before now that her ex-husband would have heard the call on the radio to go to Marianne's house. But of course, he would come. Jess stood and swallowed in anticipation. The car door opened, and Detective Chief Inspector Benjamin Morgan (handsome, still handsome, so stupidly handsome) stepped out to greet her.

'THINK OF THE OVERTIME, MATE'

Marianne had been the one to introduce them. Not long after she started working as a UCO, she came back from a job, breezing into the pub down the road from their flat with a grin on her face like she'd won the lottery.

'I've found you a man,' she said.

'I wasn't looking for one,' Jess replied.

'I know. But I found you one anyway. His name is Ben and he's my fake husband.'

'Are you joking?'

Marianne shook her head. 'Nope. He's a bit cocky. Needs taking down a peg or two. I feel like you're the woman to do it.'

'What about you? You're the one who's fake married to him.'

She gave a big belly laugh. 'No way. I'd be kicked out of Serious Crime before the bed was cold. Seriously, when we're done with this job I'll set you up. You'll like him, I promise.'

Marianne was right: Jess and Ben hit it off instantly. She made him laugh, kept him grounded; he made her feel like she was the only one in the room. They fell in love within a matter of weeks and moved in together soon after. When he was home, they spent days in bed, making love and talking, laughing, sharing their hopes and dreams. When he was gone, she simply waited, putting her life on pause until the moment he would knock on her door. Jess quickly got used to sharing Ben with his job – and with Marianne. Some weeks he spent more time with her than with Jess, and when they were home, the three of them would often still hang out together, enjoying warm summer nights at pub picnic tables until closing, or dancing the night away in the nearby clubs. But he would always find the time just for the two of them, cooking up extravagant three-course meals to gorge on, and barely ever making it as far as dessert.

That was then.

Now, Ben strode towards the cottage, his face contorted with anger and Jess shrank back, her eyes filling up at the sight of her ex-husband. Why, after all this time, did he still have such an effect on her?

'What the hell are you doing here?' He stood over her, furious, his left index finger pointed directly in her face, his right fist clenched at his side.

'I could say the same thing,' she retorted, and instantly regretted it. She knew why he was here. A tear slipped down her cheek and she rose from the step. 'Ben, I'm so sorry. I—'

He barged past her. 'Where is she?'

'You shouldn't go in there. Let someone else—' She followed him as far as the living room door and was horrified to see him standing over Marianne's body, his fingers desperately checking for a pulse. 'Ben, stop! It's a crime scene.' She swallowed guiltily, thinking of the broken glass in the kitchen bin. 'There's nothing you can do.'

'Don't you think I know that?' he said, gruffly, but he stepped away, his hands falling limp by his sides as he stared at the body in front of them.

'We should go outside.'

Ben shifted his attention to her, his eyes growing small and dark.

'Why are you here? Did you have something to do with this?'

'How could you—' Jess shook her head furiously at the accusation. 'I came to see her, to say I was sorry. I wanted to make amends—'

'Convenient timing.'

'I don't believe you'd actually think—'

'I wouldn't put it past you.' Pushing past Jess, Ben strode back out of the house. She followed him, not knowing what to say. Her eyes were welling up again, and she was shaking uncontrollably.

'I'm so sorry, Ben.'

'Are you?'

'Of course I am.'

Ben and Jess stared at each other in the doorway. It was dark now – she guessed past eleven – and the spectacle of flashing lights and police presence had begun to draw attention from passers-by. A couple more neighbours had come out to see what was going on, though none as intrusive as Rosie. One of the uniforms (pockmarked, skinny, boundary issues) cleared his throat and ambled over.

'Sir?'

Ben broke his gaze away from Jess and turned to the uniform. 'The deceased's name is Marianne Hughes,' he said, his voice hoarse. 'She's – was – one of us. Ex-UCO. Cause of death looks like repeated stab wounds to the chest. And if you don't get that torch out of my face, you'll be next.'

The uniform lowered the torch quickly. At the end of the street, an ambulance pulled up behind the squad car, the lights rolling across the walls of the houses. A paramedic got out.

'Won't be needing you, mate,' called the other uniform (chubby, young, terrible beard) from outside Marianne's cottage. 'Wasted trip.'

'Watch your fucking mouth and call it in,' Ben barked at the pair. 'You'll need a Senior Investigating Officer, murder team and forensics.' He glared in Jess's direction. 'And get the witness's details.'

'Yes, sir.'

'Ben—'

Ben ignored her and strode towards the ambulance. Uniform One pressed the button on his call radio to relay his instructions and Uniform Two looked over to where Jess stood in the tiny front yard.

'What's your name, love?'

'It's Jessica. Jessica Sinclair.'

Uniform Two looked up sharply. 'And what were you doing at the scene, Jessica?'

'I'm a private investigator.' She realised this didn't explain why she was at Marianne's house at all and tried again. 'I'm Ben's – DI Morgan's wife.'

'You don't look—'

Jess interrupted, embarrassed that she hadn't been clearer. 'Sorry. Ex-wife. Marianne Hughes was a colleague of DI Morgan's.'

'Never heard of her,' said Uniform Two.

'It was a long time ago,' Jess said, her voice shaky.

'So, an ex-colleague of your ex-husband,' he said, raising an eyebrow.

She defended herself, feeling cross. 'She was also a friend of mine. From university.'

'Can I take your address and phone number?' He scribbled the information down while Uniform One ambled back over, looking unhappy.

'Forensics are on their way. Looks like we're pulling an all-nighter.'

'Think of the overtime, mate.'

'Should we start knocking on doors, see if anyone saw anything? Sooner we do that, sooner we can go home.'

'Probably should sit tight until the SIO turns up.'

Uniform One shrugged. 'Fair enough.'

'What about me?' Jess was irritated by their lack of sensitivity. Whether or not Marianne was an old friend, surely they could see she was shaken.

They looked at Jess.

'You should probably wait too,' Uniform Two said. 'Just until the boss turns up.'

Rosie's door opened, and she poked her head out. Jess smiled gratefully. At least the old lady could vouch for her.

'Cup of tea, officers?'

'Love one, thanks. Mrs...'

'Rosie.' Rosie looked at Jess, less friendly than she'd been with the uniforms. 'You want one too? You haven't given me back my key.'

'It's part of a crime scene now, Rosie. I can't give it back.'

'Are you part of this crime scene too, then? You did practically break in.'

'I did NOT break in. You gave me a key!'

Uniforms One and Two smelled trouble and turned to face her.

'So, Mrs Sinclair—'

'Miss.'

'Hold on a moment,' Uniform One's eyes widened with realisation, as though seeing her for the first time. 'Jessica Sinclair? Aren't you that investigator off the telly?'

Jess suddenly felt weighed down by the shock of her situation. Finding Marianne, seeing Ben again... it was surreal, like it wasn't really happening to her at all. All she had wanted was to find a business partner and to potentially renew a very complicated friendship. But now, she was going to be faced with endless questioning in the absence of any other witnesses. She knew the police wouldn't let her off the hook completely, but it wouldn't hurt to try.

'Actually, I'd really like to go home if that's okay? I can come to the station in the morning to make a statement, though, if you need me to.'

Uniform One consulted his notepad again. 'Can you tell us what you were doing visiting the deceased, ma'am?'

Jess sighed; it would come out soon enough. 'There was bad blood between us. Marianne and me. From a long time ago. I'd come here to apologise—'

Uniform One gave the side-eye to his partner and then turned his attention back to Jess. 'When was the last time, before today, that you'd seen the victim?'

Jess swallowed, remembering standing at the same front door feeling her life shattering into a million pieces. 'Ten years ago.'

In the flashing of the blues and twos she could see Ben was at the end of the lane, talking to someone in jerky, urgent tones. They clapped each other on the back, and she saw Ben walk away towards the end of Penny Hill Lane. The urge to call out, or follow him, overwhelmed her. She needed to talk to him, to explain—

'You need to wait here, ma'am,' said Uniform One, touching her arm with a gentle pull. She resisted a little, and he firmed his grip slightly in response, making it clear he meant it. Ben disappeared out of sight and the second man walked towards her. It was the cocky stride of someone who knew he'd won before he even opened his mouth; as he got closer, she could see the smirk on his face, the familiar lines etched around his eyes and all hope of going home faded. Detective Chief Inspector Graham Dickson (dick by name, dick by nature) stopped in front of her.

'Well, well, well. Jessica Sinclair, as I live and breathe. DI Morgan was right, this is a *very* interesting turn of events. So, tell me, little Miss Agatha Christie... what the hell are you doing at my crime scene?'

25 March
TO: BenM0568@mail.com
FROM: JessicaS@reallifenews.co.uk
SUBJECT: Leave me alone

Ben,

STOP contacting me.

I know you want to explain things, make amends, or whatever, but I'm not interested in hearing your petty excuses and it doesn't matter how many times you say you're sorry, I will never get over what you and Marianne did.

I wish I'd never gone over to her house that night. I wish that she hadn't answered the door in your T-shirt. I wish that her guilty 'I-just-had-sex-with-your-husband' face hadn't matched yours when you appeared at the top of the stairs wrapped in nothing but a towel. I wish a lot of things, but I can't change what happened, and neither can you.

You had the affair, Ben. You slept with my best friend. YOU broke our marriage, and that's something you're going to have to live with.

You should know I've called your boss to tell him about your sordid little affair. If you can ruin my life, I can ruin yours – and hers, too. Maybe you'll have a drink later and talk about how much of a bitch I am. Maybe you won't; I don't give a shit. I hope you both rot in hell, although, frankly, even that's more than either of you deserve.

If you need to contact me again you can do so via my lawyer. I'll be filing for a divorce in the morning.

Jess

'YOU DIDN'T ACTUALLY KILL HER, DID YOU?'

Jess knew as soon as she laid eyes on Graham Dickson that he would leave no stone unturned to find out exactly what she was doing at Marianne Hughes' home. One of the 'old guard' still around from her days as an up-and-coming reporter, he'd always disliked that she was so intertwined with two of his officers and particularly pissed off when she'd married one of them – although nowhere near as angry as when she divorced him and filmed a kiss-and-tell piece for national television. It was then, as though all of his Christmases had arrived at once, to find her right there at the murder scene.

She hadn't been arrested on suspicion of anything, or even cautioned; in fact, much to Graham Dickson's annoyance, she'd *volunteered* to go to the station to make a statement before he had time to insist. But he wasn't going to let it go that easily. He made her sit in the back of the squad car for the best part of an hour while everyone had a cup of tea with Rosie and waited for forensics to arrive. Once he'd cordoned off the street and got the forensics team to work, Graham Dickson finally gave the green light for Uniforms One and Two to take her back to the station. By then the press had got wind of something serious going on and were camped out, cameras at the ready, by the police tape cordoning off both ends of the street. As Jess was driven away in the squad car, flashes of light went off in every direction. She put her hands up to her face, doing her best to shield herself from the unwanted attention, but feared the damage had been done. Not much got past this lot – it was only a matter of time before someone recognised the woman in the back seat of the squad car and she knew it.

Following their boss's lead, Uniform One and Two had changed tack, now treating her more like a suspect than a witness. She was left in an interview room and offered nothing in the way of tea or coffee for the two hours it took for some junior grunt to come and take her statement. Shift change was blamed but Jess knew it had been Graham Dickson's doing.

Still, she hadn't banked on being held all night. Jess let herself into the house and went straight upstairs, the muted colours of the dawn light leaching through the windows. She wanted a shower, and some sleep; she felt dirt and death all over her body and the image of the stab wounds to Marianne's heart seared into her brain like she'd stared at the sun too long.

She stepped into the shower and closed her eyes, letting the hot water flow over her face. They'd found glass in her hair, seen the cut on her finger. She'd been giving her statement and leaned back in her chair, sweeping and scraping her hair taut through her fingers in a bid to keep herself awake. The shard had bounced onto the table, catching the light and the attention of the officers, and her cut finger had left a smear of blood on the paperwork; they took a DNA swab, bagged the glass and just like that, she went from witness to person of interest.

What the hell was she thinking, picking up the tumbler? And then lying to the police about it? She'd said it was on the draining board in the kitchen, that she'd felt faint and had gone to get a glass of water – she didn't dare tell them she'd been poking about upstairs in Marianne's bedroom. Thinking over her reasoning now, she felt embarrassed. If she'd left well enough alone, reported the body and waited with Rosie, it would have been ridiculous for anyone to consider she killed Marianne; but now, with evidence she was involved in the crime scene and no alibi, she was the first and only lead they had.

She rinsed the soap from her body and turned off the tap. Stepping out of the shower, she heard her phone ringing. She decided to let it go to the answering service, but a few seconds later, the ringing started up again. Whoever it was, they were insistent. Jess threw on tracksuit bottoms and a sweatshirt, without bothering with pants or a bra, and hurried downstairs. The phone stopped again and Jess cursed, rubbing at her eyes; they were still sore with tiredness and grief, and she suspected she had a migraine coming. Every little sound seemed exaggerated; and there seemed to be an awful lot of it coming from outside.

Realising the noise level wasn't normal, she opened the door. It took a few seconds before she registered the gaggle of reporters standing at the edge of her property.

'Jessica! Jessica! Over here!'

'You got yourself in a bit of bother again, Jessica?'

'Any statement for the press, Jessica?'

'No walking away from this one, love!' The pack squawked like a flock of gulls, their cameras clicking away, documenting her pantless, braless state to publish god knows where. Jess stared at them, frozen and speechless.

'Did you know the victim, Jessica?' a reporter shouted out. It was then she came to.

'No comment,' she squeezed out, before slamming the door shut and putting on the safety latch, heart pounding. Her phone rang again, making her jump.

'Hello?' she said, her distress evident.

'Thank god, you've picked up.' Damon sounded genuinely relieved. 'Are you okay?'

'Not really.' Jess went through to the sitting room and pulled the curtains across the windows, blocking out the light and any photo opportunities.

'You're all over the news,' Damon said, trying but failing to keep the glee out of his voice.

'There's a bunch of press outside baying for blood.'

His concern hadn't lasted long, clearly. She knew this whole nightmare was the stuff of her agent's dreams, but he didn't need to sound so happy about it.

'They'll leave you alone soon enough. We just need to—'

'Damon, whatever PR you think you're going to weasel out of this situation, I don't want it.'

'I'm calling to see if I can help, Jess, not get you a spot on *This Morning*. They're trying to make you look guilty. They've got photos of you in the back of a squad car for heaven's sake—'

'I wasn't arrested. That was voluntary. They don't have enough evidence to pin anything on me.'

'What do you mean *enough*?' Trust Damon to have picked up on that. 'Who was she, anyway?'

'It's complicated.'

'Complicated enough to be accused of murder?'

Jess rubbed her temples. 'Probably. She was my best friend. She slept with Ben. It's why we got divorced.'

Damon was silent for a moment, clearly taken aback, but quickly recovered.

'You should make a statement. Or get the police to make one.'

Jess shook her head into the phone. 'Damon, I haven't slept. I'm still in shock. I need to process everything before I can start mounting a campaign against the press.' Her voice cracked, and she tried to clear her throat of the sadness. 'Whatever happened between us, she was still my friend. It was terrible, finding her like that.'

'I know. I am sorry for your loss, Jess, but you need to nip this in the bud—'

'She looked awful, Damon. And not just the being dead part,' Jess blurted. She sat down on the bottom stair, thinking about Marianne's cottage, for the first time trying to process what she'd seen. 'It was obvious she hadn't been taking care of herself. I think she had a drink problem. And she seemed so... unkempt. Her shoes were filthy, and her hair was all over the place, like she'd come in from a jog. But I can't imagine she ran very much.'

'I go running and you've seen the state of me. It doesn't turn everyone into a Marvel superhero.'

'Yeah, I know. But – and this is going to sound stupid – the state of her...it didn't match with the house. *She* was a mess; the house was immaculate. No sign of mud anywhere, everything so clean and tidy.' She replayed dropping the glass and swallowed guiltily. 'Even the bed was made.'

'Maybe she likes a tidy house.'

'That was never the case when we lived together.'

'People change. Did you mention it to the police?'

'I didn't think about it until now.' She paused. 'I could tell Ben,' she said. 'Not that he'll be on the investigating team, but—'

'Ben?'

'I saw him at Marianne's. He got there just after me. It didn't go very well.'

'I imagine it didn't, under the circumstances.' There was a small silence before Damon spoke again. 'You don't have to tell him.'

'I'd rather tell him than go back to the station.' She pursed her lips. If Graham Dickson found out about the videos she'd taken, how she'd snooped around the house, her next visit might end in a bail hearing. 'He could pass it onto the right people—'

'Or...'

'Or what?'

'You could use it for your own investigation,' Damon said, delicately.

'Absolutely not. My life is not entertainment fodder,' Jess snapped, thinking guiltily about the video footage on her phone. She'd convinced herself she'd taken it to help the police with their investigations, but deep down she knew she'd thought about doing the very same thing she was chastising her agent for.

'Jess, think about it. This is way bigger than anything else you've ever done. A murder case. Where *you* are the suspect. Think of the story you can make out of this. Forget death threats—'

She shook her head. She wouldn't stoop to his level. 'No.'

'But this is so much bigger than anything else you've got—'

'Damon, I investigate extra-marital affairs and tax dodgers. This is a murder case, way beyond my pay grade, and we both know it. I need to see Ben, tell him about what I saw, apologise—'

'Apologise? What for? You didn't actually kill her, did you?'

'No!' Jess closed her eyes. 'But he's the one person that might listen to me.' And exonerate her, she thought, even with the evidence piling up against her.

'It's up to you,' Damon said. 'But you've got an opportunity here, Jess. If I were you, I'd take it. The last time you walked away and blew up your career. Don't make the same mistake twice.'

Jess gaped open-mouthed at the phone. 'My life was threatened, on live TV. And now you're telling me to cash in on the murder of my best friend? What kind of animal are you?'

She jabbed at the phone and cut off the call, before turning her phone off altogether and flinging it back on the hallway table. She didn't want to hear from Damon again today, or anyone else, for that matter.

Later that night, after hours of staring at the television screen, Jess went upstairs to try and get some sleep. Unable to shake the image of Marianne from her mind, she had yet another fitful night. In the early hours of the morning, she woke in a sweat, the bed a boiling pit of tangled sheets that she'd started to become familiar with lately, as her body bent and bowed to mid-life. Realising she'd drained the last of her water hours earlier, she made her way to the bathroom to refill her glass. Pausing to look down the stairs, she realised that, in her catatonic state earlier, she'd left all the lights on. Not wanting to make her electricity bill any more painful than it already was, she went to turn everything off.

She was halfway down when she saw it. A small, white piece of card poked through the slit of the letter box, held in place by the brushes that lined the hole. Maybe that's what had disturbed her. Shaking off the last vestiges of sleep, she stepped gingerly up to the front door, yanking the card out and turning it over in her hand. Her stomach flipped as she saw the familiar script: it was another note, the same as the one she'd got all those months before at the studio. Only this time, she didn't have any doubts about it being genuine.

HELLO, JESSICA.
NOW I KNOW WHERE YOU LIVE

Her blood ran cold; she gagged and dropped the note before running to the downstairs cloakroom to be sick. Flushing the toilet after a few minutes, she gulped a mouthful of water from the sink and sank down on the floor, shaking. As the months had gone by, she'd desperately hoped her producer had been right, that that first note had been nothing but a silly hoax. But now, with the arrival of this second note – *to her home* – there could be no doubt. Someone had found her. Deliberately come to her home, broken through her bubble, *hand* delivered a virtual bomb and shattered the thin veil of lies she'd been telling herself.

Jess was suddenly aware that if the note had just been delivered, the person who delivered it could still be within striking distance. Without stopping to think, she ran to the front door and flung it open. The press pack was long gone; the trees swished lightly in the late-night breeze and even the usual humming, beeping and wailing of high street traffic was muted. She froze, realising how vulnerable she was standing at her front door, alone, with no one to protect her. The quietness felt heavy and menacing, and she stared out into the dark, not daring to go any further.

Footsteps approached and Jess shrank back, suddenly fearful that she'd recalled her assailant. The footsteps got louder and a young couple (her: long black hair, black jacket, black leggings; her: long black hair, black jeans, black boots) staggered past, holding hands. They looked at her and then smirked at each other.

'Did you see them? Did you see someone come to my door?' Her voice was shrill and panicked.

One of the girls sniggered, the other shrugged. Jess looked down at her less than form-fitting vest top, no bra, damp pyjama bottoms and wild, rangy hair. She gave the girls a lunatic glare and slammed the door shut, leaning heavily against it for a moment. Then, spying the note on the floor, she picked it up and took it through to the kitchen, slumping into a chair at the table.

It really was time to call the police. And yet, the thought of Graham Dickson questioning her, twisting her words, and somehow piling the blame onto her... It – no, *he* – made her shudder.

She poured herself some more water and gulped it down, hands still shaking and her ears and body still sensitive to every alien sound. She really, really wanted to speak to Ben. He'd been angry with her, at Marianne's house, but part of that was shock, she knew. She couldn't get Marianne out of her mind; couldn't reconcile with the idea that she'd been so close to seeing her again, to rekindling a lost friendship that meant so much. Whether Marianne thought the same or not, Jess would never know, but Ben might – and if he didn't, at least he could help her make sense of the loss.

Damon had wanted her to speak to Ben... but then again, her agent also thought she should use her life as a human-interest story. But if she couldn't make it up with Marianne, then maybe she could with her ex-husband. He was the only one who would understand how she felt, and perhaps, if she could persuade him of her innocence, he could then help her with the threatening letters too.

Jess placed the note on the table, the ugly, bold font staring back at her and wondered if her appearance as a person of interest had been what prompted the second letter. She shook her head free of the idea, refusing to let it fester for a moment longer. Because if publicity was what this person craved the most, it was only a matter of time before she'd go from a person of interest to something else altogether.

'I WASN'T ABOUT TO STICK A KNIFE IN HER'

The flat was nicer than she remembered it being. The architecture of the block was glass and grey-brown brick with little adornment and still looked modern, even though it had been built in the nineties. It had been kept well too. Trees that were pathetic-looking saplings when Jess and Ben first moved there sixteen years before, cast their mature shade over the grassy gardens at the front, while the paintwork looked fresh and clean, and balconies overflowed with wicker chairs and fairy lights. Her marriage might have disintegrated, but clearly (and rather annoyingly), the flat had not followed suit. Hardly Architecture Digest-level house porn, but it was a little more idyllic than the strings of laundry, abandoned buggies and dead plants she remembered. She looked up at what had once been their balcony and was surprised to see several pots of herbs and flowers sitting in the morning sunshine beside a little wooden table and two chairs. That was not the Ben that she'd known – he had never been one for plants, or relaxing outside on a balcony.

She checked around her to make sure no one was paying her undue attention. The press had left her alone this morning, having got plenty of footage and photos of her the previous day. Until the forensic report came back from the crime scene there wouldn't be much in the way of further speculation. Thank god. Privacy meant a great deal to Ben, the last thing she would want was to antagonise him any more than she already had, by bringing him to the attention of a bunch of journos.

The foyer door of the block had been propped open with a brick; a resident coming through every once in a while, to load a box into their car outside. Jess waited for them to disappear before letting herself in and making her way upstairs. The front door was a freshly painted green, the gold number eight standing out against it. A jaunty coir doormat welcomed her as she pushed her finger against the buzzer and a sing-song chime rang out from inside. Suddenly she felt her heart pounding. She shouldn't have come; it was too soon after Maz, it was—

'Hello?' A woman (young, pretty, pregnant) opened the door. Her dark, poker straight hair was in disarray, and she gave a little yawn, her perfect mouth stretched into an 'o' that revealed a set of white, even teeth. 'If you're selling something I'm afraid I'm not interested. Unless it's stretch mark cream.' She itched her swollen belly with long, manicured nails, painted a pale blue at the tips.

Jess looked past her and into the flat. A pair of trainers were lying in the middle of the hallway along with a few items of stray clothing. The whole place looked a bit of a mess.

'Sorry – I think I might have the wrong flat.'

The woman looked cross, her face puckering. 'Surely you saw the number on the door?'

'I did... it's just... I think someone I knew used to live here. They must have moved. I'm sorry to have disturbed you.'

'Who *are* you?' The woman looked at Jess and the green and white bouquet she held in her hand. Jess hadn't been sure if it was the done thing to buy men flowers, and she'd certainly never bothered to buy Ben any in the time they'd been together. But then she'd thought, why not? Men could surely appreciate flowers as much as a woman, in the right circumstances. She'd made sure they were *masculine* flowers: blooms that were the botanic equivalent of a pint of lager, if there was such a thing.

Embarrassed, Jess turned to leave. 'It doesn't matter.'

'Did you come to see Ben?'

Jess stopped and turned back around, staring at the woman. 'Oh, you know him! Yes. I came to give him these.' She held up the bouquet, but the woman stared blankly at the proffered blooms. 'I'm Jess. His wife. Ex-wife—' she laughed nervously. 'If I was still married to him, I probably wouldn't be turning up at his old address looking for him.' She swallowed, wondering why she was making such an idiot of herself with this woman. 'I don't suppose you have his new address, do you?'

The young woman folded her arms and narrowed her eyes. 'You're Jessica?'

'Jess. If you could point me in the right direction—'

'He lives *here.*' The woman stroked her bump again, protectively. 'But he's not home.'

Jess saw the diamond ring on her hand and lowered the bouquet. 'Oh. Oh, okay.' She felt a bit sick. This woman – this *girl* – was Ben's fiancée?

'Bye, then.' The woman took a step back into the flat and went to close the door.

'Wait! Sorry. I mean—' Jess put out her hand to stop her. 'Will he be home tonight? I wanted to talk to him about Maz. Marianne Hughes. She was a – a – friend of ours—'

'I know who Marianne Hughes is.' She tried again to close the door.

'Look, I know I'm not his favourite person – the feeling's mutual – but could you maybe ask him to give me a call?'

The woman looked behind her. Jess followed her gaze down the hallway, past the two bedrooms and the bathroom, and straight through to the living room and tiny kitchen at the end. Was he home and avoiding her? She raised her voice a little in case he could hear her.

'I know he's probably busy, but there's something... it could be important... if I could leave a message, you could tell him I called by when he comes home—'

The woman pursued her lips and shifted the weight on her feet. 'You should go,' she said.

She shut the door. Jess stood facing it, not sure her feet were going to move when she instructed them too. Her eyes started to fill with tears and she blinked them away. She wouldn't cry. Not over him. Not again. And who the hell did that child think she was, telling her to go? Determined and now angry, Jess knocked on the door again, less patiently than before.

The door swung open so suddenly that Jess nearly fell right on top of the pregnant woman. 'Jesus. Take the hint, will you?' she spat.

Jess pushed the bouquet into the woman's chest and dodged past her heading towards the living room. 'Ben?'

'What the hell are you doing?'

Jess went over to the curtains, pulling them wide open to check the balcony. She turned to the woman. 'What's your name?'

'What?'

'Your name. You didn't say it before.'

'Naomi. Not that it's any of your business,' she said. 'You can't just barge in here like this. Like you own the place.'

'I did own it.'

'It was Ben's flat,' Naomi corrected. 'Never yours.'

'Is that what he told you?' Jess said imperiously. She could see Naomi bristle with animosity.

She continued to look around the room, taking in her surroundings properly. It was filled with neutral-looking throws and vanilla scented candles, and a myriad of IKEA photo frames and predictable prints arranged in a montage pattern copied off the internet. All very *nice* with no actual character. It was also messy as hell. Magazines were strewn all over the floor, and there were piles of clothes and glasses and plates everywhere. Jess homed in on the coffee table – she knew she probably looked deranged right now but was way beyond caring. There were two cups of tea, and she felt the sides of both. The cups were still warm, which meant that someone else had been in the flat very recently. A teabag sat on the coffee table next to the mugs. There was something about the careless way it had been thrown on the wood, inviting it to stain, that infuriated Jess even more.

'Take a good look around, why don't you?' Naomi snapped.

'Whose tea is that?'

Naomi followed Jess's gaze and brazenly folded her arms over her belly, refusing to take the bait. 'Mine.'

'There are two cups.'

'One for baby, one for me,' she said, facetiously.

Jess looked closer at the mugs of tea. One – with a faint stain of lip gloss on the rim – was down to the dregs, but the other was only half drunk, the insipid, grey liquid looking more reminiscent of dishwater than anything that had seen a teabag. It reminded her of the cup that had been sat in Marianne's back garden.

'I need to talk to Ben.'

The woman walked towards her, her aggressive stance at odds with the maternal bump of her body. 'And I told you, he's not here.'

Jess scanned the room, turning to take in the kitchen.

Furious and indignant, Naomi grabbed Jess by the arm and dragged her towards the bedroom door. 'Anything else you need to see? Our bedroom? Family bathroom?' She was on a roll now; there was only one more room to go. She gestured Jess in the direction of it and pushed her forward a little, towards the door. 'The nursery?'

The door to what used to be the spare room swung open. It was done out beautifully in baby-boy blues, with bunting, a cot and a rocking chair in the corner. Unlike the rest of the house it was clean and tidy, and smelt of new furniture and talcum powder. As Jess took in the sight, she began to come back to her senses. The horror and embarrassment of what she was doing rose inside her. She shook herself free of Naomi's hand and walked unsteadily towards the front door.

'I'm sorry,' she croaked. 'I made a terrible mistake. I'll go.'

Just then, there was a noise from behind them. Jess turned to see Ben standing at the open front door, a plastic bag from the corner shop dangling from one hand and the bouquet that Naomi had dumped by the door, in the other.

'*Jess?*'

Jess swallowed. She'd wanted to see him so badly, but right now she was lost and hurting, and he was the last person on earth she wished was blocking her escape.

'What the hell are you doing here?'

'I came to see you.'

'She called me a liar when I said you weren't here,' Naomi said, rubbing her bump protectively. 'Then she barged in to look for herself.'

'You didn't mention he'd only nipped downstairs for a pint of milk,' Jess said, defensively.

Ben's eyes flashed. 'What does she mean, you barged in here?'

'That's a bit of a strong way to describe it—'

'How else would you describe pushing past a pregnant woman into a house that isn't yours?' Naomi said, her body taught with aggression.

Ben dropped the plastic bag and the flowers and went to his fiancée, putting his arm around her and kissing her forehead. 'I should have been here.'

'Oh for god's sake, Ben, I wasn't about to stick a knife in her—'

Jess instantly regretted the words but Ben pounced on them, his teeth gritted and fists clenched.

'You came to my home when you're a person of interest in a murder investigation of my best and oldest friend. To my *home*. What were you thinking?'

'I—'

He frogmarched Jess to the door. 'It's so typical of you, refusing to take the hint you're not wanted.'

Jess smarted at the spiteful remark. 'It's so typical of you to not even listen to what I have to say,' she said. 'Guilty until proven innocent, that's how it goes with you, right?'

'You were at the murder scene. You had *evidence* in your hair and a bleeding finger. You have a long history with the victim—'

'I'm fully aware of how it looks! I came here to ask you to help me prove I didn't do it. And to tell you about—' she stopped. Now wasn't the time to bring up the death threats.

'If you really didn't do it, the evidence will prove that. Coming round here won't change anything. I'm not even working on the case—'

'I know. I'm sorry. I just...' She looked helplessly at him. 'I wanted to talk to someone who'd understand. Whatever happened between us all... she's my – my—' Jess hesitated. 'My f riend.'

Ben's jaw unclenched and his eyes softened for a second, before glazing over again. 'She *was* your friend,' he said, his voice stone cold.

'Please...' Jess said quietly, the hurt edging her voice. 'You know I would never...'

'That's the problem. I don't know you at all.' He shook his head and, picking up the grocery bag, walked away towards the living room without looking back.

Naomi turned to Jess, a victory smile pasted across her face. 'It was *lovely* to meet you, Jessica.'

Jess didn't respond and walked to the front door, picking up the flowers and stopping at the threshold to face her. 'You know, it was my flat too, for a long time,' she whispered.

'I honestly couldn't give a shit.' Naomi pointed at the door and Jess shuffled out, defeated.

Making her way down the stairs and back out towards the street, Jess tried to process what had happened. Ben's lack of willingness to help her clear her name, or to talk to her about Marianne at all, had been upsetting, but it paled into insignificance in comparison to Naomi and that baby bump. Jess assumed time had stood still for Ben in the same way it had for her; that his regret that things had gone so terribly wrong would mirror hers and that they could somehow find a path through the pain, back to a place of friendship, at least. But now it was clear there was no going back.

She walked across the grass towards the car in a daze and stopped before she got in, to glance back at the balcony, with its little table and chair and the potted plants. *Ben was going to be a dad.* The thing she could never give him and the reason, ultimately, that they'd split up. His affair was never the cause, only a catalyst: their marriage had been over long before Marianne. Jess did her best not to feel bitter or angry, then gave herself permission to feel both. At Ben, for moving on with his life; at Naomi, for being young and fertile and able to bear children where Jess never could; and at herself, for letting life slip by so fast.

She felt so alone. When she'd headed over to the flat, she'd been full of ideas of how they'd sit down and talk, letting the years fall away. She'd even imagined them laughing and raising a glass to old times.

'Ha!' Jess angrily wiped away a tear. It wasn't so much knowing Ben had found someone else – he'd managed to do that before they even split up. But the baby... her womb ached with the very idea of it.

'I HOPE YOU HAVEN'T GIVEN ME A SCAR'

Jess spent the rest of the day stewing in her flat, the events of the past forty-eight hours leaving her anxious and exhausted. The press had not come back; presumably they had moved on to stalk someone else with a bigger story; still, she regularly went back to the front door to check it was locked, and upstairs, despite the boiling heat, to make sure the windows were tight. She wondered whether she should have paid a visit to the police station to report the second note after all. But nothing had happened the first time around; they had said it was probably a hoax, so why would they be interested this time? Plus, if she went to the police it was bound to get out, and she didn't want Damon or the media getting even a whiff of more scandal, or she'd never get the press to stop hounding her.

She ended up having an early dinner for something to do, eating an oven pizza she found lurking in the freezer. From over the fence, she could hear the clinking of glasses in her neighbour's garden; the barbecue had been fired up, and she was trying (and failing) to think of a reason to invite herself over so she wouldn't be home alone. Usually, she didn't mind being on her own, but tonight she wished dearly that someone was there with her, to take her mind off everything.

She helped herself to another glass of wine while she loaded the dishwasher with a solitary plate, resenting the cackles of laughter coming from next door that she knew would go on deep into the night. When she and Ben had split, she'd relied on friendships she'd made at the studio to fill the gaps in her social life. Most of her older friends had outgrown her long before, or she'd outgrown them; and now, as the token singleton and blacklisted by all her old colleagues, she was rarely invited to dinner parties and frequently passed over for family get-togethers due to a lack of kids. She'd got used to being alone, although when she moved, she'd promised herself she would try a bit harder to connect with the neighbours. She *was* a nice person, and fun too. Or at least, she used to be. She'd told herself – and anyone else who'd asked – that she was getting on with her life, but the reality was that too often she wished for her old one, or some different version of it. And as for a relationship – Christ, when was the last time she'd even had sex?

Jess drained her wine and listened to the tunes pumping through the walls. Someone new had moved in a few weeks ago; a couple of young guys, she recalled, although she hadn't paid much attention at the time. Since her face had been plastered all over the news, only Damon had bothered to reach out to her. It wouldn't hurt to nip next door, introduce herself. Perhaps, if she was really lucky, she'd find someone to keep her company through the night.

She went to put on a pair of white trainers but then, made brave by yet another gulp of wine, decided to grab a pair of stiletto heels from the wardrobe in the spare room. She chose a pair of cerise sandals that she'd never usually be seen dead in – a gift from the show's wardrobe department one time or another. She had a whole stack of similarly procured items stashed up here, most of which never saw the light of day. In a moment of total abandon, she grabbed a skimpy camisole and slid it on as well. If she made a bit of an effort, maybe her luck would change... Pleased with the overall result, she headed downstairs and out of the door with determined, slightly wobbly strides.

The house next door throbbed with life. Music and laughter pumped from it; the bare windows lit up to display the half-silhouetted bodies gyrating in the living room to house music Jess recognised from her days of clubbing, eons before. The front door lay wide open in invitation, the hallway and kitchen beyond filled with twenty-somethings toting wine glasses and chatting animatedly. Shit, these people were young enough to be her children... Feeling a bit overdressed in her heels, Jess pulled a spaghetti strap back up over her shoulder. She didn't usually just turn up at strangers' houses and invite herself in. But this wasn't exactly gate-crashing, she told herself. Rather, it was a getting-to-know-the-neighbours sort of exercise. And she didn't want to be alone right now.

Carefully positioned lanterns lined the garden path with their flickering lights, casting a warm glow over the paving stones. She took another deep breath and made her way down it, getting about halfway before her heel got stuck.

'You have *got* to be kidding me—' Straining, she pulled at it, hoping to work the shoe loose, but it was well and truly stuck. She took her foot out and sat down, legs akimbo, heaving at the shoe with the full weight of her body.

'Erm, hi, can I help you?' A man (blonde, public school, drunk) came out of the front door, looking confused.

'Oh, hi.' Jess gestured to her shoe with both hands. 'My shoe got stuck in your path.'

'I can see that.' The man blinked at her slowly. 'And who are you, exactly?'

'Oh... I'm Jessica. Jess. From next door.' She gestured with her head.

Realisation flooded his face, followed by a frown.

Jess swallowed and gave a small smile. 'I could hear your party, and thought it sounded fun, you see. So I decided—'

'To invite yourself over?'

'It was either that or be kept awake by the music,' she said, defensively, and acutely aware all of a sudden, that this was the second time in twenty-four hours she'd tried to gate-crash someone's house.

He folded his arms.

'And, I thought it might be fun, you know, to get to know my new neighbours,' she persisted. Shit, she sounded so *lame*. She tugged at her shoe. 'But I can see that was a bad idea. I'll get this free and I'll go.'

The man unfolded his arms and squatted. 'Here, let me do it.'

'No, it's okay, I've got it—'

Jess gave an extra tug and the shoe was released. The momentum spun her up and back, and her shoe-wielding fist ricocheted off her neighbour's forehead.

'What the—?' The pink missile scraped its spiky heel across his cheek. 'Ow!'

'Oh god, I'm so sorry.' Jess got up from where she had fallen backwards and hobbled towards him. 'Are you okay?'

'No, I am bloody well not,' he said, rubbing his face. 'My eye... am I bleeding?' The man blotted where the shoe had hit with the back of his hand and swore again when he saw the blood. 'I hope you haven't given me a scar.'

'Everything alright, Tristan?' Another man (short, beard, glasses) came out and clapped his hand on her neighbour's shoulder. 'I heard a commotion. Ouch. Blood. You should sue.'

'I should! She assaulted me!'

'Sounds terribly dramatic.' He grinned and dabbed at Tristan's forehead with the cuff of his sleeve. 'Hi. I'm Dev. We just moved in.'

This had been a terrible idea. 'If you could keep the noise down a little bit,' she said, clearing her throat. 'I'll take my shoe and go.'

Dev handed her the offending item. 'Here you go, Cinders,' he said. 'And we'll turn the music down, I promise.'

She gave a tight, polite smile. 'Thanks. Appreciated.'

'Sure you don't want to come in for a bit, have something to drink?'

Tristan shot his flatmate a dark look. 'She said she's going home,' he growled.

Dev shrugged and grinned at Jess again. 'If you change your mind, *you know where we live*,' he said, winking.

Thinking of the note shoved through her door, Jess whirled round to face him, gripping her stiletto. 'What did you say?'

'Woah there, psycho,' he said, putting up his hands in mock arrest. He snorted air from his nose in laughter. 'Jesus, calm down.'

'It's not funny.' Jess stared at them both, still brandishing the shoe. But the fight was leaching out of her. They looked like two normal people enjoying a Saturday night with their mates. *'Maybe,'* the little voice in her head said, *'they were just saying what people say when they recognise you from TV.'*

Tristan rolled his eyes and turned to go, clapping a familiar hand on Dev's shoulder. 'She's all yours, mate.'

'Wait—' Jess slowly lowered her arm. What was the matter with her? 'Look, I'm sorry. I've had a bit of a rough few days. I had no business coming here, invading your party. I apologise for cutting your head. And for—' For what? Being a psycho? Mortified, she shook her head, put up her hands in mock surrender and turned to leave. Hobbling away on the one shoe, she banged straight into another woman (short, round, brassy blonde hair) barrelling down the path towards them.

'Watch yourself, love,' the woman barked, pausing for a second to look at her. A spark of recognition passed across her face until she shook her head, strode up to the two men at the door, drew herself up to her full height of five foot two, and bellowed at them.

'Is one of you two responsible for this little shindig?'

Tristan glanced sideways at Dev. 'We've told her we'll turn the music down. Although it's only nine thirty, we're perfectly within our rights—'

'Don't you talk to me about your rights. I suppose you've got the right to be entertaining underage girls here as well, have you?'

'I beg your pardon?' Tristan's face turned red.

'Did you think having young, impressionable girls here would be fun?'

'I think you've got the wrong idea,' Tristan began. 'I'm—'

'Sick, that's what you are.'

'Excuse me? Mrs—'

'Don't 'Mrs' me. It's Della. Della Williams. My daughter Misha is in there and she shouldn't be.'

Tristan's mouth grew slack. 'Your daughter is Misha?'

Della nodded. 'I take it by the look on your face you thought you'd get away with having a seventeen-year-old girl in your house.'

'Seventeen?' Dev looked shocked. 'But she's so... sophisticated!'

Della's thousand-yard stare drilled into Dev. 'She gets it from her mother.'

'I'll go and get her,' Tristan said.

'No, *I'll* go and get her,' Della said. 'She needs to be fully, one hundred per cent humiliated. As do you, when I get back. Wait here.' She looked at Jess. 'Make sure they don't move.'

She barged past the two men, yelling her daughter's name. Tristan swallowed heavily and looked at Dev.

'She worked with me on a photo shoot, as an assistant. I thought she was older,' Tristan turned to Jess. 'She's so put together, not like a teenager in the slightest. When you see her, you'll understand. And we're not... it's not like we'd be interested in her... in any other way.'

Dev gestured to Tristan and then back to himself. 'We're together.'

Jess didn't know whether they wanted her to be shocked or surprised, but she was neither. Conflicted about whether to continue with her hasty retreat, or stay to watch the impending fireworks with Della, she shrugged. 'I'm sure if you explain that you had no intention of molesting that woman's daughter, she'll forgive the underage drinking part.'

Dev opened his mouth to say something else but Della reappeared at that moment, dragging Misha (slim, stunning, mother's eyes) close behind. Jess could see how Dev and Tristan could have mistaken her for older, although right now she was the epitome of a sulky teenager. Her glazed eyes and slurred speech told Jess her mother got there right on time.

'Mum! Mum, you can't do this! These are my friends; I work with them. They aren't doing anything bad. They *invited* me here. I'm nearly eighteen, I'm like, fine—'

'Don't speak to me about fine, Misha Williams. "Fine" is how I ended up pregnant with you. You're drunk already, and it's only nine thirty. It's lucky I came to get you when I did, god knows what would've happened if you'd have stayed any longer.'

'Hang on a minute,' Tristan sounded pissed off. 'I—'

Della swung round to face him. 'You,' she said, jabbing her finger into his chest, 'do not get to say anything.'

'I think I'm going to throw up.' Misha bent over suddenly and redecorated the paving stones. Tristan's lip curled in disgust.

'Serves you right,' Della said, stepping deftly over the pool of vomit to stand next to Jess. She wasn't sure whether Della was talking to Tristan or Misha.

Misha started to cry. 'My boss is in there,' she said, gulping in air. 'I'm gonna get fired.'

'You won't get fired, Misha.' Tristan said. 'I'll talk to Petra.'

'If you think you're going back to that studio you're kidding yourself,' Della said. 'You can get a job with me, where I can keep an eye on you.'

Misha gave another wail.

'Oh, stop it,' Della said. 'You got yourself into this mess. Lucky I was on hand to get you out of it.'

Jess felt a little sorry for Misha, who was still gagging in between sobs. She put her hand on the young girl's shoulder. 'Would you both like to come back to my house, have a glass of water and clean up a bit before you go home?' She gestured at her house. 'I'm just next door.'

Misha nodded, looking grateful through wet fake lashes. 'Thank you, that would be nice,' she said. 'I'm not sure... everything's quite out of my system.'

Jess looked at Della, who scrutinised her for a moment, then nodded. 'It would save messing up my truck, I s'pose,' she said, turning to her daughter. 'Although don't think you've got out of a bollocking because we have an audience. Come on. Let's go with...?'

'Jess,' she said.

'Let's go with Jess and leave these dirty old men to their party,' Della said.

'*Dirty old men?*' Tristan repeated incredulously. It was unclear which part of the sentence he was insulted by most, but Jess bet it was the 'old' part.

Della pointed at the two men. 'I'm gonna be keeping my eye on you.'

Jess led the way and, emboldened by Della's presence, called over the hedge as they reached her front door. 'Me too. After all, *I know where you live.*'

'IS THAT A BAFTA?'

Jess filled up the kettle, set it to boil and got out three mugs, teabags and the sugar. Della closed up the door to the kitchen so they couldn't hear Misha throwing up again in the downstairs cloakroom and sat down at the table.

'Nothing but trouble, that girl,' she said, shaking her head.

'How did you know she was there, at Tristan's house?' Jess got the milk out of the fridge and closed the door quickly so Della couldn't see the gaping void inside.

'I track her phone,' Della said, matter of factly. 'I don't trust that girl as far as I can throw her, never mind anyone else. I mean, would you? Look at her.'

'Probably not,' Jess admitted. 'Although she seems like she can hold her own.'

'She can't hold her alcohol though.' Della grimaced, as another retching noise came from the bathroom. 'She's eighteen in a few weeks and I'm hoping she'll grow out of it once it's legal.'

'It never seems to work that way though, does it?' Jess said, thinking of her own youthful escapades with Marianne and giving a sad smile.

Della stirred her tea. 'So, what were you doing leaving the party so early?'

Jess didn't know whether or not to fess up, but in the end, she decided honesty was the best policy. It seemed to be the only language Della spoke. 'I think I'm having a midlife crisis. My friend... died... a few days ago. And things haven't been going so well for me lately... I wanted some company, I suppose.' She spied the death threat on the table and casually pushed it under the electricity bill before sitting down and motioning Della to do the same.

Della slurped her tea as she took a chair. 'Sorry about your mate. Cancer?'

'No, it was a bit more sudden.' Jess wondered if Della was expecting her to be more forthcoming, but she didn't want to talk about Marianne to a stranger.

'Misha's a real handful,' Della said suddenly, the conversation switch taking Jess by surprise. 'She reminds me way too much of me at her age. Flighty, no self-control. I'm worried she's gonna mess up her life before she even gets started. Like I did.'

'We all make mistakes.'

'Mine's throwing up in the bathroom,' Della said, moodily. 'I was gonna be an actress, you know. Got a drama degree from Goldsmiths and everything.' Della sounded rueful. 'Blew it by getting hammered in the pub on graduation. Got pregnant that night, didn't even know until I was five months gone. Now look at me. Driving a bloody frozen fish truck around south London trying to flog twenty-four packs of salmon. Living the dream, I am .'

She took out her phone and showed Jess a picture of four children: a little boy of around six (gap-toothed, dark hair), two tweens (boy and a girl, possibly twins) and Misha.

'Here's the rest of the clan.'

'You've got four children?'

'Long story for another time.' Della looked at the clock and cocked her head towards the hallway. 'You reckon she's all done now? I need to get home, my sister's babysitting the others and she'll go mental if I'm much longer.'

Jess got up and opened the kitchen door. A greyer version of Misha stood in the hallway; her face crumpled into an attractive pout as she looked into the front room at Jess's mantlepiece.

'Are you famous?' she said. 'Is that a BAFTA?'

'I presented a reality TV show,' she said. 'It was groundbreaking at the time. And very popular.'

Della clapped Jess on the back, making her jump. 'I knew I knew you,' she said. 'You're Jessica Sinclair, P.I.'

'What's P.I.?' Misha asked.

'Stands for Private Investigator. Like Magnum P.I.'

'What's Magnum P.I.?' Misha said, again.

'A cop show from the eighties,' Jess explained.

'Oh,' Misha said, unimpressed.

Della turned to Jess and grinned. 'I reckon I could be a P.I.'

Misha laughed, bitterly. 'I thought you already were. You always seem to know where I am.'

Della ignored her daughter. 'I always fancied myself doing something like that, you know, being undercover and catching bad guys.'

'Mum, you've caught more bad guys than the rest of the female population of London put together,' Misha said, giving her the side eye. Della flicked her the finger in return.

'Poking about in people's private lives isn't all it's cracked up to be, I promise you,' Jess said.

'Ha!' Misha glared at her mother. 'Try telling that to her, will you?'

'Sounds brilliant to me,' Della said. 'Nothing I like better than figuring out someone's been misbehaving, then grabbing them by the balls to make 'em squirm.'

'I wouldn't put it quite like that,' Jess chuckled, taking herself by surprise. She hadn't laughed in a long time.

'It's getting late, we'll get out of your hair. Thanks for the cuppa and the use of your bathroom. Misha?'

'Yeah, thank you,' Misha said. 'I made sure I left it tidy, by the way.'

Jess smiled, realising she wished this whirlwind duo didn't have to leave. 'You're both welcome. It was nice to meet you. Stay out of trouble, Misha.'

Della snorted and gave her daughter a gentle shove out of the door. 'Fat chance.'

The two of them disappeared into the night and a few moments later Jess heard the heavy rumble of a truck starting up. She waited until it had driven away before going back inside, locking the door carefully and turning out the lights, save the porch light, which she decided would stay on, for now. Della and Misha had distracted her from Marianne, Ben, the death threats and the agency for a few hours, but it would be silly to get complacent.

The music from next door had quietened to a gentle, muted background beat, and Jess decided to watch a bit of television; the noise and chatter of a sitcom might divert her attention from being alone in the house again. She lay down on one end of the living room sofa, flicking through her options until she finally decided to binge *Friends* for the thousandth time. She gazed at the bright colours on the screen and let the nasal voices wash over her. Her mind drifted back to Ben. He'd looked well earlier, despite the circumstances. He'd gone grey in that sort of handsome way middle-aged men tended to do, and had a natty shirt and jeans that were fitted to show off a *very* toned physique. Not that he'd ever been unfit; since they first met, he'd always gone running and done excessive numbers of noisy press-ups in their bedroom.

She tried not to think about the extra pounds she'd piled on in the decade since they parted, or the wrinkles and bits of saggy skin that had appeared in the intervening years. Middle age was a cruel mistress. Marianne had aged too. It had been surprising to see that, and Jess wondered what had happened in the intervening years. Jess hadn't exactly had a happy ever after herself, but at least she'd survived. She might be lonely sometimes, and worried about where the money was coming from to pay her bills these days, but she was here, and relatively healthy. She thought about Marianne and her pills and wondered what had happened to cause her to need them. Depression didn't seem to fit with the girl she'd known. In a fit of nostalgia, Jess pictured her and Marianne in their early thirties and gave a sad smile. She hardly remembered what it felt like now. Those two young women, so vibrant, so *alive*.

Who the hell would want Marianne dead? Most likely it was someone from her years as a UCO who'd figured out she wasn't who she said she was, but it was a stretch to think they'd find her. She'd left the force a few years ago now and over a decade had passed since she'd worked an undercover case, and always with a different name. Maybe it was someone she'd pissed off since?

A huge sob suddenly escaped her. What a terrible end to a life. Even with no sign of a struggle, Jess wondered if Marianne died a painless, oblivious death, or if she'd been aware of what was happening, in agony and powerless to stop it. Unable to hold them back any longer, she let the tears fully flow. Marianne hadn't deserved that ending, no one did.

Her crying continued until she was finally exhausted. Mind drifting, she tried to focus on the television, but she couldn't stay awake any longer. The last thing she heard was the buzz of a motorbike outside, the fading noise as it disappeared down the road lulling her into the blissful relief of sleep.

www.sinclairinvestigations.com > *Services* > *Personal Background Checks*

Has someone new come into your family? Is your son or daughter dating a person that you don't feel comfortable with? Maybe a parent has met a new partner that you suspect might have ulterior motives? We can perform a discreet and comprehensive background check to give you peace of mind – or get you the proof you need to take affirmative action.

Contact us today to see how we can help.

'EVERYONE NEEDS A SPA, DON'T THEY, DICKIE?'

The very last thing she wanted to do on Sunday morning was to get up and go out on another job. And yet, here she was, dressed up in a flouncy shirt and skirt combo, waiting to meet Dr Angela Coleman for brunch, along with her new fiancé, Richard Whitman, and Richard's son, Simon. Work was work, and she needed the money.

'Thanks for coming,' Simon (greying hair, slight paunch, pinky ring) said, pulling her chair out for her. 'I really appreciate it.'

'You're welcome,' Jess replied. She sat down at the table and leant back while the waiter (thin, young, permanently raised eyebrow) poured her a glass of sparkling water and placed the white linen napkin on her lap. She felt incredibly self-conscious, being on a job somewhere so public, but liked to think she was on safe ground at The Wolseley, dining amongst the higher echelons of London society. With a bit of luck, anyone who did recognise her would have the good manners to leave her alone; aside from blowing her cover, she was far too vulnerable at the moment to be comfortable with strangers approaching her unchecked.

She smiled reassuringly at Simon. 'So, what have we been up to lately, fake boyfriend?'

'Oh, this and that. We played golf yesterday and had a weekend in Rome a few weekends ago.'

'Oh, I love Rome!' Jess clapped her hands together with pretend joy. 'Not that we saw a lot of it,' she winked. Simon shifted uncomfortably in his seat, so Jess stopped and gave him a sympathetic smile. She knew he was finding this all very difficult; they'd agreed that giving her a fake name and pretending to be an item was the quickest and easiest way to a seat at the table with Simon's father. But Simon was gay, and while Jess could barely believe it was still an issue in this day and age, he had spent the best part of forty years keeping it from his father by simply avoiding the subject of relationships at all.

'Angela's going to be late,' Simon said. 'Dad rang this morning to tell me she had a dress fitting. It might be the perfect time to talk to him, without her getting in the way. She never seems to leave him alone.'

The former CEO of one of the biggest hedge funds of the late eighties, Richard Whitman had recently met American cardiologist Dr Angela Coleman. They'd dated for a few months before Richard had proposed suddenly, declaring the Queen of Hearts had captured his, and there was no time like the present to do something about it. Simon was convinced it was a con.

'Did you find anything out that might help?'

'She appears to be a real doctor,' Jess said, getting her notes out. 'Got her medical degree at Harvard in 1992, according to my searches. Married in 2003 to a fellow doctor, divorced in 2006. Married for a second time in 2008 to a London property magnate and divorced him in 2010. Married again in—'

'She's been married *three times* already?' Simon's face turned purple.

Jess cleared her throat. 'Four, actually. If you count the last one. A knight of the realm by all accounts. He died on their wedding night.'

'Simon!' Richard Whitman (silver fox, clearly loaded, older version of Simon) made his way across the carpeted dining room and Jess stood up to greet him. 'So, this must be the famous Rachel,' he said, kissing her once on either cheek. He stood back and narrowed his eyes, giving her a visible once-over. Jess held her breath, hoping he wouldn't say the all-too-familiar words: 'don't I know you from somewhere?' Simon had assured her watching anything other than the BBC was considered treason in his father's house, but you never knew what people got up to behind closed doors.

However, it seemed Richard was satisfied with what he saw.

'Good choice, lad,' he said, as though picking out a racehorse. He gave Simon a sound handshake and a firm clap on the back. Jess clenched her teeth into a sort of smile, then retracted it in case he started checking them over to determine her age.

Richard took his seat opposite them. 'Angela will be along in a bit,' he said. 'She sends her apologies.'

'No need,' Simon said, grudgingly. Jess gave his foot a nudge with her own under the table.

Richard cleared his throat. 'So, I wanted to talk to you about the wedding. Angela's insisting on a big do, which is fine by me, I suppose.'

'Shocker,' muttered Simon.

'I know Simon must be very fond of you, Rachel – god knows we've never met a single girlfriend of his before now – but I'm afraid Angela has said no to you being part of the wedding party.'

Jess waved the issue away. 'That's okay. It's not like I'm part of the family.'

'The thing is... she's also suggested I might like to have her brother as my – my best man,' Richard said, not meeting Simon's eye. 'I know we said you'd be doing it, old chap, but Angela asked and, well, what the bride wants—'

'—the bride gets.' Simon sighed. 'Dad, look, Jess – I mean, Rachel—'

'Good god, man, get the filly's name right,' Richard exclaimed.

Jess tried not to show her irritation at this chauvinistic old twat. If this was what money did to you, she was glad she didn't have any.

She attempted to course correct. 'So, tell me, Mr Whitman, how did you meet Dr Coleman?'

'At a fundraiser,' he said, his eyes misting over. 'She walked up to me, bold as brass, and told me she was going to marry me one day.' He chuckled. 'I should have known she was right. She's always right.'

'Except when it comes to marriage,' Simon murmured.

'Oh, I know – divorced three times, widowed in 2020,' he replied. 'We don't have any secrets. Dear god, a woman's allowed to have a past, isn't she?' He winked at Jess. 'Especially someone as passionate as Angela.'

Simon blanched. 'Don't you think it's kind of a red flag though?' he persisted.

'What's a red flag?' Angela Coleman (slender, suited, Jerry-Hall-esque) put a manicured, proprietorial hand on Richard's shoulder as she came up behind him. 'Hello, darling.'

Her sizeable engagement ring glittered as she removed her hand and waited for Richard to stand up to greet her. He kissed the cheek she proffered and he pulled out a chair for her to sit down. 'Everything alright?'

She nodded and gave a polite smile to Jess and Simon. 'You must be Rachel. It's lovely to meet you.'

'You too, Dr Coleman.' Addressing this woman by her formal name seemed ridiculous given they were about the same age. But it's what Richard would expect, Simon had explained. To show respect.

'Simon, darling, you look tired. You should book yourself into a spa. I know just the place we can send you.'

'I don't need a spa,' Simon snapped.

'Nonsense, everyone needs a spa, don't they, Dickie?'

Simon cringed at the pet name and Richard cleared his throat. 'I just told Simon the news about your brother—'

'Ah yes, you don't mind, do you? In fact, as a little surprise...' she clapped her hands in delight and waved over at the entrance. 'Look who I invited along. Marcus, come and meet everyone!'

Marcus (tanned, tall, Ryan-Gosling-level gorgeous) strolled over. His casual khaki trouser and white shirt combo, even to Jess's untrained eye, looked expensive. On one wrist, a polished Rolex gleamed gold.

'Everyone, this is my brother, Marcus,' Angela Coleman ran her hand up and down her sibling's bare forearm. Jess frowned and looked across at Simon to see if he'd noticed the slightly odd body language. But Simon was too busy staring at his new step-brother's watch.

'Simon? Are you going to say hello?'

Simon raised his eyes to meet Marcus's. 'We've already met,' he said coolly.

Marcus's eyes widened in recognition. 'I—'

'Last week, I believe,' Simon said. 'In Heaven.'

'In heaven? What on earth are you talking about?'

'It's a gay club, Dad,' Simon said.

'A *gay* club?' Richard said. 'What on Earth were you doing there?'

Simon shook his head. 'Oh, for god's sake, Dad, what do you think I was doing there?'

Richard frowned. 'But Rachel—'

'Is a fake girlfriend, by the way,' Simon said, giving a bitter laugh. 'Only not as much of a fake as either of these two, clearly.' He turned back to Marcus. 'Was stealing my watch your own idea or did she put you up to it?'

Angela gave a tinkly laugh. 'Simon, come on now, I'm sure there's been some mistake—'

'No mistake, Angela. Your brother – if he is your brother – is a thief,' Simon said, standing up from the table and throwing his napkin down. 'And what's more, I think you are too.'

'Now hang on a minute,' Richard said, reddening. 'That's no way to speak to my fiancée. Apologise this instant.'

'I bet you're not even a real doctor, whatever the internet says,' Simon said, getting carried away by his temper. 'I bet if we asked you a question about cardiology, you wouldn't have the first clue.' He looked at Jess, expectantly. 'Go on. Ask her.'

Jess racked her brains to think of something – anything – that she could say.

'Simon, this has gone too far,' Richard said. 'Of course Angela is a real doctor. She got her degree at Harvard, for god's sake—'

'Doctor Coleman, when you qualified in Boston, which halls did you reside in?' Jess interrupted.

Angela shot her a look. 'Excuse me?'

'At Harvard. Where did you live?'

Angela looked flustered. 'I can't remember. It was a long time ago—'

'No one forgets their house at Harvard,' Jess said, turning to Simon. 'I met some students from there one summer, with a friend of mine.' She thought about the fun she and Marianne had with those all-American boys and it made her feel sad all over again, for her lost youth and her lost friend. She refocused. 'You must remember your house.'

'House? It's not Harry bloody Potter.'

'Where did you live?' Jess persisted.

'I – I – Eliot!' She said, triumphant. 'I lived in Eliot House.' She smiled at everyone. Marcus looked relieved. 'Now, can we all please sit down and act like civilised people? This is a very nice hotel and I'd like to be able to come back here some time.'

'All the medical students live in Vanderbilt Hall,' Richard said quietly.

'Excuse me?'

'My golfing partner, Barney. Had a son went to Harvard, Simon knew him, they were friends at school. He's an oncologist now. I remember him telling us about Vanderbilt when he came home for his first Christmas. They came for drinks, everyone was terribly proud of him.' He looked up at Angela, realisation dawning. 'You didn't go to Harvard.'

'Darling, I can assure you—'

Richard sat up straight and gave her a powerful stare. 'Angela,' he said. 'I may be old, but I'm not a fool.'

There was a long pause. Realising the jig was most definitely up, Angela Coleman reached slowly for her Birkin bag, looking shiftily around the room. 'I think I'd better be going,' she said. She glanced at Marcus. 'I can see we aren't welcome here.'

'STOP!' roared Richard. Angela did as she was told, looking suddenly scared. 'Ring,' he demanded. 'And the keys. House *and* car.'

She sighed and surrendered the items onto the white Wolseley tablecloth, the waiter looking on with a smug smile.

'And I'll take my watch, thank you,' Simon said huffily to Marcus.

Marcus placed the watch next to the keys and ring. He seemed to be remarkably unbothered by the whole disaster unfolding in front of him.

'For what it's worth, I had the most enormous fun,' he said, winking at Simon. 'In another life—'

Richard visibly baulked. 'If I were you, young man, I'd get out of here before I throw you out. And as for you,' he looked at Angela Coleman, 'You've got about two hours to leave the country before I call the police.'

He breathed a shaky sigh as he watched Angela leave, her hips swinging indignantly as she sashayed from the room. 'Always knew she was too good to be true,' he said. 'But she was damn fine in the sack.'

'*Dad!*'

Richard signalled for the bill. 'Rachel, I'm very sorry, but Simon and I have to go. It was... lovely to meet you, but given the bomb my son dropped, I think it highly unlikely we'll see you again.'

'Before you leave,' Jess said. 'There's the issue of payment.'

'Good lord, you were *paying* her?' Richard got out his wallet and threw five fifty-pound notes at her. 'Here. For your troubles.' He looked her up and down. 'She doesn't look like a whore,' he said as he walked away.

Simon shrugged helplessly at her. 'Sorry,' he said. 'It's probably easier if I don't tell him who you really are. It'll only make things worse if he thinks I was spying on him.'

Jess blinked. 'Sure. No problem.'

'And thanks for everything. You were a great fake girlfriend, honestly. And that thing with the Harvard house? Genius.'

'Thank you.'

'I'll leave you a review,' he said. 'I promise.'

Jess raised a hand in a small wave as father and son left the dining room. She pocketed the cash, intent on stopping off at the bar on the way out. It was amazing who and what you came across in this job.

'VERY SHERLOCK HOLMES'

The next morning, Jess woke to the sound of someone calling her name. She'd stayed for considerably more than one drink in the end and had arrived home a little worse for wear. Now, she felt lousy; her head pounded in sync with her heart and she feared she might throw up any second. Her head lolled and she gasped in horror as she realised she'd fallen asleep sitting against the front door. She licked her dry lips, rubbed the smudged mascara from under her eyes, then turned around and knelt on the doormat, pulling the letterbox open a crack.

Seeing movement, the reporters outside didn't miss a beat.

'Jessica, tell us about your relationship with Marianne Hughes!'

Jess's mouth dried up.

'Jessica, a source tells us you and Marianne weren't speaking at the time of her death.' It was this second voice that brought Jess to her senses. 'Shit!' she said out loud, and shut the letterbox. What had they found out now? Had the post-mortem been done, or maybe the forensics of the glass in her hair... she felt her stomach turn in dread at the idea that the police were out there, waiting to come in and arrest her in front of a live audience.

'I understand you and Marianne were friends at university and shared a flat together after graduation,' another voice said. 'Can you tell us how you fell out?'

It was with this third voice that the doorbell rang loud in Jess's ears. She jumped a little at the unexpected sound.

'Jess. Are you there?'

Jess looked out of the letterbox again to see Della standing defiantly, with a large package in her hands. Jess opened the door, the noise from the pack outside increasing. Della breezed in like a whirling dervish and she closed the door quickly behind her.

'It's like a bloody zoo out here. Howdy partner,' she said. 'Oof, you look rough. Thought I'd nip by to say thanks for the other night.' She waggled a package in her hand. 'This is for you.'

Jess looked at the package. It was wrapped in white plastic and smelt revolting. 'Oh right... that's kind of you.' Jess's attention was quickly being dragged back to the baying crowd outside. Should she go out there and confront them? They'd be foaming at the mouth, wondering who Della was. Maybe it was better to let them stew.

'I picked you out a couple of portions of halibut, but I've got all sorts in the back: salmon, cod, prawns, sole; all flash-frozen and packed ready for your freezer. It's on me. I saw that fridge of yours, so I know it's empty. Should have sold a load to that lot as well.' She nodded at the door and the baying press beyond. 'They look like they haven't seen a decent meal in weeks either.

Shall we go through?' Della said, barely pausing for breath. To Jess's slight irritation, she put a confident hand on Jess's elbow and steered her back through the flat, holding the fish aloft like Simba the Lion King.

'Can you put the kettle on?' she said. 'Maybe make a slice of toast? I've got time for a cuppa before my shift starts and we need to talk.'

'Look, I'm sorry, you can see what's going on outside. I don't exactly have the time for—'

'Exactly. You could probably do with a bit of a distraction.' Jess couldn't deny that. She paused, taking in the woman in front of her. There was something about Della that made her instantly likeable. And comforting. She was so... *in charge.* Before she was conscious that she'd even made the decision to let Della stay, Jess was heading to the kitchen, flicking the switch on the kettle and flinging a few slices of bread in the toaster. When she came back, Della was plonked in one of the chairs by her desk, her short legs outstretched and feet barely touching the ground.

'Lovely house you've got here, Jess. I didn't take it all in before.'

'It's not all mine – I only have two floors...'

Della nodded and peered at the corkboard propped up behind her desk, with case notes pinned to it. She shuffled a few papers on Jess's desk. 'You work out of your front room, then? Very Sherlock Holmes.'

'Della. It's nice to see you again, but what do you want?' While Jess liked this woman, she was a total stranger. After everything that had happened, she was crazy to have let her in the house, much less make her breakfast...

Della slapped her hand on the desk, making Jess jump.

'Right, I'll cut to the chase. I've got a proposition to make, and I'd like you to listen to it.'

'Now is really not a great time for propositions.' She looked down at yesterday's clothes. 'It's – it's been a rough few days.'

'I can see that.' Della motioned to where the press stood outside. 'People don't usually have the papers camped out on their doorstep for no reason, unless they got married to a royal or they're being done for something major.' She pointed at Jess. 'I looked you up. Your mate, the one who died. She was murdered.'

Rattled, Jess raked at her hair. 'It's not really any of your—'

'I saw that note, on your table.'

'Note?' She tried and failed to keep her voice light.

'The one you tried to hide from me the other night,' Della said. 'Can't pull the wool over these eyes.' She blinked, batting her falsies ferociously.

'I think you should go.' Jess made to move Della on out.

'I think you should hire me.'

'What?'

'I want to be a P.I.,' Della continued, earnestly.

Jess tried not to do a double take.

'I could help you with work, while you fend off the bastards out the front,' Della said. 'Hire me as your trainee. An assistant P.I. or whatever. I'm a quick learner and no one gives a toss who I am. I can help you.' She met Jess's gaze. 'Or at least help you figure out who sent you that note.'

Jess blinked and shook her head. Who did this woman think she was? What the hell was going on, that perfect strangers thought it was okay to barge into her life? 'I'm fine,' she said. 'I don't need help.'

Della tipped her head towards the front of the house. 'That lot being out there says different. And I'll be honest: you strike me as someone who could do with a friend right now.'

At this, Jess stopped short and looked at her, overcome for a moment. It might be painful to hear, but Della was right, she did need a friend. Jess thought about the note, Marianne's murder, and the state of her business. And then she assessed the woman sitting opposite. It would be good to have someone on her side. But could she *trust* her?

'I know what you're thinking.' Della interrupted Jess's ponderous silence. 'I'm loud, I take up too much space. People think I'm scum because I've got four kids by two different dads and I drive crab sticks around in a truck. But I am smart and ambitious and I'm a hard worker. And I owe it to myself and my family to do something more with my life. It's time to get out of that rut, make the kids proud of me, use my skills to do something a bit different. This seems like a good opportunity for that.'

She reminded Jess of Marianne: hugely likeable, and a force of nature. But she shook her head, knowing this wasn't really the opportunity Della thought it was.

'I could do with the help. But I can't pay you,' she said, resigned. 'I'm sorry.'

'We can come to an arrangement,' Della said. 'Maybe if I bring in some business, or solve a case, I can take a cut – but in the meantime we'll call it work experience. I can keep doing the fish sales: I get discounts and I've got four kids at home need feeding, plus we'd have the truck. For stakeouts. No one gets suspicious of a frozen fish truck. No one looks at it twice.'

Jess sighed. It wasn't the worst idea in the world; she needed help, and Della was good company, too. Jess could almost hear Damon salivating, treating it like a social experiment to throw in sometime around chapter seven. *If nothing else, she'd make a great addition to the book.*

'I could start on Thursday.'

Jess didn't know whether it was the fact she'd barely slept a wink in the last seventy-two hours, or whether she was actually losing the plot, but she accepted the circumstances of fate.

'Fine, welcome on board. Do you want jam on your toast?'

'I DIDN'T KNOW YOU WENT TO PARTIES'

Della had been gone about half an hour when Jess's phone rang.

'I'm outside,' Damon's voice said. 'I'm taking you for lunch.'

'I'm not dressed—'

'Get some clothes on and get out here quickly, before this lot consume the car like a pack of piranhas.'

'I've already eaten—'

'Jess, it's not about the bloody breakfast! Just get in the car!'

She did as she was told and left the house. The baying of the press increased as she approached them, and, shaking, she fended off their hostile jostling and finally reached Damon's car.

'It's like you have an inbuilt antenna,' she said, foregoing any real greeting.

'For what?' Damon replied. 'I don't need one to find out how you're doing when every online news station is beaming live images of your front door to my computer screen.' He pulled away from the curb quickly, waving at the reporter taking their photo as he passed. 'I know we said there's no such thing as bad publicity, but—'

'I don't know how to make them go away,' Jess knew she sounded worried.

'Look, don't worry, we can turn this around,' Damon said. 'They've got nothing except some vague story about a bit of bad blood between you and the dead girl. The forensic reports will be back soon.'

Jess swallowed. 'That's what I'm worried about.'

'Why?' He looked across at her from the driver's seat and Jess swallowed.

'Why don't we wait until we get to—'

'Jess, what's going on?'

'I swear to god, I only broke a glass—'

He leaned heavily on the brakes. 'You did *what*?'

'It was upstairs by her bed, there was nothing on it.'

'Upstairs? You went *upstairs*? Jesus Christ, Jess. I hope you've got a good lawyer.'

'I can't afford any more lawyers.'

'So you're just going to wait for the police to turn up and arrest you for tampering with a crime scene?' Damon said. 'Or worse, murder?'

'That's a huge assumption. They could have found other evidence, of the actual killer—'

'This has gone too far.' Damon pulled off again, accelerating. 'You need to get out there and talk to the press, beat them at their own game. You know the rules. Change the narrative.'

'I don't have a narrative!' Jess said.

'Maybe you should.' He turned the car onto the main road.

They sat in the booth of the quiet basement coffee shop, Damon perusing the extensive menu of toasted ciabattas.

'What do you want?' he said.

'I'm not hungry. Just a coffee. And a slice of carrot cake.'

Damon nodded and went upstairs to order at the counter. While she waited for him to come back, she thought about her situation. She was hardly in a great position. Forensics were bound to turn up all manner of secrets, she was sure, if the killer had been careless enough to leave evidence behind. If they hadn't, she was screwed. She knew from living with Marianne and being married to Ben, that the worst of humanity could still get away with murder, literally, because of lack of forensic evidence.

'*A source tells us you and Marianne weren't speaking at the time of her death.*' The reporter's words from earlier rang in her ears. She knew how every investigation ran: consider the most likely scenario and use the evidence to help prove the theory. *She* was the most likely scenario, currently, and all they needed to do was dress up the evidence a little and they'd have their man. Or rather, woman. Jess sighed. She needed a story – but more than that, she needed to give the police something else to focus on, to push her away from the epicentre. Maybe Damon was just the person to help her.

'All ordered.' Damon arrived back and slid into the seat opposite. 'Right. Let's start from the beginning. Who the hell *is* Marianne Hughes?'

Damon was polishing off the last of his glorified cheese and ham toastie when she finished explaining the very complicated history of her, Marianne and Ben. He wiped his mouth with a paper napkin, looking aghast.

'Well,' he said. 'On the one hand, everything you say sounds completely innocent and your actions and reactions justified. On the other hand, you've put yourself squarely in the frame for murder.'

Jess cleared her throat. 'I hired someone,' she said, hoping to placate him. 'That's good, right?'

'You did?' Damon's voice filled with interest.

'I met her at a party on Saturday night,' Jess said. 'Her name's Della.'

'I didn't know you went to parties,' Damon said.

She tried not to sound indignant. 'Well, now you do.'

'So, is she qualified? Has she done this before?'

'Not at all.'

Damon laughed. 'At least it will make for an interesting chapter in the book.'

He was *so* predictable. 'She's going to help with stakeouts and so on, like we talked about, while I—'

'While you try to make bail?' He signalled for the bill.

'That's not funny.'

'Oh, I know, darling.' He turned to face her. 'None of this is funny.' He pushed his plate away, irritated. 'Is there anything else you've not told me?'

Jess hesitated then pulled out the second death threat from her handbag, encased in a clear plastic bag. 'This came last week. It was delivered by hand.'

Damon took it and raised his eyebrow. 'Another one?'

'Yep.'

'That lot in your front yard don't know about it, I take it?'

Jess shook her head. 'No. At least, I don't think they do. But someone's feeding them information about me. That's why the reporters were all back again today. They got a tip-off that Marianne and I weren't speaking to each other when she died – and that makes me look even more guilty than I did before.' Jess pursed her lips. 'It might only be a matter of time before one of them finds out about the notes too. How will I ever go back to living a normal life after this? Everywhere I go, people recognise me. It used to be exciting when I was on the show, I'd get a real buzz from it. But since I left, it's been exasperating – and now it's become downright dangerous.'

'We can get a court injunction; tell them they have to leave you alone—'

'If we do that, it will make me look even more guilty,' she said. 'I didn't kill Marianne, but even if I have all the proof in the world, that won't turn the tide of public opinion if they say

I did. And if I'm killed by some crazy fan, they'll probably say it was justified and I deserved it.'

'We'll find out who it is,' Damon said, reassuringly. 'More often than not people give themselves away eventually.'

'Are we talking about my letter writer or Marianne's killer?'

'Either. Both,' Damon said. 'Maybe they're the same person.'

'Unlikely.'

Damon paused. 'Jess, I fear that if you leave it up to the police, you won't get the answers you're looking for. And you might end up in a world of trouble.'

She racked her brains to think of anything that might exonerate her. Maybe the police would find something in their search; but Damon was right: if it didn't fit with their theory, they'd just as easily dismiss it. Perhaps it wouldn't do any harm to do a little digging of her own, too. There'd been a case, years ago, where she'd helped to put a man in prison thanks to her due diligence. It had been her big break – the one that got her noticed. Ben had been annoyed with her about it, telling her to leave the police work to the police. But sometimes, looking at things through the lens of a storyteller revealed more than good old-fashioned detective work would ever do.

She thought about the video she'd taken at Marianne's house, that she'd conveniently left out of her story to Damon. If she wanted the police to look at more than the evidence laid out in front of them, she had to prove her innocence and get them to see things from a different perspective. When she got home, she'd get started.

MARIANNE HUGHES – *Notes from crime scene video*

- *Marianne had stab wounds to the chest and heart that had caused heavy bleeding. No signs of struggle.*

- *The murder weapon was missing, probably a knife of some kind.*

- *There was blood to the front of her clothing, the sofa and the living room floor below where she was sitting, indicating she bled out in situ.*

- *Time of death was estimated by forensics as approx. 9 p.m. on Tuesday evening. The front door was locked, the back door was open, no sign of forced entry.*

NOTE: There's no clean exit from the house this way. A killer would have had to go through a bunch of other gardens to get in or out the back. On a warm night in June, it was likely there would have been plenty of people sat in their gardens, even if the ones on either side were unoccupied. It wouldn't be worth the risk. So the killer must have left via the front door. (Witnesses?)

- *There was a mug of tea on the patio, undrunk, and cigarettes in the ashtray, one without lipstick stains. The killer's? Could he be known to Marianne? (Would tie in with lack of struggle and unforced entry).*

NOTE: Three bottles of vodka at the scene (one empty in the bin) and a bottle of diazepam in the bathroom cabinet. Alcohol / substance addiction issues? If she was incapacitated, that may have contributed to her lack of defensive wounds.

Living room contents: sofa, armchair and small coffee table with a TV remote on top. Desk in the window with a laptop and iPhone plugged in. The TV in the corner was switched off. It was clean and tidy, no obvious evidence of disturbance to anything.

NOTE: Could there be evidence on the laptop or phone?

'I'M AFRAID WE'RE NOT AT LIBERTY TO SAY'

The uniforms swept past her as she opened the door to them, nodding as they passed. 'Mind if we come in?'

Jess could hear the frenzied rabble of the press pack behind them, all smelling blood.

'Hello, hello, hello, what's all this then, Jessica?'

'You here to arrest her?'

'Did you do it, Jessica?'

'Jessica, anything to say to the press before you go down?'

Jess ignored them and swallowed hard, suddenly feeling damp with sweat.

'What can I do for you both? Did you find Marianne's killer?'

'I'm afraid we're here to ask you to accompany us to the station,' Uniform Two said.

'Am I under arrest?'

'Not exactly.'

'So I don't have to come with you if I don't want to?'

Uniform One cleared his throat. 'DCI Dickson sent us, ma'am. He asked us to tell you that you could come in for questioning or he'd have you arrested for breaking and entering.'

'Those weren't the exact words—'

'—but we've left the bad ones out.'

'He was very clear—'

'Breaking and entering? I don't understand.'

'—he said you'd been bothering DI Morgan at his home.'

'I went to give him some flowers.' Jess was indignant now. What had Ben been saying? She'd pushed her way in, yes; but she'd hardly call it breaking and entering. 'Why does DCI Dickson want me to come in, specifically?'

'I'm afraid we're not at liberty to say,' Uniform One said.

'Of course not. It's just that I've been rather harassed myself this past week.' She indicated outside. 'And I do mean actually harassed, rather than nipped round with a sympathy bouquet.'

The two police officers shuffled their feet.

'We were just told to come and get you,' Uniform One said. Uniform Two tipped her handbag off the hallway table, making the contents spill out onto the floor. 'Whoops.'

Jess frowned. 'You need a warrant to search that.'

'It was an accident. I'll clear up.' He waggled the clear plastic bag with the anonymous note in it. 'What's this?'

The dark letters stood out clearly even from where she was standing. 'It's private.'

'Got something to hide, Ms Sinclair?'

'No,' Jess said sharply. She decided to play ball – she didn't need any more suspicion heaped upon her. 'It arrived last week, in the night.'

'Have you had any other messages like this?' Uniform One looked interested now too.

'Once,' she said. 'A while ago now. I was frightened at the time, but I had hoped it was nothing. When this one arrived I was going to report it, but—'

'Why didn't you?'

'She's been busy with other things, mate,' Uniform Two said, putting the rest of her belongings back into the bag. 'Discovering dead bodies, tampering with crime scenes, harassing police officers, that sort of thing.'

Uniform One gave a small smile and turned back to Jess. 'It's most likely a hoax. Celebrities have this sort of thing happen all the time. We can log it if you want.'

She shook her head. 'No, thank you. It's fine – as you say, it's probably nothing.'

Uniform Two picked up Jess's house keys and dangled them in her face. 'Ready?'

They exited the house, the uniforms waiting behind Jess as she double-locked the front door. The noise from the press pack grew louder.

'Where's her handcuffs?'

'Jessica, how are you feeling?'

'What's the charge?'

'Did you get in trouble for trying to crash another party?'

Jess stopped dead in her tracks and looked over the hedge. Dev was on his way up next door's path. His grin gave way to a concerned look. 'Hey. Are you okay? Do you need me to call anyone?'

'Leave me alone.'

'I'm only trying to help. I'm—'

'I don't need your help,' she said, raising her voice over the din of the press.

'Let me know if you do. That's what friends are for, after all!'

Exasperated, Jess turned to face him again. 'We are *not* friends, Dev. And I'd appreciate it if you would mind your own business.' She spun on her heel and marched on, the officers trailing behind her.

The airless, windowless room she was placed in for questioning was even less inviting than the one she'd been in on the previous occasion. A dirty chair was waiting for her, covered in questionable stains, and she sat down gingerly, picking at her fingers and waiting for Graham Dickson. When he finally rolled in ten minutes later, she found her mouth was dry from lack of water and she needed the bathroom. She wasn't about to ask for either.

Graham Dickson flung a file down on the desk. Jess knew it was an old police trick, to make people feel uncomfortable. Ben had told her that when they first met. A thick file full of nothing, to intimidate people into talking. Had Graham Dickson forgotten who she'd been married to? Who she'd been best friends with? She folded her arms defiantly.

He opened the file and pulled out three pieces of paper. Jess resisted the temptation to look at them; she didn't want to give him the satisfaction of knowing she was curious. Whatever their contents, he'd get round to telling her in his own time. She wasn't going to beg him.

'Forensic report on Marianne Hughes's house made for interesting reading,' he said, smiling at her. 'You, Miss Sinclair, are all over it. And all over the news too, I believe. If they didn't think you were guilty already, wait until they get their hands on this. You should have been more careful.' He tutted, as though disappointed and Jess reddened slightly, cursing herself for feeling guilty for no reason.

'The glass shards we found in your hair were a match to the shards we found in the bin,' he continued.

'We've been through this before. I was upset, I needed some water,' she lied. 'I got the glass out of the cupboard and my hands were shaking so much...'

'Yes, so you said in your witness statement,' Graham Dickson peered at the paperwork. 'But I'm afraid we have far more than that to discuss.' He placed a printout in front of her.

'What's this?'

'This is one of the many pill bottles we found in Marianne Hughes's home. There were several placed around her home, in the bathroom, the bedroom, and most notably, the living room.'

Jess frowned. She didn't remember seeing any pills in the living room.

'Rather unfortunately for you, we found a partial print on one of the bottles.'

'Not of mine.'

'Of course it's yours.' Graham Dickson grinned, maliciously.

Jess remained silent.

He pushed another piece of paper towards her. 'Let me explain. When you came in to make your witness statement, you agreed to provide us with a set of fingerprints to rule you out of the crime scene. But instead, I'm afraid it's placed you right at the heart of it.'

Jess looked at the photo. 'But I didn't touch anything.'

'You just told me, you opened a cupboard and got out a glass. You used a dustpan and brush, you opened the bin to put the broken shards in,' Graham Dickson said. 'You cut your finger and left blood at the scene. I think we're long past the point where you can claim you didn't touch anything.'

'But I was wearing—'

'You can see for yourself the print on the pill bottle is a match,' Dickson said. 'My officers inform me that you showed a great deal of interest in how we are handling this case. That you wanted to know details.'

'I asked if they'd found Marianne's killer. She was my friend—'

Graham Dickson sucked at his teeth. 'I'm not stupid, Sinclair. I know you had a good look round that house before we arrived.'

'I didn't kill her. And I'll prove it.'

'You'll stay the hell away from this investigation, do you hear me?'

'But if forensics haven't—'

Graham Dickson leaned towards her, putting his mottled and pitted face close enough for her to feel his breath. 'Look, Miss Marple, I'll level with you. At the moment, things aren't looking great for you. We're still waiting on the post-mortem results, but early indicators are that it was a combination of pills and alcohol that rendered Marianne Hughes unconscious before the killer stabbed her to death. Your prints are on a bottle of antidepressants. Your blood is on a glass at the scene. We can't convict you on that alone, which is why we haven't arrested you yet. But I've got you at that crime scene. And I've got a motive. A nd if *that* doesn't put you in the frame for murder, I don't know what does.'

'I'M NOT THE ONE WHO WAS STALKING HER'

On Wednesday, she woke late again. The weather had turned cloudy and cool, and the press had disengaged yesterday; mercifully the forensics results hadn't been leaked and with no further story, or movement to or from the house, they disappeared. Jess knew better than to relax; they had already set her up as the guilty party, making her out to be the deranged ex-wife with an axe to grind. They'd be back again, she was sure, if they got so much as a whiff of the evidence mounting against her.

She dragged herself out of bed and downstairs to check her phone. Damon had sent another barrage of messages, saying she should PLEASE CALL HIM URGENTLY. Jess replied to the most recent, sent at quarter to one this morning, saying that she was busy writing a book and if he kept interrupting her, she'd never get it finished. She couldn't deal with him right now; she needed space to think – plus ready herself for Della starting work the next morning. There was a lot she needed to get done today, before she had someone else watching her every move.

She sat, scrolling her phone, her mind drifting back to Monday, at the police station. She hadn't been able to stop thinking about what Graham Dickson had said – that he'd got nearly enough to put her away. But Jess knew the evidence wasn't real. She'd been wearing gloves: there was no way her fingerprints could have been on a pill bottle, partial or otherwise. And she was sure there hadn't been any pills in the living room – she'd spent hours yesterday scouring the video she'd taken and hadn't spotted them. Which either meant Graham Dickson was framing her, or someone else was.

She flicked to the photos of the crime scene again, combing the frames to see if she'd missed anything. Not that she could present it as evidence – if the police discovered all this on her phone, they might change their minds very quickly about charging her. She should leave things alone and let them take care of finding the killer. But what if they didn't? Or what if she spotted something that they couldn't?

There had to be another way. A less *forensic* way. She couldn't get access to Marianne's phone or her laptop to see if there was anything on those, but she could ask the neighbour, Rosie, about the comings and goings on the street leading up to the day Marianne was killed. The older woman seemed like the sort of person who would keep an eye on the people going past her house.

'You're not asking her anything, you fool.' Jess shook her head to clear it and closed up her phone. What was she doing?

Yet another message from Damon came through.

'Stop messaging me!' she typed, stabbing at the phone screen. Hitting send, she was about to give up when something occurred to her. She might not be able to access Marianne's phone, but... she scrolled down her messages, pausing to look at the ones she'd sent to Marianne. She had no reason to keep them, but they were the last contact she'd had with her friend, and she couldn't bring herself to get rid of them, even if they'd gone unanswered.

She checked the 'last seen' timestamp and drew a breath. Flicking to her calendar she checked the dates to make sure she wasn't going mad. But there, plain as day, was the proof that she wasn't. Marianne's phone was 'last seen' on Wednesday, well after she died and well before her body was discovered. The little blue ticks by her message told her that someone had read them. But whoever it was, it couldn't have been Marianne. Jess's heart banged wildly. With shaking hands, she checked back at the photos she'd taken of the crime scene. The phone was plugged in and charging, placed out of the way of the blood flow. Jess would bet that it too, had been cleaned and tidied. The killer had been meticulous about clearing up after themselves, and in doing so, had removed their DNA from the scene as well as destroying the timeline of events. But maybe they hadn't banked on Jess noticing the slip.

Marianne was killed on Tuesday, but the 'last seen' timestamp told her the killer must have gone back the next day.

It was a huge risk to take, to return to the scene. What if someone had come to visit, not knowing she was dead already? Christ, Jess's own text message even suggested as much... She shuddered. Had they known she was coming? Was the whole thing a set up? Jess grunted and shook her head. Marianne had been dead a full day before she sent her final message. They couldn't have known she'd come to the house.

Still, someone had returned to the scene. It was true that paying another visit to Penny Hill Lane probably wasn't what Graham Dickson had in mind when he told her to stay away from Marianne's case. But Jess couldn't help herself; if the police were going to pin the murder on her, she had to do something, fast.

At the front door, Rosie eyed her suspiciously. 'You lied to me. You told me you were her friend. The police said—'

'It wasn't a lie. I was her friend.'

'It's false representation.'

'I want to help find who killed her.'

'That's the police's job.' Rosie pursed her lips and folded her arms. 'Do I need to call them to get rid of you?'

Jess held out her hands. 'No! No. I'll go.' She turned and walked down the path, then stopped and looked back at Rosie's front room window.

'What is it now?'

'You said you were always seeing her coming and going.'

'That's right.'

'You seemed to know her quite well.'

'I didn't say that.'

Jess raised an eyebrow. Rosie sighed.

'We used to have a chat over the fence once in a while.'

'You said you hadn't seen her since the day before she was killed. Monday. Is that right?'

'Mmm.'

'But you have a key to the house.'

'*Did* have it. It's in police custody now, remember?'

Jess paused. 'Rosie... Did you – did you let yourself in to Marianne's house, after she died?'

'Of course not! That key was only ever in case of emergencies, in case she locked herself out. Which she did, from time to time.'

Jess nodded. If Marianne was drinking heavily, there was no doubt Rosie would have been called on more than once.

'I wasn't the only one with a key, though.'

'What do you mean?'

Rosie stared for a beat, an ever so slightly smug smile appearing on her face. 'That copper had one.'

'Ben?'

She waved her hand. 'That the one you had the beef with? Yes, him. Seen him let himself in a bunch of times over the years, usually after she'd been on a bender.'

'He's always been very protective of her.' Jess felt a stab of jealousy and pushed it away. 'I didn't realise they'd stayed such close friends.'

Rosie snorted. 'If that's what you want to call it.'

Jess tensed her jaw. 'He's engaged to someone else. Having a baby.'

'I know. That's what the argument was about.'

'What do you mean?'

'He came the day she died.'

'But you said you hadn't seen Marianne since Monday.'

'I remembered wrong.' She paused. 'Sometimes that happens. Age, you know.' She nodded to herself. 'No, I definitely saw him on Tuesday morning, because it was free paper day and I was putting it in the recycling. He was prowling about outside like a bear with a sore head, but she'd gone out.'

'Do you know where?'

Rosie shook her head. 'I'm not the one who was stalking her,' she said pointedly.

'I wasn't stalking—'

'When she came back, they had a row, really ugly it was.'

'What about Wednesday, or Thursday? Did you see Ben then as well?'

Rosie frowned. 'She was already dead by then. Now you're getting your days confused.'

'Silly me.' Jess smiled encouragingly. 'Let's go back to the day she was killed. You said they were arguing about Naomi?'

'That new fiancée, the pregnant one. I heard Marianne calling her a bitch. And later, a slut. It was all rather ugly.'

'Rosie, why didn't you tell the police about this?'

'I told you. I forgot.'

Jess didn't believe her. The older lady didn't seem like the sort of person who forgot anything.

'He's one of them, isn't he?' Rosie cleared her throat, but Jess was pretty sure the way she had said the word 'them' was tinged with...distaste. 'They'd never have believed me if I said he'd been over here arguing with her the day she died; it would be my word against his and they'd assume I'm just some old biddy who didn't know what she was talking about.'

Jess sighed. Rosie was right. If Ben denied being at Marianne's that morning, Graham Dickson would have taken his word over Rosie's and written it off as the ramblings of a gossipy old lady who'd got her days mixed up.

'Is there anything else you remember about his visit?'

'Not really.'

'Did he see you? Does he know you were there?'

Rosie shrugged. 'I went back inside after I'd thrown away the paper. He looked very angry standing there, and I'll be honest, quite intimidating for such a good-looking man. I got on with cleaning the bathroom, although I could hear the shouting through the wall clear enough. I didn't see him leave.' She looked concerned. 'Do you think he's the killer?'

Jess shrugged hopelessly. 'He was the last person to see Maz alive. He has a door key, and he didn't tell anyone he'd been to see her.' Jess let Rosie fill in the blanks. 'You have to tell the police what you know. Without saying I said so,' she finished hastily. The last thing she needed was for Graham Dickson to know about her little visit today.

Rosie shook her head. 'I'm sure the information will find its way into the right hands,' she said, folding her arms. 'You do it. You can say an anonymous source tipped you off. I don't want to have to go through all this nonsense with the police again. I've got better things to do.'

Jess sighed. 'Fine. But if the police do pay you another visit, you never spoke to me about this, okay?'

'I'm not making any promises,' Rosie said, and shut the door. Jess waited a moment, wondering if the woman would drop her in it. She could be calling Graham Dickson right now; Jess wouldn't put it past her.

She hurried her way down Penny Hill Lane, keen to put some distance between her and the crime scene. What Rosie had said, rattled her. Could Ben have killed Marianne? He had an opportunity – and he could have easily gone back to the scene on Wednesday to clean up and then again on Thursday night when she had seen him, visiting the murder scene in front of witnesses to make sure his DNA was discounted. Maybe he'd stopped for a cuppa after he'd cleaned the place and that's why the back door was open... Jess thought about the insipid tea left on the patio outside and it jogged a memory of a near-identical mug of tea growing cold on Ben's coffee table when she'd been there. But surely, he wouldn't have been so careless? And in any case, what would be his motive? Was calling his fiancée a slut strong enough to push Ben over the line and commit actual murder? He'd looked so shocked when he saw Marianne's body and she found it difficult to believe he'd be capable, but then, as she knew from years as a journalist, stranger things could happen.

A man (tattoos, bearded, moody) passed her on the narrow part of the lane, walking with quick, sure-footed steps that belied his height and girth. She barely had time to dodge out of his way and would have taken a normal person to task over it, but she wasn't about to tackle this mountain of a man; he looked like he'd soon as pick her up and throw her into the allotments than move out of her way. Instead she stood, passive aggressively staring at his back as he walked. She assumed he was using the lane as a short cut to get to the level crossing beyond, but to her surprise he slowed down as he neared the halfway point. She couldn't tell precisely from where she was standing, but it looked like he'd stopped outside Marianne's cottage.

'Excuse me,' she called, taking a few steps back towards the house. 'Hello?'

The man-mountain glanced back at her briefly, put his hood up and moved on at a pace. Jess shrugged. Maybe the police incident tape wrapped over the front door had caught his attention. Still... she waited for him to turn right out of the lane and then followed him, half jogging to catch sight of him. At the top of the lane, she looked left and then right, to where the level crossing had its barriers down, waiting for the train. The man wasn't there, which meant he had to have turned right... she searched the busy pedestrian street for him but couldn't see where he had gone. Just as she was about to give up, the loud rumble of an engine disturbed the eerie peace of the level crossing. There he was, helmet shielding his face, but unmistakable thanks to the sheer size of him, sat astride the motorbike waiting for the train. Quickly and carefully, Jess snapped a photo of the number plate. She doubted this guy was in any way relevant, but at least she had something in case he was.

She walked back to her car, wondering what to do next. The most sensible thing would be to go back to Graham Dickson, confess she'd been back to the murder scene and tell him about the man lurking at Marianne's house, Ben's visit the day she died and their argument about Naomi. But what evidence did she have to offer him? Aside from being angry with Marianne for telling Ben his fiancée was a bitch (which Jess wholeheartedly agreed with), she couldn't prove Ben had done anything wrong. Making derogatory comments about his pregnant girlfriend probably wasn't enough to incite a police officer to murder – but even if it was, it wasn't wise to start accusing him of being a killer without cast iron evidence to prove it. And the man stopping at Marianne's house could be complete conjecture on her part. He could have simply been trying to get a better phone signal. She started the engine and pulled away. There was no way she could go to Graham Dickson with any of this. Not least, because he might use it all against her.

SINCLAIR INVESTIGATIONS
NEW CASE INFORMATION

Please fill out the form below with as much information as you can.
Note: Contents of this form are confidential and will not be shared with anyone outside of Sinclair Investigations without prior consent of the Client.

NAME: ~~MR~~/MRS/~~MISS~~ JOANNA LITTLEWOOD
ADDRESS: 24, HEMLOCK AVENUE, CLAPHAM, SW4 7FH
OCCUPATION: HOUSEWIFE

HOW CAN WE HELP? PLEASE GIVE AS MUCH INFORMATION AS YOU ARE ABLE, TO ASSIST US WITH OUR RESEARCH.

My husband, Paul, has never been perfect, but he's always provided for us. He works in insurance, runs his own business. It's his passion – says it always pays to be careful. And my husband is a careful man. That's why we've always had a roof over our head, food on the table and a nice holiday in the sun once or twice a year. We've never gone short, but we've never been what you'd call flush with money either. A few weeks ago, he came home with gifts for all of us: a PlayStation for the boys, a big TV for the sitting room, a nice pair of diamond earrings for me. When I asked, he said things were going well at work and we could afford to treat ourselves a bit.

But I don't understand where the money's coming from. Yes, he's running his own company, but it's never been big money, despite the long hours. I started to worry, I tried to look for bank statements but they're all online. Then my friend Caroline said she saw him in a pub one lunchtime, miles away from his office, with a woman. I was sure it was just a client, but Caroline said they looked... close. I mentioned it to him, and he went all quiet and told me to mind my own business. The next thing I know he's brought home an enormous diamond ring for me. I told him it was too much, but he kept going on about how much he loved me, as though it would somehow distract me from asking difficult questions. I might only be a housewife, but I'm not stupid. I know something is the matter, it's not like him to be secretive, we've always shared everything. I need to know where he's getting that money and why he's lying about it. And I want to know who that woman is.

'IT WOULD HAVE MELTED BEFORE SHE DIED'

Jess parked in a space on Ealing Common and cut the engine. It was a cool night, although pleasant; the sky was still light and the fresh green of summer trees swishing gently in the evening breeze made it feel more like Provence than Ealing.

'Just follow my lead,' she said, turning to Della. 'And remember, if you find yourself in a difficult situation, excuse yourself, go to the ladies and I'll meet you in there.' Jess had been embarrassed to admit she'd forgotten all about her new assistant starting in the excitement of her discovery and subsequent visit to Rosie yesterday. After the initial shock of finding her at the front door, they'd begun the case with a forensic examination of Paul Littlewood's publicly available information. In this instance, social media didn't seem like the place she would find the information she was looking for and they'd skipped over it in favour of running a search on the Companies House website.

'PJL Insurance Limited,' Della had murmured over tea and toast. Paul Littlewood's photo was clipped to the top of the case notes, and Della prodded at it with her finger. 'He has a business registered to his address. Not his home address, though,' she observed. 'Him and Joanna live in Clapham. But this address is Ealing.'

Jess nodded, pleased she'd picked up on the anomaly. 'It's why I always check with Companies House first, to see if there's any other place I might find people, before I start trying to follow them. I checked it out on Google Maps. It's a two-up two-down near the pub he was seen drinking in.'

And now here they were, right outside. The Cricketers Inn was one of those grand, old Victorian corner spots, sat opposite the grassy expanse of the common, and in lieu of her camera, Jess took a few photos on her phone as evidence of where they were before tucking it away. Propping her shades onto her head, she pulled her hair into a ponytail, ready for action.

'Okay?' she said to Della.

'Let's get this bastard,' Della replied.

Jess didn't expect to find Paul Littlewood in the pub – that would have been too good to be true – but it didn't hurt to try, or at the very least ask around and see if anyone knew him.

They got out of the car and walked slowly across to the pub, Jess going in first, while Della stood outside making a fake phone call. Jess ordered a white wine spritzer and went to sit in a corner, pulling a magazine out of her bag. A few minutes later, Della came in and pulled up a stool at the bar. The barman – possibly the landlord (bald, bristly, bags under the eyes) – was clearly not interested in stopping to chat, so Della sipped on her pint and checked her phone occasionally.

From her vantage point Jess could see most of the pub. It was a sea of empty tables, and she wondered if they'd have had better luck coming on a weekend. Tuesday evenings weren't notoriously busy for pubs, although she personally tended to like them much better when there was less likelihood of being asked for selfies or having to banter with drunken *I Know Where You Live* fans.

A man (stubble, suit, satchel) approached the bar. Jess bet he worked in the media, or real estate; she couldn't tell which, but probably the media. Estate agents didn't tend to carry man-bags, and she didn't remember seeing the estate agent-staple Mini Cooper parked nearby.

'Hi,' he said to Della, gesturing at the stool parked a few feet away from her. 'Do you mind?'

Della shrugged. Jess wondered if it was a pickup line; this bloke was about twenty-two, if a day, but Della was hardly unattractive, even for a woman fifteen years his senior. The man took a seat and ordered a pint and a shot.

'Bit early in the week for shots,' Della said, engaging him in conversation. Her accent had morphed north of the Watford Gap, landing somewhere around Sheffield, Jess guessed.

'That depends on what you've got to celebrate,' the man said.

'I take it you're celebrating then?'

'I've got a new job, as an account exec at an advertising company.'

Jess smiled to herself. She'd been right about the media type.

'Congratulations,' Della said, holding out her hand for him to shake. 'I'm Katy Slater, by the way.'

Jess cringed at the forced introduction. There was no way he'd reciprocate—

'Chris Littlewood,' replied the man. 'Nice to meet you, Katy.'

Jess's head shot up at the name and very briefly she caught Della's eye. Littlewood? It couldn't be a coincidence. But what possible relation could he be to Paul? When Joanna had spoken to her, she'd mentioned her children were still in their teens.

Della carried on the conversation. 'So are you celebrating with anyone or just drinking alone with only this old lady for company?' She gave a short laugh, and he joined in with a friendly 'ha'.

'You're not old,' he said. 'But no, I'm waiting for my mum and her friend to join us. And my dad, if he bothers to come.' There was an edge to his voice that suggested there was an unspoken tension between the man and his father.

'I'm sure he'll be made up,' Della said.

'Maybe.' Chris Littlewood gulped on his pint. 'It's Mum needs cheering up, anyway.'

'Oh?'

He shook his head. 'Oversharing. My dad says I should stop it.'

Della smiled. 'There's no harm in talking if there's a friendly ear to listen.'

Chris took another sip of his pint. 'We had a break-in a few months back. Dad said he got home from work and found the door wide open. He called the police, filed a report. Loads of stuff got taken, Mum was devastated. He didn't seem all that bothered, though. Says we can claim on insurance and get new.'

'Men don't always understand the emotion behind this sort of thing,' Della said. 'No offence.'

'None taken. I think Mum was most upset about the jewellery because of the sentimental value, you know? She didn't notice until ages afterwards.'

'That's horrible. What went missing?' Della asked.

'Mum's diamond earrings. And her engagement ring.'

Jess choked on her drink, sucking an ice cube into her windpipe by accident. She tried to cough but it was stuck whole and refused to budge. The noise of her gagging in panic must have caught Della's attention because suddenly she was at Jess's table and performing the Heimlich Manoeuvre. After three goes, the ice cube torpedoed from Jess's throat and across the pub, skittering to a halt in front of two women (one: wiry, tall, great hair; the other: blonde curls, skinny jeans, muffin top) who had walked into the bar at that moment. Paul Littlewood (short, thinning brown hair, check shirt) followed them in, oblivious, tapping something intense on his phone.

'Mum!' Chris said. 'You're here.'

'Of course I am,' said a woman who *definitely* wasn't Joanna Littlewood. Jess drew a sharp breath.

'Hello, Chris!' said the taller woman, obviously pleased to see him. 'Congratulations on the new job.'

'Thanks, Aunty Darcy,' Chris said.

'Sally, what do you want to drink? This round's on me.' The woman Chris referred to as Aunty Darcy addressed her friend.

'Don't be silly, he's my son. I'll get them.' Chris's mother, Sally, smiled politely at Della and Jess. 'Who are your friends?'

'Mum, this is Della. She just saved that woman's life.'

'Nonsense. It would have melted before she died,' Della said.

Jess smarted at the casual way Della dismissed her near-death experience and clutched her throat. Chris, keen to get the introductions over with, gestured towards Jess hopelessly.

'I'm sorry, I don't even know your name.'

Darcy stared back at Jess, open-mouthed. 'I do. You're Jessica Sinclair. The private investigator.'

'WHAT A NOB'

Jess smiled to hide the panic rising inside her. There was nowhere to hide. This woman had either seen her on the show or worse, seen her on the news.

'Yes, you're right. It's me. Hi.' She gave a small wave.

Darcy's gaze took her in. 'You're on a job,' she said, bluntly.

'No, no... I'm in here for a drink.'

'No, you're not. You don't live around here, and I've never seen you wear your hair like that before. I had to check twice to make sure it was you.'

'It could be because she doesn't want to draw attention,' Della said. 'She's been all over the news because of that murdered woman in Barnes.' Jess cringed and shut her eyes. Della was trying to be helpful, but letting the whole pub know she was being accused of murder perhaps wasn't the best course of action.

Darcy strode towards Jess and then nodded towards Della. 'Are you working with her?'

'Shit. I did think she was asking me a lot of questions,' Chris piped up.

'What did I tell you about oversharing, Chris?' Paul Littlewood was still tapping away on his phone as he spoke but stopped and turned back towards the door. 'Just got to take a call,' he mumbled. 'Back in a mo.'

Darcy turned to face Jess. 'Is it Paul you're investigating?' she whispered.

'Darcy, what on earth are you talking about? Have you gone mad?' Sally's face was screwed up in astonishment.

Darcy pointed at Jess. 'This woman investigates extra-marital affairs. Clearly, Chris isn't the target, which leaves Hamish, and I can hardly imagine *he's* the object of anyone's desire—'

'Oi,' the barman said. 'I can hear you, you know.'

'—and there's no one else worth investigating in here. Except us,' she said. 'And I know my ex-husband couldn't give a hoot about me. Which only leaves you and your dear husband.' She jerked her head towards Paul, who was pacing about outside, barking into the phone. She turned to Sally. 'Did you hire these women to spy on Paul?'

'I've never met them before in my life,' Sally said, her lips set tightly into her face. 'Darcy, you've got to stop projecting your own problems onto everyone else. Paul and I are fine, I don't need a private detective to tell me that.'

Darcy set her mouth in a grim line. 'I am not projecting my problems onto you, Sally. But the facts speak for themselves. Jessica Sinclair is not just here to drink a white wine.'

It was like watching a skinny, well-heeled Hercule Poirot. Jess sighed inwardly.

'Darcy, I absolutely refuse to sit and listen to any more of this nonsense.' Sally hoisted her handbag over her shoulder.

'Wait!' Jess had a horrible feeling she knew *exactly* what Paul Littlewood had been doing, and she wasn't looking forward to breaking the news to either Sally or Joanna. She took a deep breath and stood up. 'Darcy's right. There's something you should know.'

Sally turned to stare at her. Chris went pale. Darcy folded her arms, looking smug.

'Paul's wife *did* hire me.'

'What are you talking about? *I'm* his wife, and I've never met you!'

Jess took a step towards her. 'His other wife,' she said, gently.

'Holy shit,' Della said.

'Holy shit,' Darcy echoed.

'Fuuuuck.' Chris sat heavily on his stool.

'Shots, everyone?' The barman lined up some glasses and began to pour.

'Paul... is a *bigamist*?' Darcy's lip curled up in distaste. 'He's a cheating, lying *bigamist*?'

'Darcy, calm down—'

'He's your husband! Why aren't you as angry as I am?'

'I'm sure there's a perfectly reasonable explanation. Or am I supposed to take the word of this total stranger?'

'Yes!' Darcy's fists were clenched so hard the knuckles had turned white. 'She's Jessica Sinclair! She does this for a living.' Darcy looked at Jess. 'What do you know?'

Jess swallowed hard and used the voice she normally reserved for interviewing traumatised guests on the show. 'Sally, your husband Paul is married to Joanna. They live in Clapham and have two teenage sons.' She paused. 'I know you had a break-in recently. You should be aware... Joanna and her family recently got given gifts by Paul. A PlayStation, a television, diamond earrings ... and a new diamond ring.'

Sally's face froze. It was difficult to tell which way she was going to go with this information.

'I'm really sorry,' Jess said. 'I'm going to have to inform his wife – his other wife – this evening. And the police too. What he's done is illegal, and there's the robbery and insurance fraud on top that could land him in a lot of trouble.'

'Dad could go to prison?' Chris sounded like all the wind had been knocked out of him.

Jess nodded. 'Up to seven years for bigamy.'

'Christ.' Della shook her head. 'What a nob.'

Jess was going to have to reign in Della's commentary. It was unprofessional to give your opinion on the scale of dickheadedness a person had achieved, particularly if you needed to appear in court as a witness.

'*What* a nob,' Darcy echoed again, just as Paul Littlewood walked back into the bar.

'What did I miss?' he said. 'Hello, son. Well done on the job—'

In a heartbeat, Darcy strode towards him and punched him, hard, in the face. Paul Littlewood staggered backwards, tripping over a bar stool and landing on the sticky pub floor.

'Darcy!' Sally ran towards Paul.

'What the fu—?' Paul's nose was bloody, and he reached up to wipe it, leaving a red smear on his face.

'You utter, utter bastard. I thought Andy was bad, running off with his secretary, but *you*. You're despicable.'

'Darcy, please, don't.' Sally looked up at her, pleading.

'How can you even think about defending him?' Darcy said. 'I'd kill him.' She looked at Jess. 'Do you do that too?'

'No,' Jess said, firmly.

Hamish slammed a fist down on the bar. 'Out!' he shouted, his gravelly voice powerful enough to stop everyone. 'You and her—' he pointed to Della and Jess '—get out of here. You've caused enough trouble here tonight. And you,' he said to Darcy, 'you're barred. Get your bag and go.'

'But—'

'I said, get out of my pub!' Hamish roared.

There was no arguing with Hamish. Darcy picked up her bag. 'I'm sorry, Sally,' she said. Sally didn't look up from where she sat clutched to Paul, shellshocked and angry but holding onto him for dear life. Darcy turned away, hurt. She put a hand on Chris's arm as she left. 'Call me, if you need to talk,' she said. 'I'm always here for you. And your mum, when she's ready.'

Jess collected her rucksack and motioned to Della. The two of them trotted out of the pub after Darcy.

'I'm sorry you got caught up in all that,' Jess said, out of breath trying to catch her.

Darcy stopped and turned, her blonde blow dry bouncing to a halt a few moments after. 'It's okay. It's a shame it wasn't my ex-husband I punched, but I'll make do.' She paused, her pretty face crumpled for a moment, before it cleared into a smile. 'Sorry, we were never formally introduced. Darcy Campbell. Huge fan.' She stuck her arm out. Jess was so surprised at the forthright introduction she gripped the woman's hand and shook it.

'Jessica Sinclair. Jess.'

'Formerly of *I Know Where You Live*; latterly of Sinclair Investigations.'

Jess frowned. 'Gosh, you really are a fan.'

Darcy shook her head. 'Oh god, that sounds so stalkerish. I mean, I was – I am – not a stalker – a fan, I mean – I watched your show all the time, but I didn't know you were running your own agency until they said it on the news a few days back.'

Jess gave a polite smile and Darcy took her voice down to a whisper.

'Did you do it? Did you kill her?'

Jess drew in a breath. 'Excuse me?'

Darcy's eyes widened. 'Sorry, I shouldn't have asked that.' She paused, then laughed. 'I mean, *obviously* you'd tell a total stranger, though, right?'

Della folded her arms. '*Obviously* she'd have to kill you too, if she did.'

Darcy's laughter dwindled.

'Darcy, this is Della, my assistant.'

'Hi, Della.' Darcy flicked her a smile. 'Thanks for everything you did in there.'

Della nodded.

Jess checked her watch. 'I need to call in and report to our client. I'm sure she will want to file charges. Nice to meet you, Darcy.'

Darcy tapped a French manicured finger against her lips in thought and then shook her head. 'No. It's a stupid question,' she said.

Jess raised an eyebrow in enquiry.

'I'm looking for something to do,' Darcy said. 'I'm getting a divorce and I need something to fill my days to stop me from sending angry emails to my solicitor, or worse, my cheating bastard of an ex-husband.' She flushed. 'Or punching people in pubs.'

'Ah—'

'I caught him red-handed, you know. Found a photo on his phone, of his personal assistant spreadeagled on a bed in nothing but a red lacy bra and a very nice Brazilian wax.'

'I'm sorry,' Jess said.

'He said it was nothing serious, but I'm not sure if that's better or worse. They carried on seeing each other anyway, and a matter of months later they're all over social media, labelling each other with affectionate pet names that frankly make me want to barf. And the kids *love* her. Keep telling me how fun she is and how Daddy's chilled out since they got together. As if I need to hear any of that.' She smiled serenely. 'Anyway, it's a bit of a stretch, but god, I loved your show...' She took a deep breath. 'I don't have much in the way of work experience; but I'd work hard for you and all that snooping about I did to catch my husband —' she lowers her voice, '—and on the kids, online and all that – you have to keep your wits about you with teenagers these days... well, I think I'd make a good investigator, with a bit of training.'

Della cleared her throat heavily. Jess took the hint. 'The thing is, I already have—'

'I thought about trying to date, you know, to get my mind off things. But I'm not ready for that. I need to do something for myself – get a job, have a career, even.' She paused. 'Please?'

Jess looked across to Della for a cue and got a huge eye roll for her troubles. But while Jess knew Della wouldn't be thrilled to relinquish the kudos of being her only assistant, she had to consider Darcy's pitch. The woman had skills and could come in handy for some of the jobs where Della's cavalier attitude might land them in deep water. Plus, with the two women out in the field, she would be free and clear to investigate Marianne's murder, figure out who sent the death threats, and write Damon's god-damn book. But how would she ever afford another trainee? And what made her think she could even train them to be any good?

Darcy took her hesitation as a sign that she should pile on more reasons to hire her.

'Look, I just want to make sure other women like me don't suffer. He gave me chlamydia, you know.' She went quiet, and Jess saw a flicker of emotion in her eyes betraying her otherwise confident exterior.

'It's not that I don't think you'd make a good P.I.,' she said carefully. 'Only, I can't afford – I mean, things are tight, at the moment.' That was an understatement.

'I don't need the money. Think of me as a volunteer – an intern. You'd be doing me a favour, honestly.' She looked at Della. 'I promise, I won't steal your job. I'll create my own. Maybe do some business development for you. I know so many people with marital issues, it can't be that hard.'

Della tipped her head to either side slowly, deliberating. 'Might be good to have three of us,' she said. 'You got a lot on your plate at the moment. Darcy and I can learn on the job together, we've got each other's backs that way. We can both help get the clients in. She can offer to spy on her rich mates and their husbands, and I can deliver flyers when I'm on my fish rounds, and try and drum up a bit of business that way.'

Jess looked at the pair of them. They might make a good team: Della with her devil-may-care attitude and Darcy's acerbic wit and solid right hook. She shrugged. If it wasn't going to cost her anything – and of course, as soon as she could, she'd pay both of them, no matter what Darcy said – then what was the harm?

She stuck out her arm. 'Welcome to Sinclair Investigations'

Darcy's mouth fell open. 'Really?'

Jess smiled. 'If you want it.'

'Oh my goodness, thank you!' Darcy flew at her, causing Jess to step back involuntarily into the street. A car drove by and leaned on its horn, loudly.

She pulled away from Darcy. 'Give me your number and I'll message you with my address. Come about nine tomorrow.'

'Sounds amazing! Oh – what shall I wear?'

'Something comfortable, that you can move in,' Jess said, turning to leave with Della in tow.

'Something that won't make me look like the dumpy one,' Della murmured.

'You're gorgeous and you know it, Della.' Darcy blew a kiss before checking both ways to cross the street. 'Thank you, Jessica. You won't regret it, I promise.'

As she and Della walked to the car, Jess considered Darcy's parting words. She wasn't entirely sure she wouldn't regret every last decision she'd made in the past week. Was she being foolish to think that taking on two women with no prior experience and a litany of potential shortcomings could save her from financial ruin, death threats and quite possibly, a murder charge? There was only one way to find out.

'WHAT DO YOU EAT WHEN I'M NOT HERE, THE FURNITURE?'

The next morning, Della was at the door bang on nine o'clock; Jess watched her from upstairs, and saw, to her dismay, that a bunch of reporters were back.

As soon as she opened the door, they began shouting.

'Morning, Jessica!'

'Jessica, tell us how you're doing today!'

'Jessica, how did your DNA get on the pill bottle?'

'Are you the Penny Hill killer?'

'Why did you have broken glass in your hair?'

The *Penny Hill Killer?* That was a new one. Clearly the forensic report had been leaked. Jess closed her eyes with heavy resignation; it was only ever going to be a matter of time. She ushered Della into the house and was about to close the door when she saw Dev chatting to one of the photographers. She narrowed her eyes. What was he doing, hobnobbing with the pack? Was he one of them? Or maybe he was the one who'd tipped them off... she thought back, trying to remember when she'd last seen him. He'd been lurking about the day the police came to take her to the station; in fact, it seemed like he was always around lately. But how would he know about her and Marianne, or the contents of the forensic report? She shook her head and ushered Della into the house. As she was about to close the door, she caught Dev's eye. He stared at her with a grim fascination, his attention gone from the photographer and his gaze laser-focused, drilling into her with chilling intensity. Jess felt herself grow uneasy. Did she know Dev, from somewhere else? Was he doing more than tipping off the press?

'Pull yourself together, Jess,' she said to herself, and swung the door shut with a slam. Della was waiting in the living room.

'You okay, boss?'

'I'm sick of them. It's frustrating, not being able to come and go without being hassled, and they're getting information they shouldn't that's making things worse. And now there's Dev—' She stopped short, reminding herself that Della was her employee, not her friend. 'I'll be fine. Thank you for asking though.'

Della eyed her up doubtfully. 'Tell you what, I'll make us a cuppa,' she said and left the room.

'I told you, I'm fine—'

Jess heard the crashing and banging of cupboards in her kitchen as Della searched for mugs, teabags and a spoon. A few minutes later, she came back bearing two mugs of steaming tea, on a tray which Jess had only a faint recollection of possessing, along with a jug of milk, sugar and a pack of Jammie Dodgers.

'Bought the biscuits with me in case I got hungry,' Della grinned and placed the tray on the coffee table, gesturing to Jess to help herself. 'Lucky I did. What do you eat when I'm not here, the furniture?' She took a seat opposite Jess and picked up her tea, lumping two spoons of sugar in and stirring noisily. Job done, she slurped and sighed with satisfaction.

'So, what are we doing today, then?' she said. 'Are we going on a job?'

'Not today.' Jess glanced at the window. 'We need to wait for Darcy.'

Della laughed. 'She's a crazy bitch, that one.'

'Do you think I made the wrong decision?' Jess asked, feeling anxious.

Della shook her head. 'Not at all. She needed to get out of the house, and I get the feeling you could do with another pair of hands.' She waved towards the window. 'Let's see what she makes of this lot when she gets here. You never know, she might karate-kick them all to the curb for you.'

The doorbell chimed. Jess set her tea down and went to answer the door to an angry-looking Darcy.

'When you see this sort of thing on the television, you don't stop to think about it being real,' she said, turning and giving the press pack a hard stare. Someone wolf whistled.

'Oh for goodness' sake,' she said, flicking her hair and stalking down the path back towards the press.

'Darcy, wait—'

'Look, you lot. This woman has done nothing wrong. *Nothing.* You should go.'

'Who are you, her lawyer?' someone piped up.

Jess craned to see if she could see who it was who'd asked, but the voice was coming from the middle of the pack. She scoured the faces, realising she had the opportunity to take a good look at them all while Darcy was distracting them. She took each journalist in, one by one. Not a single one of them was looking her way. They only had eyes for Darcy.

It was hardly surprising. Tall and slim, her legs were wrapped in those patterned leggings that pretended to be for yoga but were really for showing off what amazing legs you still had at fifty. A royal blue bandana held her lustrous hair back and her ringless fingers were freshly manicured with pale baby pink varnish. She put her hands on her hips.

'I'm not a solicitor. As a matter of fact, I work for Jessica. In her P.I. agency.'

There was a barrage of questions.

'Where were you at the time of the murder?'

'What do you know about Marianne Hughes?'

'What's it like working for a cold-blooded killer?'

'Are you worried you'll be next?'

Darcy raised her chin a little higher and pointed a finger at them. 'You are all crazy,' she said, 'if you think this woman could harm anyone like that. She's spent years righting the wrongs of some of the most despicable people, seeking out justice for their victims.'

'Maybe she's taken the justice thing a little too far,' a journo said. 'Got a little angry with someone for something...'

'What on earth would Jessica Sinclair have against Marianne Hughes?' Darcy barked.

'That's a good question.' The journo gave them a wry smile. 'Jessica? Care to tell your friend what we know?'

'Darcy,' Jess croaked, 'will you please get inside?'

Darcy retreated up the steps to the front door and stepped inside the hallway. 'It's intense out there,' she said. 'What a bunch of bastards. How much longer do you think they'll stay? It doesn't seem like they're going away any time soon.'

Jess thought about the reporters. She couldn't have them digging too deeply into her relationship with Marianne, or anyone else for that matter; and whoever their 'source' was, feeding them information, needed to be careful too. The Metropolitan Police didn't take kindly to people revealing the identities of their undercover officers, even former ones, and thanks to this latest leak, if they had a mind to, the press wouldn't have to look too hard to find out about Ben and how he fit into the equation. If they printed his photo – which they would, if they made the connection – there'd be every chance his life would be at risk too.

'Just ignore them if they're there again tomorrow,' Jess said, firmly. 'Don't engage. They'll twist anything you say to make it fit their story.'

'That's easier said than done. Someone has to set the record straight. You're not a killer, Jess. Why would they want to make out you are?'

'It's complicated,' she said, thinking of Graham Dickson and the false evidence against her.

She showed Darcy into the front room. Della was busy dunking a Jammie Dodger into her tea, but on seeing them, shoved it whole into her mouth. She was the opposite of Darcy in every way, resplendent in cargo pants and a tight Nike running top that stretched across her breasts and made the swoosh so long that Jess could probably ski down it. Surprisingly delicate tattoos spiralled around her wrists and up her forearms, with the names of her children stencilled into the patterns, and when she smiled, her bright white veneers threatened to make them all snow blind.

'I was thinking,' Della said, through a mouthful of crumbs. 'That we need a new name.'

'Good morning to you too, Della.'

'Oh, hi Darce. So, what do you think?'

'Hmm?' Jess was checking the curtains were closed tight against the photographers.

'Our name. We've got to have a name. Sinclair Investigations is boring.'

'I hadn't thought about it, to be honest.'

Della wagged her finger. 'It's gotta be called something catchy. What about "Something Fishy" if we're using the van? Or "Hook, Line and Sinker"?

Jess wasn't sure she wanted to change the name. She liked Sinclair Investigations; it was unassuming and did what it said on the tin. But she didn't want Della to think she was an arsehole. 'I'll think on it, okay?'

Della shrugged. 'If you say so. You're the boss.'

Della was right. She was the boss, and she needed to act like it. 'So,' she said, in a decisive tone. 'Thank you both for braving the press pack.' She was surprised to find she was nervous, her heart banging in her chest as though it were her first day on live television. It had been a long time since she'd worked with anyone and she didn't want to mess it up. She liked both these women a lot, and badly wanted them to like her too. She took a deep breath and gave them her warmest smile.

'Let's get started.'

'FOR THE RECORD, THERE WILL BE NO AVENGING ANYONE'

They worked the whole morning, Jess going through the outstanding enquiries, Darcy offering potential clients meeting slots in the diary, and Della updating the website and designing some flyers. Jess felt a great burden lifting from her. Now she wasn't worried about manpower – or womanpower, even – she could line up a couple of jobs a week, maybe more if Della and Darcy had the capacity. With Darcy going through her old messages, Jess realised how much work she'd been losing. By lunchtime, she felt happy for the first time in ages, and when Della suggested they go for a quick drink to celebrate, it didn't take much for her to be persuaded. Joanna Littlewood had given them a bonus for not only capturing her duplicitous husband in the act but knocking him to the floor as well, and Jess suggested they escape in her car and treat themselves to a glass of wine.

They sat in a booth at the rear, well hidden from the view of any passing cameras.

'Here's to a successful first day!'

Della, Darcy and Jess clinked their glasses. Jess hadn't intended on getting a bottle, given she was driving, but Della had ordered it and she felt it would have been churlish to refuse. She sipped at the dry white wine before placing it back on the table.

'So, how many children do you have, Darcy?' Jess said.

She nodded. 'Two. Daughters, fourteen and sixteen. They hate me most of the time.'

'I hear you,' Della said. 'Misha is seventeen going on twenty-five and still being a pain in the arse. Anyone want some chips? I'll order some.'

'In fairness, they've been through a lot. The divorce... it's not been easy.'

'How did you find out about the affair?' Jess asked.

'My husband told me he'd joined an amdram society.' Darcy sounded like she'd swallowed a glass of lemon juice. 'He said he was going from work to rehearsals twice a week. It's how I caught him, in the end: I went to see the show at the local theatre to surprise him and he wasn't in it. And when I asked, no one had ever heard of him.'

'What did you do?'

Darcy twirled her wine glass, her voice half-pride, half-shame. 'Followed him to a dodgy two-star hotel round the corner from his office. Sat in the lobby until they came down from the room. Took photos of them getting off with each other by the lift.'

'Didn't they notice you?' Della looked astounded.

'Never even looked my way.'

Jess could see that this was what hurt Darcy the most.

'Men don't look at you the same when you get older,' Darcy said.

Della shook her head. 'Wankers, the lot of 'em.'

Darcy laughed. 'Della, you don't know the meaning of the words. You're what – thirty-five?'

'Thirty-eight,' Della replied. 'But that don't mean much. My boyfriend – the one that got me pregnant with Misha – he scarpered when she was two months old. Just got up one day, said, "I can't do this," and left.'

'That's terrible,' Darcy gasped.

'That's not the worst of it. Bastard came back a few years later, wanting to be part of Misha's life and all that bollocks, and stupid me, I let him. We got back together, I got pregnant again. Same thing happens, except this time he leaves me before I've even had the baby.'

'You were still pregnant?'

Della nodded. 'Seven months. With *twins.* He said my arse was getting too big and he didn't like fat girls. He went off with some skinny cow from the estate. Left me with three kids under five to look after.' She shook her head. 'I was twenty-four.'

'Does he ever see the kids?'

Della shook her head. 'Not really. Aaron, my ex who I had Sammy with, is the one that brought them up.'

'What happened to him?'

She shrugged. 'We drifted apart. It was amicable.' She looked at Jess, narrowing her eyes. 'So, what about you?'

'I'm divorced,' Jess replied.

'What happened?' Della asked.

Jess hesitated. 'Marianne Hughes was my best friend, we met at university.' She took a deep breath. 'She slept with Ben – my husband. Ex-husband.'

Della whistled. 'Your fella was a bit of a wanker, then.'

'No. Not really. I mean, yes... but... it's complicated.'

'It always is, with men.' Della gave a bitter laugh and Jess shook her head.

'I'd actually gone over to her house to apologise.'

'Apologise?' Darcy's face coloured and her nostrils flared, like a horse about to rear up. 'You've got nothing to be sorry for.'

'Actually, I do. I was really out of order after I found out about their affair. Our marriage was basically over anyway,' she said, glossing over the details. 'They made a mistake, a heat of the moment decision that cost all of us, and I put the blame on Marianne, which was stupid. I wasn't nice to her. She quit her job because of me; she was an undercover police officer and a good one too.'

'That's very generous of you,' sniffed Darcy. 'I'm not sure I'll be as forgiving of Nancy.'

'Nancy?'

'My husband's lover, or whatever she wants to call herself.'

'You might feel differently in time, Darcy. It was ages ago now, for me – a whole decade's gone by since then.'

Darcy sipped her drink. 'Was she dead when you found her?'

Jess nodded.

'I've never seen a dead body before,' Della said, chomping on the stale nuts sitting in a pot in the middle of the table.

'Me neither,' Jess said.

'Not on your show?' Della said, incredulous.

'We never covered anything as heavy as that,' Jess said. 'It was all affairs and fraudsters and the occasional missing person.'

'What was it like, being on telly?' Della said. 'I thought you'd be loaded, but it doesn't look like it. No offence.'

'None taken,' Jess lied, smarting at the comment. She shrugged. 'It's complicated. I got sued for breach of contract, and it's been harder than I thought to get the P.I. business going. I can't make a move without being asked for a selfie, or an autograph.'

'I bet you're always going to parties. That's what I'd like about being famous. All the parties, meeting people you see in the magazines. And the clothes. Do you get free clothes? I always thought that would be the best thing, getting all that free stuff.'

'Yeah, well, free clothes don't pay the mortgage,' Jess said, bitterly. She paused for a moment, deciding whether or not to trust them with more information. 'The night I found her... Ben was there too, at the cottage.'

Darcy sat up straight. 'Your ex? Why? *Clearly* he—'

Jess cut her off. 'He's a detective inspector. He responded to the radio callout. I had a feeling he would, if he heard the address, but I wasn't really prepared for it.'

Della's eyes widened. 'Were they still together?'

'I don't know. Maybe. He has a fiancée, but...' She thought about what Rosie had told her. 'They were work partners... friends... it was complicated.'

The three women sat silently for a moment before Della spoke again.

'So you're in the frame, because of what happened with you and her and Ben,' Della said. 'And because you were at the crime scene.'

Jess nodded. She might as well tell them everything now. 'The police say they found my fingerprints on a bottle of pills, but I was wearing gloves.'

'You think someone planted it?' Darcy looked shocked.

Jess shrugged. 'It's the only explanation.'

Della set her empty glass down. 'We need to find out who did this. We need to open our own investigation and figure out who really killed her.'

'I've already started,' Jess said. 'But I haven't got very far. I do know that she and Ben argued the same day she died. The neighbour told me.'

'So it could be him,' said Darcy. 'Typical man, blaming everyone else for something he did.'

'Anyone else?' Della said. 'What about his fiancée?'

'Naomi?' Jess said. The thought hadn't occurred to her before now. 'It's possible. They were arguing about her. But she's pregnant. I don't think—'

'Motive,' Della said, firmly. 'Put her on the list.'

'And the police,' Darcy said, pointing at Jess. 'What's the name of the officer who produced the fingerprint on that pill bottle?'

'DCI Dickson,' Jess said. 'But there's no way we can take on the police—'

Della gasped in delight, making Jess and Darcy jump. 'Oooo...you're a celebrity who needs to clear their name and avenge their best friend. It's like something off of the telly. *For real.*'

'For the record, there will be no avenging anyone,' Jess said. 'I've already got a stalker sending me death threats as it is.'

'Death threats?' Darcy said, looking alarmed. 'Are we in danger?'

Jess shook her head. 'It's personal. Probably a hoax.'

Della huffed air out of her nostrils. 'It didn't read like a hoax to me.'

'It doesn't matter about the letters. If the police find out we're poking our noses into a murder investigation I'm being framed for, and it turns out they're the ones framing me, I'm as dead as Marianne anyway.'

'Then we'll start with Ben and Naomi,' Della said. 'He could be the one who's framed you. It all adds up. He knows Marianne, he was at the crime scene, he could have planted the evidence.'

Jess shivered. 'Maybe,' she said. 'But I can't see that Ben would do that to Marianne in the first place. He's a good man – or at least, he was...' she trailed off.

'Right up until the moment he nobbed someone else while you were married to him,' Della said.

And pregnant, Jess thought briefly, before pushing the memory away. She opened her mouth to protest, but Della and Darcy were right: Ben was hiding something, although she couldn't imagine him killing Marianne. 'I think Naomi's the more likely candidate,' Jess told the two women. 'She seemed like the sort of person who'd be capable of stabbing someone if the mood took her.' She didn't mention the bit where she'd barged into the woman's home uninvited.

'Maybe Marianne knew something about Naomi, and she killed her to shut her up,' Della said.

'Or maybe Marianne still had feelings for Ben and couldn't bear him being with someone else?' Darcy countered, her eyes flashing. 'Maybe—'

'Jessica Sinclair!'

Jess swung round and a flash went off in her face.

'There's me thinking I had nothing to take back to the boss tonight, and then here you are.' A reporter from outside the house (ruddy face, beer gut, leather jacket) was looking like all his Christmases had come at once. He whipped out his phone and started recording. 'You never answered my questions before, but maybe we can do this the civilised way, over a drink.'

'I don't want a drink with you, and I have no comment.' Jess put her hand up. She could feel herself getting angry.

'Who are these lovely ladies you're with today?' The reporter gestured to Della and Darcy. 'I saw them at your house, but we never got introduced.'

'Della Williams,' Della said. 'And this is Darcy Campbell. We're trainee investigators with Kiss Me Quick Investigations. It's a working title,' Della said, casting a hasty glance at Jess.

Jess raised an eyebrow.

The reporter turned to Darcy. 'What do you know about Jessica's relationship with the deceased, Marianne Hughes?'

'I—'

'She has no comment,' Jess said, her tone clipped.

'Is Jessica still assisting the police with their enquiries?'

'It's none of your—'

'She has no comment.'

'Why did the police visit Jessica's house?'

Jess growled. The reporter turned to her. 'Your DNA and fingerprints were recovered from the scene.' He looked back at Della. 'Are you concerned for your safety? How do you feel about working alongside a potential murderer?'

'I said *no comment*!' Seeing red, Jess flew at the reporter suddenly, pushing him and knocking him over.

'Jess!' Darcy jumped out of the booth and stood watching with her hands over her mouth as the reporter's camera landed with a dull thud, followed by his phone. While he reached for his camera to assess the damage, Jess picked up his phone and dropped it into the large water jug sat on the table. Darcy gasped. Della chuckled.

The reporter pulled himself to a standing position. 'What the hell—'

'You think that by harassing me I'm going to give you what you want? You think that it's okay for you to vilify me, make my life a misery? All I want now is to be left alone. Leave me alone! God, I can't believe I used to be one of you.'

The reporter leant over and lifted his phone out of the water jug, shaking his head. 'Quite a temper you've got there, Jessica. That's destruction of property.'

'What it is,' scowled Jess, 'is me telling you to back off. And you can tell all your scumbag mates the same. Here's your statement for the press: I didn't kill Marianne. But I'd give anything to know who did. Whatever the nature of our relationship, she didn't deserve to die. So I'm going to make it my mission to find out. Is *that* good enough for your boss?'

Jess stormed out of the bar, shaking, leaving Della and Darcy behind. Driving home and recklessly dumping her car in the street, she stalked past the press pack and stared up at the place she called home. It wasn't a castle, but it was hers, and Sinclair Investigations was hers and she'd be damned if she was going to lose either because the police had made her 'a person of interest' and the press were determined to vilify her. It was time to have a chat with Graham Dickson and set him right about a few things.

As it happened, Graham Dickson agreed. Shortly after she got home, the uniforms turned up again and arrested her for assault.

'MIND YOURSELF, LADS, SHE'S GOT A TEMPER'

'Please tell me why I shouldn't charge you right here and now,' Graham Dickson barked, coming into the interview room she was currently being held in. 'I thought I was clear that you needed to stay out of trouble.'

'I can't help it if the press won't leave me alone,' Jess said. 'If you'd just tell them I'm no longer a person of interest then they'd move on and find someone else to pick on.' She stared him down, defiantly. The man could be such a prick.

'Neil!'

Uniform One popped his head around the door. 'DCI Dickson?'

'Did that journo make his statement yet?'

'Yes, sir.'

'Bring it in here, for god's sake!'

'Sir.' Uniform One skidded out of the room and reappeared some minutes later with a file in his hand. Graham Dickson opened it and read with what Jess could only guess was deliberate slowness.

'Destruction of property and common assault.' He closed it up. 'Give me one good reason not to speak to the judge and get you the maximum community service time and a whacking great fine.'

She couldn't afford a fine. She couldn't afford the criminal record. She momentarily closed her eyes to calm down. Reopening them, she made an attempt at looking contrite. 'I'm sorry, I really am. He was harassing me, in a public place, after I'd said "no comment" a million times. They won't leave me alone,' Jess said. 'All I want is to get on with my life.'

'Was that what you were thinking when you stuck the knife in Marianne Hughes?'

'You and I both know I didn't kill her,' Jess snapped. 'Like I said to Ben at the crime scene, if I'd wanted to kill Marianne, I'd have done it years ago. I was there to make amends. And those fingerprints – they couldn't have been mine. I'm being framed, can't you see that?'

'The problem I have, Jessica, is that you keep showing up like a bad smell. First at my crime scene, then uninvited to an officer's house, then here, under arrest, because you couldn't keep your temper in check. There's no one who can vouch for your whereabouts the night Marianne was killed. You and she have bad blood between you. You left evidence at the scene. You can see how all this might look to even the most casual observer.'

'But I didn't kill her.'

'You keep saying that. But carry on like this and you'll make it impossible for me not to charge you anyway.'

The door to the interrogation room swung open.

'DI Morgan. What can I do for you?'

Ben nodded at Jess. 'Are you charging her?'

Graham Dickson shook his head. 'I'm not going to give that scumbag reporter the satisfaction.'

'Can I have a word with her then?' Ben said. 'Alone?'

They all knew a formal interview between ex-spouses would be considered inadmissible and a huge violation, but Jess knew she'd pissed Graham Dickson off enough that he'd give Ben the all clear for a quick chat. He picked up his files and handed them to Ben. 'She's all yours.'

Ben sat down opposite her and gave her a hard stare. Jess swallowed. He wouldn't dare touch her in a police station, of all places. There must be cameras everywhere—

'What did you do to her, Jess? I want the truth.'

Her eyes widened – of all the nerve. 'You have got to be kidding?'

'Then why are you all over that crime scene?'

'I'm not.'

'Come on, Jess. You and I both know—'

Jess straightened in her seat and looked around. 'Are we being recorded?'

Ben shook his head.

'I wanted to know what happened,' she said, quietly.

'We all want to know what happened. But it's Dickson's job to work it out, not yours. You're lucky he hasn't found out about your little visit to the next-door neighbour, or he'd have you banged up already.'

'You know about that?' Jess felt all the blood drain from her.

'Of course I do,' he barked. 'You think she didn't report you for poking around and asking her questions? You're lucky I took the call.'

'She said she wouldn't say anything,' Jess said, defensively.

'Never rely on an old busybody. Rule number one of being a good detective.'

She leaned into him. 'It's you who should be worried. She told me you had a key. That you'd been over there and had an argument with Maz. That you were the last person to see her.'

Ben smiled. 'And you think I'm going to share all that with Dickson?' he said, sitting back in his chair. 'Why would I do that?'

'Because if you don't, I – I will,' Jess stammered.

Ben laughed. 'And you think Dickson will believe you? Or that Rosie will change her statement, so you come off as innocent?' He slammed his fist on the table. 'You should be thanking me that I haven't filed the report yet. If he finds out you're witness tampering, he'll get a warrant for your house and find something to bang you up for good. You'll need a bloody good solicitor to get you on the right side of the bars again, Jess.'

She gritted her teeth. 'You haven't explained to me why you lied. Why you haven't told anyone about being there, about the argument with Maz.'

He stood and pushed his chair away. 'That's the great thing about being a cop,' he said. 'I don't have to explain.'

Della was waiting for her outside the station.

'I parked around the corner in a loading bay,' she said.

'Thanks Della.'

They walked around to where the fish truck was parked. Darcy sat in the passenger seat and shuffled over to make space when she saw them approaching. 'They let you out then,' she sniffed, wrinkling up her nose. 'You smell awful.'

Jess gave her a rueful grin and slid in beside her. 'I'm sorry I flew off the handle like that.'

'I totally get it,' Della said, sliding in the driver side and starting up the truck. 'I wonder how those journos would like it if you hung outside their house for days giving you nothing but grief.'

'I used to be one of them,' Jess said. 'They're only doing their job, but they'll do literally anything for a scoop on a story. A has-been TV presenter being involved in a murder case is like feeding the Gremlins after midnight.'

'I hope they go away soon,' Darcy said. 'I don't want to end up on the news. It wouldn't look good to the judge, and god forbid Andy gets full custody of the girls.'

'Don't worry, Darcy. I think we've had enough run-ins with the media for now,' Jess said.

'So, what happened?' Darcy said. 'How come the police let you go?'

'They don't like the press any more than I do, I suppose.'

'That doesn't sound like a reason.'

'I know.' Jess looked out of the window at the passing rows of houses. There was something wrong that Jess couldn't put her finger on, about Graham Dickson's reluctance to charge her for assaulting that journo – or for murdering Marianne. She didn't want to be arrested for anything, but if he was so convinced she killed Marianne, why not take the opportunity to at least question her some more about it, and try and force a confession? It wasn't like she'd had a lawyer in with her; he could have given it a go. But he didn't. Why not?

'I have a hunch Graham Dickson is hiding something too,' she said.

'Maybe he's in on things with Ben,' Darcy said. 'Maybe Ben has already confessed to killing Marianne, and he's protecting his own.'

Della shook her head. 'Nothing worse than a dirty copper.' She grinned lasciviously. 'Or nothing better, depending on the circumstances.'

Darcy threw her a look.

'Whatever their motivations, I don't trust either of them right now,' Jess said, 'but I don't have a clue how to begin investigating Ben or Graham Dickson.'

'We'll find a way,' Della said. 'There's always a way.'

Jess let herself in the front door to the current rolling soundtrack of her life – journo questions and flashing bulbs. She flicked off her shoes and placed her keys in the little trinket tray on the hallway table, and was about to head for the kettle when there was a knock at the door. Jess studied the shape through the glass. It didn't look like the police and the hacks hadn't dared knock on her door yet.

She opened the door to find her neighbour Tristan, holding a small package.

'Hi,' he said.

'Oh! Erm... hi.'

They hadn't spoken since Jess had put her shoe through his forehead and she felt rather awkward. 'I'm sorry – you know – about the rabble outside. They must be annoying you too.'

Tristan shrugged. 'They don't bother me. Dev deals with them, mainly. I ignore them.' He held out the package. 'This was mistakenly left on our doorstep last night. A motorbike courier dropped it off. It's addressed to you but easily done, I suppose.' He gave the package an extra thrust towards her. 'I haven't opened it. Dev said we shouldn't.'

She took the proffered package as a thought occurred to her. 'Was Dev there, last night, when it was delivered?'

Tristan nodded. 'He was the one who found it, actually. He went outside to have a cigarette – I won't let him smoke in the house – and he came back in with it.' His face coloured. 'We... we saw you'd been arrested, so we thought we'd keep hold of it until you came home.'

'Thanks.'

'I'd better go,' Tristan said. The press were beginning to get restless again, the noise slowly building behind him. 'Dev says he thinks you—'

She didn't care what Dev thought. 'Thanks again, Tristan.' Swinging the door shut, she took the package into the kitchen and put the kettle on to boil. Intrigued and not willing to wait until she was sat down with a cuppa, she pulled at the Sellotape holding the package together and ripped open the paper. Inside was a small letter knife, with an intricate black and white china handle. It was pretty, a trinket you'd keep in the hallway to open the mail. She wondered who it was from and tugged at the white piece of card stuffed in with it.

YOU'RE NEXT

The knife and the note clattered to the floor and Jess gasped in horror. Was that *the* knife? She picked it up again. It looked clean, save for her fingerprints which were now all over it. But she could guess that somewhere, lurking in a cut or a crevice, was all the evidence anyone needed that this was the knife that killed Marianne. She gave a huge sob, realisation coming over her in nauseating waves. Whoever was sending the notes, had sent her Marianne's murder weapon. Whatever she'd assumed before, had been wrong. The two cases were linked, the death threats were real and she had to find out who was behind them before it was too late.

'IT'S NOT HOW PEOPLE USUALLY GHOST THEIR EXES'

She pulled up outside a shabby looking 1930s terrace and cut the engine. The row of houses was what Jess could only describe as 'busy', with leaded light windows, porch extensions and a plethora of garden gnomes, plastic windmills and abandoned furniture. Della's tiny, gnome-free house sat in the middle and was as neat as a pin. The pebble-dashed front gleamed with fresh, white paint and the front door was painted with a rather fetching deep yellow gloss. There was a small front garden that was just large enough to cram in the wheelie bins and still have room for a small patch of manicured grass.

'It's not much, but it's home.' Della motioned Jess inside. Jess set her small overnight bag in the hallway. She could hear the faint put-put of electronic gunfire and kids' voices carried out into the hallway from the living room.

'We have a guest!' Della announced, to no one in particular. 'They'll come once they smell food,' she said to Jess. 'Come on, let's get you a drink. Wine or beer?'

'I wouldn't say no to a cuppa, actually,' Jess said.

Della gave a gentle stroke on her arm. 'Whatever you want, Jess.'

She'd been hysterical after she'd opened the package, throwing clothes and a toothbrush into a Tesco carrier bag and practically running out of the door. She'd barely noticed the press pack as she ran to her car, not caring that they saw her open the garage, not answering when they demanded to know what was going on. In a panic, she'd called Della, telling her about the note and the knife; in her haste to leave, she now realised she'd left both abandoned on the floor of the kitchen. She felt sick, wondering how long it would take for Graham Dickson to find it if he got that warrant Ben threatened her with. She was pretty sure Dickson was the sort of man who'd find some way to use that note against her.

They went into the kitchen, a tiny galley with pristine worktops that were lined with blue and white striped jars. The over-counter cabinets were decorated with certificates, awards and children's artwork, each item stuck with care to ensure a curated, rather than overcrowded look. A calendar hung on the wall, with five coloured pens dangling from the nail. Della caught Jess looking at it and grinned. 'Five people in a tiny house, you've gotta be organised with your chaos.'

'I'm impressed,' Jess said, and she meant it. A single mum of four working two jobs, Della was totally bossing it.

'We've got fish for dinner,' she said.

'We've always got fish for dinner,' grumbled a teenage boy (spotty, gangly, uncoordinated), stumbling into the kitchen and searching the cabinets. 'Have we got any crisps left or did Misha eat them all?' He stopped and looked at Jess. 'Hello.'

Jess smiled. 'Hi.'

'This is Jess. She's gonna be staying with us for a few nights. This is Liam.'

'Not in my room I hope.'

'Rude,' said a teenage girl (spotty, gangly, full of attitude), crowding into the tiny kitchen.

'Actually she's gonna be in yours, Maya.'

'Are you kidding me?'

'Now who's rude,' Liam said, grinning and pulling out a packet of crisps from the back of a cupboard.

'Don't ruin your dinner!' Della called after him.

'I can sleep on the sofa,' Jess said. 'I don't want to put anyone out.'

'It's not putting us out, is it?' Della glared at her daughter. 'You can bunk in with Misha.'

'But   '

'It's either that or share with the boys,' Della said.

'This is so unfair!' Maya stomped off.

Della shook her head. 'One day they won't be quite so revolting,' she said. 'Meanwhile, hey, meet my lovely kids. Aren't they great?'

Dinner was delicious. Jess couldn't remember the last time she'd had a decent home-cooked meal, but the cod fishcakes Della had rustled up were so tasty she found herself asking for the recipe.

'You need to get some of that fish I already gifted you out of the freezer first,' Della half-joked as she wiped the last of the plates clean. She leant down and gave her youngest's hair a ruffle. 'Bath time, Sammy,' she said, matter of factly. Seven-year-old Sammy pouted and ignored her, racing a car around the legs of the kitchen table.

'Sammy, I said it's bath time,' Della said, in a voice Jess had never heard her use before. It was a sort of meditative, hypnotic hum. 'Up you go, I'll be there in a minute, okay?'

'Yes, Mummy.' He obliged without a word, getting up and heading for the door as if he'd been programmed. Jess's lips formed a small 'omg'.

'Oh, that? Yeah, he's going through a phase where he does everything I tell him,' she said. 'It won't last, if the others are anything to go by, but I'm making the most of it while it does.'

'The others aren't as bad as you make out.'

'You can tell you've never had kids.'

Jess gave a small smile through pursed lips. She knew Della wasn't meaning to be hurtful.

'What's wrong?'

'Nothing.' She widened her smile. 'I was thinking about Ben.'

'And that made you smile?'

She straightened her face. 'No. No, it doesn't.' She sighed.

'Do you think it was Ben? Who sent you the notes, I mean?'

'There's no proof, Della.'

'But it all adds up that it was him.' Della paused. 'He's threatened you already. And clearly there's history there, between all of you.'

'But that's the thing. It's history – ancient history.'

'Is it?'

Jess thought about how angry he'd been with her, when he found her at the cottage, and again when she went to his flat. 'He had access to the crime scene, as a police officer,' she said, still reluctant to even think of Ben framing her for murder. 'He could have taken the knife, planted my fingerprint...'

'—and gotten away with all of it because he's the police.' Della's lip curled.

Jess sighed. 'I know he's the logical choice; he's the only one that links to both cases. But there's no actual proof,' she said, 'and no real motive to kill Marianne, that I'm aware of.

'Except their argument,' Della replied.

'Except their argument.' Jess felt herself get teary. 'How could he kill his best friend? How could he send those letters to me, threaten me? And why?'

'He's got a baby on the way. Maybe he needed to tie up some loose ends.'

'It's not how people usually ghost their exes.'

Della stretched and sighed. 'I have to go up and do Sammy's bath,' she said. 'When I come back down, we'll talk about how we're going to spy on Ben.'

'I already told you—'

'We don't have the resources, blah blah. Except as I already told you, we do. I've made a couple of calls. Get yourself an early night, because tomorrow, we're pimping my ride.'

'IF WE EAT ALL THOSE, WE'LL NEVER GET OUT OF THE TRUCK'

Jess opened up Della's toolkit and began taking out the necessary items.

'It's like being in the A-Team,' Della exclaimed. It was Saturday and the depot where they were parked was empty; according to Della, it would be 'filled with the elite of the frozen fish world' restocking their trucks later on, but this morning, the dock was deserted, and they were offloading, not restocking.

Darcy wrinkled her nose up as she pulled another cardboard box from a shelf in the truck. 'How long has this been in here? It smells like it last swam the Atlantic around the same time as the Titanic.'

'Oh that'll be the smoked haddock,' Della grinned. 'Never very popular. I keep it at the back so it doesn't put the customers off when I open up the doors to get stock out.'

'I can see why.' Darcy passed the offending box down to Jess, who placed it on the stack with the others.

'That the lot then, Della?' A man (rugged, piercing blue eyes, muscles from Brussels) in blue overalls tied at the waist and a

'Canning's Fish' T-shirt stood with his hands on his hips. Darcy looked like she was going to dribble all down her dress.

'Thanks, Bill, yeah that's it. I'll be back for it all on Monday, I promise.'

Bill glanced at Jess and the cordless screwdriver she was checking over. 'Just take care of the truck, yeah? The boss'll come down on me like a tonne of bricks if he finds out what you're doing.'

'The boss is your dad, and you know that gruff old sod will forgive me anything,' Della grinned. 'Don't worry, though, I'll look after her.'

'Did you need a hand, with, you know, the modifications?'

Darcy looked hopefully at Della and Jess. 'Maybe it would be good to have a man around to help with any heavy lifting.'

Jess grinned. 'You could help us get the top off the refrigeration unit,' she said to Bill. 'We could do with the help as long as you don't want paying.'

'I'll gladly give up my morning for free to help you three ladies,' Bill said.

Darcy tittered. Della rolled her eyes.

'Come on then, Bill. Make yourself useful and start lugging those boxes over.'

'I'll help you,' Darcy said, rushing over to join Bill.

Della and Jess surveyed the pair.

'Darcy seems quite smitten,' Jess said.

'Bill's recently single.' Della looked at him. 'Bit young for her, mind you. I'd had him pegged for myself to be honest, but Darce is probably in greater need of a shag than I am so I s'pose I'll give him up. Plus, his dad is my boss. Family and business don't go well together.'

They began unpacking the boxes as Darcy and Bill brought them over to the truck. A couple of office chairs appeared first. They were padded and had arm rests, and once Della had fitted the castors to them, she and Jess lifted them up into the truck.

'Look Darce, we've got ourselves some FBI chairs,' Della said.

'What's an FBI chair?'

'You know, on the telly, you're always seeing them in the back of trucks, with their fancy screens and headsets and stuff. We're like the *Female* Bureau of Investigation!' Della looked around, proud of herself. 'Come on, admit it, that's a good one.'

'It's a big improvement on the other names you've come up with,' Darcy said, carrying over another box. 'I was terrified you were going to suggest the A-Team earlier. What's in this one? It's very light.'

'What do you think, Jess?' Della grabbed the box from Darcy and picked up an imaginary phone with the other hand. 'Good afternoon, this is the FBI, how can we help you?'

Bill laughed. 'I reckon the real FBI might have something to say about that.'

'Maybe.' Della put the imaginary phone down and started opening the box Darcy had carried over. 'Yes! They arrived!'

'What did?'

Della held up two tins of McVitie's Family Circle biscuits. 'For emergencies.'

Darcy shook her head. 'If we eat all those, we'll never get out of the truck.'

'I'm sure you would.' Bill winked at Darcy, and she flushed.

Della climbed into the truck and slipped the biscuits onto a shelf that had formerly held the prawns. 'It's starting to feel a bit less parky in here now. It'll be a good few hours yet before it's warmed up properly though.'

'You can hook the compressor back up if it starts getting too warm in there,' Bill said. 'You might be glad of that if the weather stays like this.' He wiped a trickle of sweat from his brow. Darcy looked like all she wanted to do was lick it off.

'We should probably tackle getting the lid off the condenser and install the cameras next,' said Jess, looking up at the roof of the truck.

'Should be pretty straightforward,' Della said, clambering up onto the roof via a ladder they'd found in the corner of the warehouse. 'They're magnetic and wireless, work off an app. Darcy, did you bring your iPad?'

Darcy nodded. 'I'll go and get it now.'

'Good job. Bill, get up here with a screwdriver and let's see what we can do.'

Some hours later, they had forward, side and rear facing security cameras installed inside the grills of the refrigeration system and images of the warehouse from three different angles on Darcy's iPad.

'There.' Della wiped her hands and jumped down from the ladder. 'Sorted.'

'It's not perfect,' Jess said, 'there's a bit of shadow from the grills. But I think we should be able to see well enough. This was a brilliant idea, Della.' She looked inside the truck. 'You've done a great job setting up in here too, Darcy.'

Two wheelie chairs were pushed neatly underneath the shelving on one side of the truck which was doubling as a desk. A plastic storage box with a kettle, mugs, coffee, tea and little pots of UHT milk inside sat on a shelf above. A couple of throws and an old blanket decorated in dinosaurs were stacked on the shelves further back, as well as some kitchen roll, a box of tissues and a first aid kit. The makeshift desk had a small box on it filled with pencils and pens and a stack of notebooks underneath. It didn't look homely, exactly, but it was functional and most importantly, could all be removed at a moment's notice to restore Della's truck to its primary function.

Della plonked herself on one of the chairs and spun herself. 'Miles better than sitting in the front of the cab,' she said and wheeled the short distance to the far end of the truck.

Darcy brushed imaginary dust off her hands. 'Are we finished here? Only it's getting late and I want to take a shower and get something to eat before tonight.'

Della chuckled. 'You make it sound like we're off to a party.'

'It's the most exciting Saturday night I've had in months. The kids are with their father all weekend and I'm a free agent.'

'You divorced, Darcy?' Bill enquired.

Darcy swallowed hard. 'Not quite. But nearly.'

Bill shook his head. 'Nasty time. I remember when my missus left me, I wanted to punch something. Not her. But something.' He flexed his arm muscles involuntarily. 'It's what got me into working out. Do you work out?'

A flush crept over Darcy's face. 'Not really,' she replied in a small squeak. 'I do a bit of yoga, though. I find it calms me.'

'So does punching people,' Della quipped. Darcy flung her a stern look.

Bill nodded with appreciation. 'You've gotta find things that keep you calm.'

'I'd love to keep listening to you two lovebirds chatting,' Della said, jumping down from the truck. 'But it's time to go. Got a long night ahead.'

Jess took her cue and shook Bill's hand. 'Nice to meet you, and thanks for your help.'

'No problem.' He reached into his rucksack. 'Sorry... Della said not to, but I was wondering, would you mind?'

A copy of the Radio Times was in Bill's meaty hand, along with a sharpie pen. Jess laughed. She was pictured with a pair of binoculars and a spyglass and dressed vaguely like Sherlock Holmes. It must have been from the first episode of *I Know Where You Live,* when Damon had managed to call in a favour to the editor and get her on the cover.

'My dad keeps all of them,' Bill said, looking bashful. 'When Della told me she was working with you, I had a look through to see if you were on any of the covers. I'm a big fan, you see.'

'You'll have made my agent's day,' Jess said. With all the running from the press lately, for rather different reasons, she'd almost forgotten she used to have actual fans.

She signed the magazine cover and handed it back. 'So you enjoyed the show?' she said.

'Up to a point.'

'Oh.' She was taken aback. 'I'm sorry. Those last few months, they weren't the best quality—'

'Oh no! Not like that. I found out my wife was having an affair, you see. With my best friend. Couldn't watch it, after that.'

'Me too,' Darcy said. 'I mean, not my best friend. His secretary.'

'That's rotten,' Bill said.

Jess looked at Bill and Darcy. Each with their own experiences, each a victim of someone else's selfishness. Adultery itself wasn't the worst crime but it cut deep, nonetheless. She knew of too many people whose lives had been wrecked by deceit, while the perpetrators had simply moved on with their lives. She knew that as well as anyone. On bad days, she believed wholeheartedly that Ben had completely ruined her life. He'd left her skint, childless and incapable of trusting anyone enough to provide her with the family she'd craved. Years down the line, it appeared to have had almost no effect on him at all. He was the one settling down, having a baby, while she was the one trying to make ends meet to pay the bills until she died alone and got eaten by next door's cats.

'I'm sorry you went through that, Bill. And you, Darcy. And Della too.'

Della grinned. 'Got a better life now because I didn't put up with that shit.' She looked at Bill and Darcy. 'You will too.' Smiling, she walked towards the driver's side of the truck. 'Cheers, Bill. Look after my stock, yeah? I'll be needing it back.' She got in the truck, gesturing to Darcy who was headed for the passenger side. 'And don't wait too long to ask this one out,' she called. 'It's her birthday tomorrow and she could do with the distraction, whatever she says.'

'Della!' Darcy flushed again, ran to the truck and climbed in, slamming the door shut behind her.

'Nice one, Della,' Bill muttered.

'Just ask her!' Della waved a hand out of the driver window as she started the engine. Jess slammed the rear doors of the truck closed and banged on them before jogging round to take her own seat in the cab. They were good to go.

SURVEILLANCE: SUBJECT DI BEN MORGAN AND NAOMI WILLS

Saturday 22 June

DI Ben Morgan and fiancée Naomi Wills at their flat

6.00 p.m.: Naomi and Ben confirmed as home
7.00 p.m.: No movement
8.00 p.m.: No movement
9.00 p.m.: No movement
9.12 p.m.: No—

'I NEVER KNEW FROZEN FISH WAS SO UNPOPULAR'

'I hope you realise we're missing out on a hot date with *Love Island* and a bottle of pink fizz tonight,' Della said, as they parked up near Ben's flat. 'We had the TV all to ourselves while the kids are all on sleepovers.'

Jess felt guilty. 'If you don't want to stay I can take the truck—'

Della grinned. 'Nah. It's worth skipping for a bit of bona fide spy work.'

'Surveillance, Della.'

'In hot pursuit of the truth,' Della continued in a Hollywood-style American accent. 'Oooo... Hot Pursuit. What about that for a company name?'

'I think it sounds like a porn site.' Darcy sat in the middle seat, dressed from head to toe in black: leggings, running top and a black cap perched on top of her ponytailed blonde locks. She rearranged her legs around a bulging bag in the footwell.

'Move that rucksack if it's in your way,' Della said.

'Christ, Della. What have you got in there?'

'A few snacks. Some Pringles, couple of packs of chocolate bourbons, sausage rolls, a pack of Celebrations...'

'What about the biscuits you stashed earlier?'

'I assumed we'd be gone a few hours and you don't want to see me hungry. You strapped in?' She stepped on the brakes and pulled up between two streetlights, far enough away from the block that they couldn't be seen with the naked eye.

'So, quick question,' Darcy said. 'Just to get this straight: we're spying on your ex, right?'

'It's surveillance.' Jess said.

'So we're *surveilling* your ex.'

'Yes. And his fiancée.'

'And he's police,' Darcy stated.

'Yes.'

'Undercover police,' Darcy persisted.

'Yes.'

'So, won't he be kind of a specialist when it comes to being watched?'

'Yes. But he's not on a job, he's at home. He's not been a UCO for years, and even when he was, he never worked out of his home address. No one knows where he lives.'

'You do.'

'He won't be expecting anyone to be watching him.'

'Unless he killed your mate, in which case he might,' Della said.

'You have a point,' Jess said. 'But that's what we're here to find out. And if we don't, I'm not sure anyone else will.' She looked around. People going to and fro across the area in front of the flats paid almost zero attention to Della's truck, some even went out of their way to avoid it.

'Told you, it's the perfect surveillance vehicle,' Della said. 'No one will even catch my eye in case I try to palm them off with a pound of prawns.'

'It is quite incredible,' Jess replied. 'I never knew frozen fish was so unpopular.'

'You have to be a certain type of personality to do the job, that's for sure.' Della switched off the ignition and stared across the street. 'So which one is he in, then?'

Jess pointed. 'Third floor, balcony on the left.'

'The one with the poncy wicker chairs?'

'That's the one.'

'Hmm.'

'What's that supposed to mean?'

'You were right. It is nice here. If he wasn't such a dickhead you'd have been well sorted.' She opened the window and sniffed. 'Smells of sausages. What I wouldn't give for a nice charcoal smeared sausage with a dab of brown sauce...' Della heaved the rucksack onto her lap and located a six pack of sausage rolls from Tesco. 'This'll have to do, I suppose. Want one?'

'No, thank you.' Darcy said, turning up her nose. 'Anyway, shouldn't we get in the back before you start your midnight feast?'

'Good idea,' Jess said. 'I'll get set up in the back with you; maybe Della can take a walk around the block so we can test out the equipment and make sure we have eyes where we need them.'

They made sure the coast was clear before they got out of the cab and climbed into the converted rear of the truck.

Della fished a bunch of leaflets out of her bag. 'See you in a bit, then.'

'What are they?' Jess asked.

Della tapped her nose. 'Figured I could drum up a bit of business while I'm here,' she said. 'I'll do the rounds, check out your man, and deliver a few leaflets while I'm at it. Never one to miss a sales opportunity!'

'But Della, we're supposed to be incognito.'

'Exactly,' Della replied. 'If I was driving around in this thing and *not* trying to sell frozen fish, that would be more suspicious. Right, Jess?'

Jess nodded. 'You make a good point,' she said. 'Go and deliver the leaflets; we'll see you back here in half an hour.'

Thirty minutes later there was a tap on the truck door and they let Della in. She was looking a bit sweaty and was out of breath.

'Phew! It's warm out there this evening.' She flopped herself onto one of the chairs which promptly wheeled itself into the side of the truck with a heavy thud.

'Shhh!' Darcy said. 'You'll draw attention to us.'

'We could be having a karaoke stripper party in the back of this truck and no one around here would be interested,' Della said. 'Everyone's sauced up from drinking too much rosé in the sunshine and the football's on. Looks like a good match too—'

'What about Ben and Naomi?' Jess interrupted.

'Oh yeah, they're in,' Della said casually.

'You saw them? Both of them?'

Della nodded. 'Ben answered the door. Bit of a looker.'

Jess blushed. 'I'm aware.'

'I gave him a flyer. He called to Naomi to ask if she'd be interested; I heard her answer from down the hall. They weren't, by the way. No one was.'

Jess nodded to herself. 'So, they're both home.'

'Yeah. They looked pretty bedded in for the night, to be honest. He was wearing joggers and an old T-shirt, really showed off his pecs, I mean—' she made a motion with her hands. 'Phwoar.'

'Alright, Della,' Jess said, flustered. 'We get the idea.'

'So, now what?' Darcy asked.

'We'll keep our eyes on the door just in case.' Jess checked her watch.

'Just in case what?'

'They leave.'

Jess's stomach gave a long, large rumble.

'Bloody hell, Jess. Thought there was a thunderstorm in the truck for a minute.'

'Sorry.' It was nine o'clock, and everyone was getting restless.

'I'm starving, too,' Della said. 'I saw a chippy around the corner when we got here. Shall I go and get us something?' Della made a move to get out of the truck and Jess stopped her.

'No, you stay here; I'll go. Darcy? Want anything?'

'Nothing for me, thanks.'

'Chips for me,' Della said. 'No vinegar though. Do you need some cash?'

'My treat.' Jess opened the doors wide enough to fit through then jumped out, putting the hood of her jacket up to hide her face. 'Call me if you need me.'

Della nodded. 'Aye, aye, boss.'

Jess shut the truck door as quietly as possible and jogged around the corner to the chip shop. She knew from when she'd lived here that the fryers would be going deep into the night, staying open to catch the last of the stragglers from the pubs. But on a footie night, this was the best time to come, just before the end of a game, to get a fresh bag of chips without the queues. She and Ben used to do it all the time, back when she'd shown more than a passing interest in the football; it had been a post-match ritual of sorts. They'd wait until the final whistle blew, then make a dash to the chippy to beat everyone else to it. They'd come back and eat the chips in bed and make love afterwards, their greasy lips and fingers clamouring for each other.

She'd never eat chips in bed these days. But she hadn't had wild greasy sex for over a decade either, so maybe it was difficult to judge exactly what she'd do, given the opportunity. She rounded the corner and saw with satisfaction that the chippy was still there, the blue and red signage encouragingly familiar and the same old discoloured 'Open' sign flapping against the door. She squinted at the sharp fluorescent light as she went in, and then smiled at the familiar bubbling of oil which meant a fresh batch of chips had just gone in. She'd lost none of her timing.

She didn't know the girl (spotty, spiky hair, lots of earrings) behind the counter. She wouldn't have expected to, after a decade. It was odd, visiting a place you once lived and spent so much time in: familiar, like you'd been before, but without the sense of belonging.

'Two portions of chips, please.'

The girl nodded and began shovelling chips onto the paper stack by the side of the fryers. Her fingers were red raw and chapped. Jess tried not to look at them too much, for fear they'd put her off her food.'

'Salt and vinegar?'

'Just salt, please.'

The girl packaged up the first portion and moved onto the second. The bell rang behind Jess, and she instinctively turned a little, just enough to see Ben approaching the counter.

'THESE ARE GOOD CHIPS'

Shit. Jess's heart leapt in panic. She turned her head back sharply, pulled the hoodie a little tighter over her head and hoped to god he hadn't been paying attention to her face. Yes, she wanted to talk to him, but she wasn't a big fan of a restraining order.

'That's five pounds eighty.'

Jess handed over six pounds in coins and nodded farewell. Her phone was ringing loudly in her pocket – no doubt Della or Darcy. She grabbed the chips off the counter, bundled them under her arm and tried to act as natural as possible while flicking her phone to silent. She couldn't afford even the smallest of glances at Ben and certainly couldn't let him hear her voice; she had to trust that he hadn't seen her and get out as quickly as possible.

Another woman (twenties, smoker's cough, greasy hair) came into the shop. So much for avoiding rush hour. Jess gave her a half smile in thanks as she moved past her through the open door. As she passed, the woman's eyes widened. 'Hey, aren't you—'

A horrible realisation came over Jess – the woman recognised her from the television. She had to get away before she said anything that would give her away—

'Fish and chips twice please. And a couple of gherkins too, if you've got them.'

Ben's voice rang out, and Jess used it as an opportunity to escape the chippy and scurry down the road towards the truck. Not daring to get too close until Ben was safely back home, she looked around quickly, then took the opportunity to dive into a large bush. The aroma of her chips was overpowering and making her drool, but she didn't dare unpack them. She held them to her body instead, the heat seeping through her hoodie. She waited, crouched uncomfortably, for Ben to go by.

After a few minutes, Ben left the chippy and walked back towards the block of flats. He was on the phone, complaining about something. She listened, trying to make out what he was saying.

'...There's nothing new to report, she's not home, she's not been home for days....' he paused to let the other person speak. Jess strained to hear. Was he talking about *her*?

'Fine. I'll go by tomorrow, see if I can get in and look around.'

Jess swallowed, thinking about the knife and the note on the floor of her kitchen. Surely he wouldn't – he couldn't—

'Okay, okay... I'll be there in an hour.'

Where? Was Ben going to break into her house? She watched helplessly as he ended the call and began to jog towards the entry door of his block of flats. Breathing a sigh of relief as it closed behind him, Jess stood up and made her way quickly back to the truck.

'Where the hell have you been? Oooo... those chips smell brilliant.' Della grabbed her portion and sniffed them. 'You left off the vinegar. Good girl.'

'We tried to call you,' Darcy said. 'Ben left the flat. We were going to follow him but you told us to stay here.'

Della shoved a handful of chips in her mouth. 'These are good chips.'

'Ben was in the chippy.' The smell of the food was making Jess feel sick.

'What?' Darcy said. 'Oh my god, did he see you?'

Jess shook her head. 'I don't think so. It was a close call though.'

'Lucky you didn't walk right into him,' Darcy said.

'So the big news of the night is that Ben and Naomi got some fish and chips,' Della said, chewing viciously on a chip. 'What do we do now? Wait another two hours for him to take out the rubbish?'

'Sitting here breathing in chip fat does seem to be a bit of a waste of time,' Darcy said. 'He's clearly home for the night.'

Jess didn't want to admit that Ben might be leaving again shortly, or that he was most likely headed over to her house, where he'd find everything he needed to arrest her. These women had only just met her, and she'd already dragged them into an operation that wasn't strictly legal. She didn't want to make them accessories to murder as well. 'Why don't you both go,' she said, resigned to the fact that if he was on his way to break into her house, there was absolutely nothing she could do about it – certainly not appear there in what suddenly felt like the world's most recognisable truck. 'Get a taxi home, both of you. I doubt anything else is going to happen tonight.'

'Are you staying?'

She nodded. 'Just in case. But there's no need for all of us to be hanging around. I'll bring the truck back in the morning, if that's okay?' She gave them both a handful of twenty-pound notes. 'Here. For tonight.'

'You don't have to do that,' Darcy said. 'I told you; I'm not doing it for the money.'

'I am,' Della said.

Darcy shot her a dark look.

'It's fine.' Jess shrugged, nonchalantly. She'd increased her overdraft earlier that day, but she didn't want them to know. 'I don't want you being out of pocket for the taxi.'

'Cheers, boss.' Della pocketed the cash, opened up the back doors and let the fresh air and the rumbling of London's nightlife flood in. She and Darcy eased themselves off the tailgate and Della fished inside her impossibly tight leggings to retrieve the keys to the truck from a pocket on her thigh. She tossed them at Jess, who scrambled in the half-light to catch them. 'Bring it back in one piece,' she said, in a terrible stage whisper that threatened to wake half the neighbourhood. The pair took off down the road, silhouetted against the streetlight, and Jess closed up the tailgate again, resuming her watch on the flat.

Not long after, a movement on the monitor caught Jess's eye. She squinted at the figure coming from the block. It was Ben, dressed in what Jess would call his 'cop clothes': jeans, shirt and leather jacket – a completely unnecessary accessory on a warm night like tonight, worn more out of habit than anything. He walked across the grass, his features lit up on the grainy screen image with every streetlight he passed.

He scouted the area as he moved, keys in hand. As he passed the truck, it felt like he was staring right at it. Jess involuntarily shrank into her seat, as though Ben had x-ray vision. She felt completely powerless, watching while Ben got on his motorbike and listening to the revving of the engine. She couldn't follow him – he'd see the truck and guess immediately that something was up. She wrung her hands, not knowing what to do, watching the monitor helplessly as he sped by.

Ben's motorbike.

She felt like she'd been run over by the words, as she recalled the noise of the bike engine she'd heard the night of her next-door neighbours' party. And Tristan's words too, about the package with the knife being dropped off by a courier. Had it been him? Her heart broke a little bit more. She had so wanted to believe that Ben wasn't capable of this, but it was looking more and more like he might be the monster she was looking for.

It wasn't even five minutes later that the lights in the living room went off. Jess guessed Naomi had gone to bed following Ben's departure and sighed. She may as well call it a night too. She jumped down onto the road, closed the back doors as quietly as she could, and was walking towards the front of the truck to drive home when the entry door to the block swung open again. Jess spied the exaggerated silhouette of a pregnant woman.

'Now, what are you up to?' Jess murmured.

Naomi moved across the grass towards the road where the truck was parked and Jess suddenly realised she was completely exposed. With as much stealth as she could muster, she crept around the back side of the truck and peeked over the bonnet to where Naomi was still standing. She held a phone in her hand, illuminating her face and tapped impatiently at the screen. After a few minutes, a Toyota Prius pulled up, and she got in the back. Jess looked at her watch. Where on earth was Naomi going at ten o'clock at night? It didn't matter, for now; more significant, was that Naomi's surprise departure meant the flat was empty. If Ben was going to break into her house – well, two could play at that game.

'IT'S FIVE O'CLOCK SOMEWHERE'

Jess stood at the door of Ben's flat. The post-match, post-pub traffic to and from the block had made it easy for her to slip inside the foyer, the adrenaline caused by the unexpected opportunity propelling her through the entry door and up to the third floor so fast that she barely remembered how she got here. She checked once more to make sure no one was looking and took a key out of her pocket. It was a bit of a gamble that Ben hadn't changed the locks in all these years, but when she inserted the key, the door to the flat swung open. Jess shook her head. For a police officer, Ben was pretty slack when it came to home security. More fool him.

The hallway light was still on and she made her way inside, taking in details that she hadn't been able to the last time she visited. Without Naomi's watchful eye on her, she could spend time searching for clues that might help her figure out what was really going on. Not that a hallway would be the place to leave evidence lying about. Sure enough, apart from the usual aspects of domesticity, she didn't see anything suspicious.

She made her way towards the back of the flat and poked her head into the galley kitchen that sat to the left of the living room.

Even in the dim light, she could see it was a mess. Dirty plates and mugs accumulated in the sink and the bin was overflowing with the night's fish and chip wrappers, giving the whole area a slightly funky aroma that was part gym locker and part wheelie bin.

She withdrew back into the living room and used her phone torch to check the drawers in the sideboard. Apart from a few tealights and a box of matches, they were sparsely populated. Jess had taken their wedding gifts when she left – the good china, the cutlery canteen and serving plates, vases, and so on. It looked like Ben had failed to replace any of it, although why Naomi hadn't, she couldn't say. Maybe they were waiting for the wedding gift registry. Maybe it was all in the sink waiting to be washed up.

A phone sat in one of the drawers, along with a charger. It was what Ben had called a burner – a phone for his jobs, that was untraceable and easily disposed of. A painful recollection of a younger Ben clutching one rose to the surface, and pain and regret surged through her. They'd been so happy, once upon a time, and he'd spoiled everything... she pushed the memory away. She shouldn't have allowed Ben to make her feel this way for so long.

She tried turning the phone on, hoping Ben was as slack with his phone security as he was with his home. It was completely dead, so she plugged in the charger. With a bit of luck, it would have enough charge to turn on before she left. She moved into the bedroom, reluctantly. The duvet looked like it had been in a fight; she didn't want to think about why. She checked the wardrobes and cupboards; they didn't reveal much else, except, Jess noted, surprisingly little in the way of maternity outfits. Things had obviously moved on from when she was trying for a baby; in those days, she would wander the shopping centres gazing longingly at maternity wear in the windows of Mothercare and wondering if she'd ever get the chance to wear it. But today's clothes were softer, baggier; Naomi was slightly built, and she obviously didn't feel the need to 'dress the bump'. She still had a few months to go, though; that might all change by the time autumn rolled around.

The bedside tables were sparsely populated with a pregnancy book on one side and on the other – Ben's, she presumed – a stack of redundant condoms. She fished further into his drawer and, lodged right at the back, found a book with a photo tucked inside. She pulled out the photo and was shocked to see it was of their wedding day, from over a decade previous: him dressed in a tux, proud as punch next to her, his blushing bride. Jess's eyes filled. Why would he keep hold of this, of all things? She placed it gently back inside the book, and shoved it into the drawer, shutting away the memory.

The bathroom light shone brightly, making her squint. It was as disgusting as the kitchen, hair everywhere and the dried scum of soap and toothpaste clinging to the sink. How was Ben putting up with this mess? He'd been fastidious when they'd been married. She thought about Marianne's pristine crime scene and wondered whether he or Naomi would ever be remotely capable of leaving it that way, given the evidence in front of her.

There was only one room left. Jess took a deep breath and made her way into the spare room. The nursery was exactly as she'd seen it the time before, the only tidy room in the whole flat. A desk she hadn't noticed on her last visit was pushed against the wall behind the door, the remaining remnant of the room's former life. Jess took some photos and had a look in the filing drawer that was tucked under one side of the desk. It was mainly bills, insurance certificates and so on; the majority were Naomi's, with no obvious joint accounts. Jess wasn't surprised: it had been the same when she'd been married to Ben. He'd told her when they moved in together it was because he never completely trusted anyone with his money.

'Do you ever really trust anyone with anything?' she'd asked.

'Only Marianne,' he'd replied.

Jess looked at the photo montage hung over the desk, with various shots of Ben and Naomi together, plus a few more from Naomi's younger days: a picnic in a park, a black-tie event and a group of friends lying about on beds in what looked like university halls. Jess took a few shots of the montage and the paperwork on the desk before gathering it up to take back to the living room. Ignoring the baby paraphernalia, she left the room quickly and closed the door behind her.

She sat on the sofa, feeling more depressed than she had in a long time, about the state of her life. Naomi might be a terrible housekeeper, but Ben didn't seem to mind, which meant he was probably happy – happier than he'd been with her, certainly. She put her phone down so that the light shone onto her lap and began looking through the credit card bills she'd picked up from Naomi's desk. She couldn't read them in the dim light and didn't want to risk putting a light on, so she took photos to look at later, at home. Jess glanced at the phone charging. It was an old-fashioned flip phone, and it would need a bit of battery life to turn on. While she waited, she put the paperwork back in the nursery and went to sit back on the sofa. She closed her eyes, and remembered how a phone just like this one had once saved Marianne's life.

Jess didn't know the details. Ben and Marianne had always been tight-lipped about the cases they were on – in part because they weren't allowed to say much, and in part, she knew, because she was a journalist and they suspected she wouldn't be able to help herself.

She and Ben had tried another round of IVF, just before they split up. Jess had felt obliged to give it one last go, even though her heart was heavy at the idea of it. Ben wasn't due home for another day, but out of a sense of duty, she supposed, he'd come back early, to go with her to the doctor for the final consultation. He'd turned up at home after four days on the road, looking tired and smelling of cigarettes and stale beer. She suspected he'd spent at least one night in the cab of a truck, although the clothes he'd slept in would be bagged up and left in a car park somewhere, along with the rest of the remnants from his secret life.

He'd taken his jacket off and flopped down on the sofa, staring into space, his mind obviously elsewhere. Jess had busied herself making tea. When she was done, she perched on a dining chair, not wanting to squeeze in next to him.

If all this was a massive inconvenience, she'd rather he'd have stayed away.

'You didn't have to come, you know. I could have done it by myself.'

Ben immediately prickled. 'Do you need me at all, except as a sperm donor?' he'd asked stiffly.

'It seems like you don't want to be here.'

'Of course I do. What kind of question is that?' He stood up, walking to the sink and dumping the tea out. 'Just give me five. I need a shower before we leave.'

A few minutes later, his phone rang.

'Ben! Your phone.'

'Which one?'

'What do you mean, which one?'

'What kind of ring is it?' He appeared at the door wrapped in a towel, his torso dripping and covered in goosebumps. Jess tried to focus. Despite their estrangement of late, he still looked hot.

'I dunno. Like an old-fashioned—'

'Shit!'

Ben shoved her aside and ran into the living room in three or four giant strides, shaking out his jacket until a small, ancient looking phone tipped out.

'Shit.'

'What is it?'

'I have to go.' He pulled on the clothes he'd left on the bathroom floor, catching his feet in the joggers and swearing as he battled with his T-shirt. Barefoot, he grabbed his trainers from the hallway. 'Sorry. I'll call you.'

He'd gone, as suddenly as he came, and Jess stood in the empty flat feeling lost, and wondering who or what had sent him running. Certainly, someone who mattered an awful lot. Which meant it could only be Marianne.

He'd returned the next morning, ashen-faced, with Marianne trailing behind him. She was bruised, the right side of her face swollen from her eye to her jawline; she had a slight limp that made her wince as she walked.

'Maz! What happened?'

'I'm fine.'

'She's going to stay with us for a night or two.' Ben took his phone from the back of his jeans pocket – old, ratty jeans Jess didn't recognise – and plugged it into a charger. 'You can have the spare room,' he said to Marianne. 'I'll stay home with you today, make sure you're okay.'

'I told you, I'll be fine,' she said. 'Go in and make the report. I don't need a babysitter. I'm fine.'

Even Jess could tell she wasn't being truthful. She tried to change the subject. 'Does anyone want a cup of tea?'

Marianne swallowed. 'Have you got something stronger?' she said.

'It's ten o'clock in the morning.'

'It's five o'clock somewhere.'

Ben grabbed a glass and a bottle of Scotch from the tray on the sideboard. 'Here.'

Marianne poured herself a drink with shaking hands and downed it in one. 'Thanks.' She poured out a second one and downed that too. Ben watched her carefully and held out his hand to Jess when she moved to take the bottle.

'Leave it. She can have it all, if she needs it.'

Jess couldn't help herself from asking. 'Are you okay? Do you want to talk about anything? Are you hurt? Do you need to go to a doctor? I could call, make you an appointment—'

'Got my medicine right here.' Marianne lifted the bottle of Scotch and gave her a rueful smile. 'And thanks, Jess... but you know I couldn't talk to you about it, even if I wanted to.'

Jess's eyelids fluttered as she heard a clunking noise. It was light outside; she must have been asleep for hours. She rubbed her eyes, disoriented. She could smell chips. Something wasn't right—

She was still in Ben's flat; and fully aware, now, that the noise that woke her was the unmistakable sound of a key in a door. She was only frozen with fear for the briefest of moments before she leapt up and away from the sofa. There was no way down, and nowhere to hide. Except... heart thumping, she headed for the patio door that led to the balcony, mentally crossing her fingers that it wasn't locked. She pulled at the patio door, relieved when it slid open with a heavy, whispered whoosh. She stepped out on the patio and closed the door again.

'Ben?'

Naomi's voice filtered down the hallway and Jess stood stock still outside the patio door. There was no way to lock it from the outside, but mercifully, the curtain had fallen back into place and she was hidden, for now. She made her way to the far end of the balcony and crouched low, behind the wicker armchair. As hiding places go, it was crap; if anyone came out here she'd be toast.

She willed Naomi to stay inside. It didn't help that it was a glorious morning. Sure enough, Naomi could have only been in the flat for a few minutes when she opened the patio door. Jess felt sick.

A phone rang.

'Hey you,' Naomi said, taking the call. 'Missing me already?'

'Just checking you didn't want to stay in bed with me a bit longer.' A male voice, a vibrating baritone, filtered outside. Naomi must have put him on speaker.

'You know I didn't want to leave.'

'You were *filthy* last night...'

Naomi gave an uncharacteristically girlish giggle and opened the curtains slightly to let the breeze in. Jess attempted to make herself even smaller, praying she didn't open them all the way and expose her.

'Talking of filthy, I need to go and have a shower. Ben will be home soon from the nightshift.'

'You should've had one here before you left.' The man's northeast accent was strong but soft, similar to Naomi but less gentrified. 'You could still come back, you know. I don't have to leave for a couple of hours.'

'You know I had to get home, Jake. If Ben finds out—'

'Who cares? It's going to come out soon anyway.'

'I know. But—'

'I don't know why you're dragging your feet telling him.'

'I've got to go.'

'When am I gonna see you? I'm leaving town on Wednesday, and it's gonna be a month before I can get back again.' He chuckled. 'That baby bump's gonna be enormous. We'll have to do it doggie style.'

Naomi tittered. 'I can meet you on Monday. Tuesday's the funeral.'

'You're going?'

'It would look pretty odd if I didn't.' She sighed. 'I'll call you, okay? I love you.'

The call ended and Jess's heart thumped so loudly she thought it might be trying to join the conversation. Naomi was – what? Having an affair? But she was *pregnant*.

Music started up inside the flat. After five minutes or so, Jess thought she could hear the sound of running water. Crawling slowly across the balcony, she held her ear to the edge of the open patio door. Sure enough, the shower was running, and from the uneven slapping of water against the tiles, Jess deduced Naomi was already in it. She bit her lip. She had no idea if Naomi was fast or slow in the shower, but it was the best opportunity she was going to get to make her escape. She waited another few moments before daring to begin the somewhat risky journey, crawling across the living room on her hands and knees. She edged down the hallway, past the nursery and then the part-open bathroom door, staying below eye line and listening carefully for any signs that Naomi was about to come out. She prayed that the steam would hide any hint of movement from the hallway beyond. Past the door, she slowly got herself up – slower than ideal, thanks to her stiff legs and cranky back. She got as far as the front door before she remembered the phone plugged into the wall. But it was way too late to go back. The shower turned off and with her heart thumping, Jess tiptoed quickly to the front door, opening and closing it with the expertise that had come from years of letting herself in and out while Ben slept. Breathing a sigh of relief, she bolted down the stairs, raced across the grass and threw herself into the truck.

'THERE'S NO SUCH THING AS BAD PUBLICITY'

Jess woke up later on Sunday afternoon, the long, late night taking its toll. Sitting up in Maya's bed where she'd collapsed earlier, she rolled her head from left to right, feeling a satisfying snap of gristle as she loosened off the muscles in her neck. She stretched, scrunching then releasing her toes, and rotating her wrists and ankles to wake them up too. She wanted a shower to freshen herself up and wash the greasy smell from her hair, but she needed a bath; it would ease the aches in her body and help her think through her next move.

Her phone rang before she'd had the chance to decide one way or the other. She rolled over and grabbed it from the bedside table.

'Jess.'

Her agent was the last person she wanted to hear from. She mentally kicked herself for not paying attention to the screen before answering.

'Sorry to disturb you on a Sunday but I wanted to make sure you were still alive. It's all been very quiet lately.'

From anyone else, Jess would think this was a voice of concern, but she knew it was Damon's pointed way of telling her she hadn't been taking his calls.

'I've been a bit preoccupied.'

'Well, it's time to focus. When you've got a book coming out there's no such thing as bad publicity. Remember that.'

How could she forget? 'I don't have a book coming out.'

'Actually, you do. That's why I called. All these rumours about you seeking bloody revenge on your nemesis, it's raised your profile significantly. The publisher moved your dates up, they want to see your manuscript ASAP.' He paused. 'We can ask them to hold the last few pages. The murder accusation would make a fantastic final chapter, especially if you found the killer.'

'I'm not accused of anything, Damon.'

'Not *officially*...'

There was no way she was telling him about her escapade the night before. 'I'm not allowed anywhere near Marianne's murder case, as you well know.'

'Of course not, darling. But if you *did* happen to find the killer—'

'You'll be the first to know, Damon.'

'Atta girl. And how are your new minions doing?'

'It's a work in progress.'

'Like your book, I assume.' There was a short silence. 'The publishers are putting the pressure on to get it out there while you're still hot news. I need to get that manuscript, Jessica.'

'I *know*, Damon.'

'Can you at least tell me the title?'

She had to think quickly. One of Della's crazy name suggestions came to her, and, knowing Damon wanted something from her, she decided it would have to do.

'It's called Grime Scene Investigation,' she said.

There was a silence, followed by a howl of laughter.

'I love it, darling. Grime Scene Investigation! What a great title, I can almost see the cover now—'

'Gotta go, Damon.'

'Of course, dear. I'll call you again next week, maybe you can send me the opening chapters?'

'Yeah, maybe.' She crossed her fingers and gave silent thanks Damon couldn't see her face. 'Later, Damon.'

'Ciao.'

Della had left a note outside her door, telling her she'd taken the kids out for the day. Jess took the opportunity of having the house to herself to run a bath and try to relax, but it was easier said than done. Since the revelation of Naomi's affair Jess couldn't shift the nervous energy bubbling away inside. Her thoughts were constantly on Ben. When was he supposed to be getting married? And when was the baby due? By the looks of Naomi, Jess guessed the autumn sometime, maybe October. A wave of sympathy swelled inside her. Jess had certainly seen a smorgasbord of infidelity in her time on TV, but the awfulness of this situation almost made her feel sorry for Ben.

Almost.

As Jess got out of the bath, her mind started to sharpen. Ben had been going to check out her house, she was sure of it. But he wouldn't find the knife unless he let himself in without a warrant, and if he did that, whatever he found would be inadmissible. If he wasn't the killer, and wasn't trying to frame her, then there's no way he'd break in. But what did this all mean for Marianne?

Rosie had said Ben and Marianne were arguing about Naomi... had Marianne found out about the affair? If she'd seen Naomi and Jake together and confronted them, told them she was going to spill their secret, *that* would certainly be a motive. But accusing Ben's pregnant fiancée of murder on the face of a single phone call she overheard seemed like a long shot, in terms of building a solid case. Because then she'd have to explain how she'd broken into her ex-husband's home and hidden on a balcony. She'd need a lot more before she went to Graham Dickson with *that* theory. She gnawed at her lower lip. Things – and by things, she meant her obsession with solving this case – had spiralled a little bit out of control. She needed to calm down and apply a bit of logical thinking to the situation.

The heat had disappeared out of the day and dusk was already creeping across the sky when she winched herself off the bed. Cursing her stiffened legs, Jess went downstairs to the sitting room with her laptop and looked again at the photos of the bank statements she'd found on the desk in the nursery. Naomi's surname caught her eye; maybe she'd find out more by running a trusty Google search. She typed Naomi Wills and found a LinkedIn profile, but it was with great annoyance that Naomi's Instagram was locked and her Facebook page revealed little more than a profile pic. Jess had assumed Naomi would be the sort of woman with a prolific social media presence, but maybe Ben had put a stop to that. When they'd been living together, he'd asked her to do the same thing, to keep his identity safe. A decade on, he wasn't in that line of work anymore, but there'd still be people around who'd be very interested to know Ben wasn't who he said he was.

Maybe there'd be something pre-Ben though. She dug further until she found a small news article in a trade magazine about Naomi from 2018, when she'd taken over as operations manager for a large advertising agency in west London. Naomi was accomplished, which meant she was intelligent, and not as young and stupid as Jess had hoped her to be; circling back to LinkedIn, she managed to trace a more comprehensive breakdown of Naomi's career. She'd worked for several different companies in the decade prior, firstly as a receptionist and later as an admin assistant for a graphic design firm in Durham. Jess noted she'd been in London for nearly six years, since she was thirty-one. She wondered what had driven her to move south.

She looked again at the pictures she'd taken, of the montage above Naomi's desk. She must have met Ben almost immediately after she'd arrived in London. At forty-four, he would have been thirteen years older than her, which was quite a gap. Jess wasn't sure she'd have fallen for someone that old in her early thirties, even if he was devastatingly handsome. She thought of Ben again. Maybe she would have. A man in his forties wasn't *unattractive*; although that was then. A vibrant, sexy forty-four-year-old bachelor was a stark contrast to the grumpy, bitter fifty-one-year-old in the throes of a midlife crisis Naomi would be faced with these days. Maybe that was what had led her to cheat on him.

Jess still found the whole idea unbearable. The irony wasn't lost on her, that Ben was the victim of an awful affair; maybe she should have felt vindicated, but instead she found herself feeling sorry, not for him, but for the baby that he and Naomi were bringing into the world. It wasn't the best of starts to family life, particularly not if one of them was arrested for murder. And it would only be one of them: with their relationship as disparate as it now appeared to be, Ben and Naomi couldn't possibly have been in on things together. More than ever, Jess found it difficult to imagine the murderer was Ben. Marianne had been trying to tell him a truth he didn't want to hear, but that wasn't a reason to kill her. Whether Naomi felt the same way about exposing her affair with Jake... that was another thing altogether.

TO: Jessica@Sinclairinvestigations.co.uk
FROM: Ninafoster72@aol.co.uk
SUBJECT: Help required

Dear Jessica,

I read that you've started your own P.I. agency and I hope you can help me. Some time ago I found a hotel room booked on my husband (Adam)'s credit card, on three different occasions, each a week apart. At first I thought maybe he'd booked for a client, so I gave him the benefit of the doubt and almost forgot about it. When he sent me a dick pic (attached), though, I realised something was very wrong. Why would your husband of twelve years send you a picture of his penis from the train toilet? He deleted it quickly, of course, but it was too late: I'd already seen it (and saved it), and deleting it made him look guilty. One Sunday afternoon not long after, while he was asleep in his chair, I used his Face ID to get into his phone. I learned that trick from someone on your show – very handy! I found a chat thread, from a woman called Clare Hathaway. The entire affair was laid out in text messages (attached as a PDF). As you can see, they met on platform two at Reading station and spent the next four months sexting each other on the 6.52 to Paddington before deciding to take things to the next level. They had sex in the train toilets for a while, but now they use a hotel. It's always on a Monday, always the same time and place.

I could have confronted Adam about this a while ago, of course, given I have the proof sitting on my phone. But you see, Clare is married too, and why should our marriage be the only one to suffer? Hence, I'm emailing to ask you for help. I want more, better photos, dirty bed sheets... anything else that will prove that the two of them are having the most sordid of affairs. And then I need you to find Clare Hathaway's husband so I can show him.

Finally, in case it's of use, I attach a photo of Clare also. Although I wouldn't say it's all that flattering, it appears to be the only one Adam has dared to keep on his phone.

I look forward to hearing from you.

With kind regards,

Nina Foster

'I TOLD YOU THESE WERE BRAIN FOOD'

Della yelled up the stairs at decibels only mountains were built to withstand.

'Maya! Get off your phone and get your shoes on, you're going to be late!' She then handed several lunchboxes to Jess. 'Here, give them to anyone under eighteen.'

Jess stood by as the morning chaos that could only come with kids in the house ensued, and watched as Della herded, cajoled and barked at her offspring to get shoes on, brush their teeth and grab their bags, before yelling up the stairs again.

'Misha,' she shouted. 'It's time to go.'

'Coming.' Misha, deeply unhappy about being made to get out of bed, made her way downstairs and slipped on her trainers.

'You can't take me in your pyjamas,' Sammy said.

Misha shrugged. 'It's this or you don't get to school on time.'

Sammy looked annoyed. 'Mu-um, tell Misha.'

Della looked at her eldest daughter. 'Put a sweater over that vest top at the very least. Don't need the headmaster having a heart attack at the sight of your nipples greeting him at the door.'

Misha rolled her eyes. 'Way to body shame me, Mum.'

Della rolled her eyes back and proceeded to shoo Sammy, Maya and Liam, who appeared out of the living room like a rabbit out of a magician's hat, out of the house. 'See you all later and Misha, when you get back, can you tidy up the kitchen?'

'Am I getting paid for this?' Misha said.

'Are you paying rent, or bills? Love you!' Della countered, then promptly shut the front door on her kids. She turned her attention back to Jess. 'Let me get changed and we'll be off.'

'You're fine as you are, Della. You don't need to worry about—' Jess found herself standing in the hallway alone before she'd even finished her sentence. Ten minutes later Della reappeared, resplendent in a strappy sundress and hat.

'Weather's so lovely today, I wanted to make the most of it. Don't worry, I'll put some sensible shoes on, in case we have to run anywhere. Shall we get going and meet Darce?'

Darcy was waiting for them at the tube station, dressed in a floral, sleeveless trouser suit with flares so wide you couldn't see her feet.

Della whistled. 'What a stunner!'

Darcy straightened imaginary creases from the front of her outfit. 'I've had it years; Andy never liked me wearing it, but I thought I'd give it an outing seeing as I don't really care what he thinks anymore.'

'You look great,' Jess said, and meant it.

'Thank you, Jess.'

They found an empty set of seats at one end of the train, far enough away from anyone else that they could talk, at least until they reached Earl's Court and things got busier.

'So, our very own "brief encounter",' Darcy said, rubbing her hands together.

'Oooo… Brief Encounters Limited,' Della replied, her eyes lighting up.

'No.' Darcy and Jess spoke firmly in unison.

'Nina Foster sounds like a woman after my own heart,' Darcy said. 'Although I'm not sure about the whole ruining someone else's marriage part.'

'It's not our decision to make,' Jess replied. 'Our client is paying us to collect the proof and put her in touch with Clare's husband. What happens afterwards is their business.'

'Yes, I *do* get that, but I'm not sure I'd appreciate someone sticking their nose into my business like that,' Darcy commented. 'I mean, she doesn't know their circumstances. Maybe the husband already knows about the affair. Maybe he's doing his best to ignore it. Or maybe he doesn't have a clue and finding out will be the worst thing to ever happen to him.'

Della interrupted. 'Why are you taking their side, Darce? If you hadn't found out about Andy yourself, but someone else knew, wouldn't you want to be told?'

'I'm not sure,' Darcy said, her voice small. 'Probably. But life was so much simpler before.'

'Really?' Della said. 'Or did you just pretend it was, so you didn't have to change?'

The question was left unanswered as they reached the hotel, the façade covered with scaffolding that hid the nineties bold lettering and flaking paintwork. It clearly wasn't anywhere near as glamorous as the website had made it sound. In Jess's experience, hotels rarely were. The fictitious sites of Hollywood movie affairs, with dazzling lights, beautiful people and exotic décor were in stark contrast to the hotels and motels she'd been in during the past months of playing P.I., where sticky carpets, badly dressed tourists and the stench of desperation were more the norm. This one was no different.

'Hang on,' Della said. 'Are you coming in with us?'

Jess nodded. 'I thought I might.' She didn't elaborate and Della looked confused.

'But I thought you wanted us to do things without you? I thought that was the whole idea?'

'It was. It is,' Jess said. 'But this is your first proper job and I want to make sure it goes well. We're in central London; no one pays attention to who you are here, unless you're Madonna or the Queen. It'll be fine. We're going to order a nice late breakfast to eat in the lobby and it will look like three friends meeting, one of whom happens to have been on the television.'

'You could have made a bit more of an effort, Jess. Here's me and Darce in our Monday best and you look like you got dressed in the dark.'

Jess looked down at her unwashed cropped jeans and T-shirt. It was a nice T-shirt – or had been, before it got one of those annoying holes in the front near the button fly of her jeans that always seemed to happen after a few months of wear. Della wasn't wrong: she'd let herself go a bit lately. 'This is all I had clean. All my good clothes are at home.' Along with the murder weapon, presumably, as there'd been no warrant put out for her arrest, sitting on the floor where she'd left it.

'Maybe stop by later on to pick some up,' Darcy said gently. 'Especially as it's Marianne's funeral tomorrow.'

They went in through the door and stopped at the glossy, black reception desk. It looked swish enough from the outside, but like the façade, it was older than it first appeared: Jess could see the chips and dents in the lacquer and the blotches of grubby finger marks that had been left all over the surface by customers leaning over on their way in and out. There were numerous armchairs in the reception area, on a carpet that had seen better days, and behind that, an open-concept café-cum-bar that looked like a glorified Costa.

'Can I help you?' The receptionist (young, sullen, too much makeup) looked up from behind the desk, assessing the three of them. Her eyes settled on Jess, her disapproval of the scruffy jeans and T-shirt combo abundantly clear. Jess turned on her best TV celebrity charm.

'Jessica Sinclair. We're here for breakfast. I believe my agent booked us, the name of Damon Brown. Table for three.'

The girl checked her computer. 'We don't have anything in here, I'm afraid.'

'That's disappointing,' Jess said. 'But you don't seem busy. Is it okay if we just—' she gestured to the lobby.

'Of course.' The girl could hardly say no, although given half the chance she looked like she would have. 'Come right this way.'

'We'll sit by the window, please. This will be fine.' They took a spot on a trio of low-slung chairs. Jess noticed a ring mark on the table; on closer inspection, the chair upholstery was tired and there was a stain on one of the seats. Not that it mattered to her, but she was always surprised at how much wear and tear these so-called five-star hotels got away with.

'We've got a great view of the lobby from here,' Darcy said.

'They've got pancakes,' Della salivated as she poured over the menu. 'I love pancakes. Can never get them right myself. Always too doughy.'

'Can I help you?' A waitress (Nordic, blonde, complacent) came over, balancing an iPad in one hand.

'We'll have a pot of English breakfast tea, please. And a croissant for me.' Jess said.

'We have a breadbasket that's got a croissant, a pain au chocolat, sourdough toast and a muffin in it?' The girl's voice lilted upwards, so that she made it sound like a question.

'Sure.'

The girl's long, acrylic nails tapped on the screen. 'Anything else?'

Della raised her hand. 'American pancakes please. With bacon and maple syrup and a side of berries. And a latte.'

'Jesus, Della.'

'What?' Della glared at Darcy. 'It's brain food.'

'Anything for you, madam?'

'A fresh orange juice, please.' Darcy looked at the menu. 'And a granola with yoghurt.'

Tap, tap, tap. 'Thanks,' said the girl, whisking away the menus. She came back moments later with a jug of water stuffed with mint leaves, cucumber and a lemon, and poured a glass for each of them.

Jess waited until she was gone to get out the client file from her backpack. She passed Della and Darcy a mugshot of Adam Foster.

'A reminder of who we're looking for.'

'He's a dickhead,' Della said. 'You can tell by the goatee.'

'I don't think you can judge someone's moral standing by their facial hair,' Darcy said.

'Don't you?' Della replied.

Their teas and coffees arrived, served in colourful bone china cups with a complementary floral pattern sugar bowl and milk jug. The teapot was enormous; Jess hoped the stakeout wasn't completely ruined by them all needing the bathroom halfway through.

She poured a cup for herself and Darcy. Della stirred a couple of lumps of sugar into her coffee and was taking her first sip when she choked and put her napkin up to her face.

'Della, what are you doing?'

Della tried very hard not to draw attention by coughing. She shook her head at Jess, eyes wide. 'Don't... turn... round...'

'What on earth is the matter?'

'It's Naomi!' Della said, hissing from behind her napkin. 'I went to their front door; she recognises me and we'll be screwed!'

'Come and sit next to me, she won't recognise you from behind. Darcy, can you get some photos?' Jess said, calmly. 'Darcy? All good?'

Darcy picked up her phone and motioned them to squash together. 'That's perfect, I can pretend I'm taking photos of the two of you,' she said, tapping away furiously.

'Is she on her own?' Jess asked.

Darcy nodded, her eyes never straying from Naomi. 'Maybe not for long, though. She's got a room key and she's headed for the lift.'

'Follow her. Find out the room number.' Jess's voice was low and urgent and Darcy immediately sprang into action, tucking her phone in her pocket.

'Hang on a minute,' Della said, 'I thought we were here for Adam Foster?'

Darcy hesitated and Jess jerked her head towards the lifts. 'Go. We'll cover things down here.'

Jess didn't dare look as Darcy sailed away from them and across the lobby. When they heard the lift ping, she breathed a sigh of relief.

'So my guess is you didn't come just to keep us company,' Della said, raising an eyebrow.

Jess paused, knowing she'd have to confess to being in Ben's flat the night of the stakeout. 'I found a couple of spa treatments from this place on her credit card statement. When I found out we were headed here anyway, it seemed like too good an opportunity to miss.'

Della folded her arms and narrowed her eyes. 'How the hell did you get hold of Naomi's credit card bill?'

Jess pursed her lips and came clean about the whole sorry story, ending with her hasty retreat while Naomi was in the shower.

'Huh,' Della said, when she'd finished. 'Well, your motives were sound, even if your method was a bit... kamikaze. You're lucky she didn't find you. Or that Ben didn't come home.'

'I know.' It didn't bear thinking about. Ben finding her in his house, uninvited, for a second time, would definitely lead to an arrest.

'You really think she could have killed Marianne?' Della said.

'It would certainly make sense. But if I go to Ben, or Graham Dickson, with my theory, I need proof that I'm right. There's no way he'd believe me about this unless I've got concrete evidence.'

'We know she doesn't have the murder weapon,' Della said. 'So, how will you prove it was her? And what's she got against you, that she's sending you death threats?'

'I found our wedding photo in Ben's bedside drawer,' she said. 'Maybe Naomi thought he still had feelings for me.'

'But she's sleeping with someone else. She could have left Ben anytime.'

'She's clearly not a rational person,' Jess said, getting a little annoyed at all Della's questions. 'And we don't know that she sent the first note. She could be a copycat.'

Della nodded. 'True, I suppose. So, what's next? Apart from sending Darce into a lift with a psycho.'

'Darcy knows to be careful,' Jess said. 'I only asked her to follow Naomi in case she's meeting this 'Jake' guy she was on the phone with. If we get the evidence, Ben will have to believe me.'

'Better make sure she doesn't kill you before then. What if—'

'Pancakes?' The waitress had arrived with their food. 'And a breadbasket. The granola's on the way.'

'Thank you.' Jess smiled at her, although it wasn't returned.

Della resumed her seat across the table. 'This looks amazing,' she said, digging in.

'Anyway, Della, remember why *you're* really here,' Jess said, watching Della make eyes at her food. 'If we don't get the photos of Adam, Nina Foster has to wait another agonising week for them.' Della made a non-committed noise. 'Do you want to swap places? I can watch while you eat.'

'I can do two things at once, you know,' Della finally said, her mouth full to bursting. She took a huge swallow then suddenly her eyes widened.

'What's the name of that bloke you said Naomi was shagging?'

'Jake. I don't have a surname, I—'

'Jesus Christ.'

'What?' Jess turned around to see what the fuss was.

Della shook her head. 'It can't be—'

'Can't be what?'

'Jake Lemmon. From Pink Lemonade.'

'Who?'

'You can tell you don't have kids,' Della said, taking out her phone. 'Here. See? They're huge YouTube stars. Misha idolises them.'

Naomi was having an affair with a YouTube celebrity? Jess felt suddenly indignant. 'I can't sit in the back of a police car without reporters camping outside my front door for a week. How is the press not all over this?'

'Hush money, I expect.' Della quickly wiped her mouth, brushed herself down and got up from her seat.

'Where are you going?' Jess hissed.

'Scuse me. Jake! Jake Lemmon!'

Della had put on her best Scouse accent and was headed towards the reception area.

Jess slid down in her seat, gazing out of the window. It was about then that Adam Foster (slim, stubbled, spectacled) and Clare Hathaway (busty, blonde, botoxed) chose to walk by. 'It never rains but it pours,' Jess muttered. She shifted round to Darcy's vacant chair and watched the mess unfolding in the lobby. Jake Lemmon (mussed hair, leather jacket, skinny jeans) stood at the reception desk, pinned in place by a short, crazy lady.

'I'm a huge fan,' Della was gushing. 'At least, my kids are. You'd make my day if we could have a selfie! I know you're probably busy and everything but—' she wiggled about, the good foot in height between the two of them allowing him a bird's eye view of her cleavage '—I'm worth it.'

Jake Lemmon smiled easily and nodded to Della's phone. 'Sure.'

Della handed her phone to Adam Foster, who was waiting impatiently to check in. 'Would you mind doing the honours?'

'Actually—'

'We should get one of you, too!' Della said. 'I bet your kids – do you have kids? Maybe not, you're quite young – anyway, if you do have them, they'll love it—'

'We don't,' Clare Hathaway spoke, her definitive tone taking the edge off Della's enthusiasm slightly.

'Ah well,' she shrugged, then turned her attention back to Jake. 'Ready? One, two, three, cheese!'

Adam Foster handed the phone back, and Della checked the image. 'Perfect,' she said, fiddling about a bit with the screen. 'So sorry to have disturbed you. I hope I didn't keep you from anything important. Or anyone,' she added, winking at them both, and then again at Jake.

Jake Lemmon looked uncomfortable, and Jess wondered if Della had pushed things too far. But he quickly plastered a smile on his face and nodded at her. 'Nice to meet you... ?'

'Maggie,' Della said. 'You can write a song about me if you like.' She grinned. 'Although Rod Stewart's kind of got the market cornered already.'

Adam Foster cleared his throat. 'Excuse me, but we'd like to check in—'

'Sorry, yeah, I'll get out of your way,' Della said.

The receptionist handed Jake Lemmon a key card. 'Your guest is waiting for you, Mr. Lemmon.'

Jess watched Della's eyes flick down to the number scrawled on the little card folder. Jake instinctively palmed it.

'Don't worry,' she chuckled. 'I'm here celebrating my friend's birthday,' she waved over at Jess, who gave a reciprocal hand gesture. 'I won't turn into some weird stalker and try to break into your room or anything.'

Jake grimaced and walked away. Della strode back to the table.

'I hope my pancakes didn't go cold,' she said.

'What the hell were you thinking?'

'I was thinking, it was time to put that drama degree to good use,' she said, handing over her phone. 'Check that out. A photo of Jake *and* one of our brief encounter.'

'How did you manage that?'

'Took it when I pretended to check the photo with Jake,' Della said. 'Now you got two for the price of one. And Jake's room number was 701,' she added. 'If that tallies with Darce when she gets back, you've got them in the bag too.'

'It tallies perfectly,' Jess said, waving her phone. Darcy had sent a photo of Naomi disappearing into a hotel room, and another of the closed door: room 701.

'Amazing work,' Jess said.

Della grinned and shoved another mouthful of pancakes in. 'I told you these were brain food.'

'I JUST NEED A MOMENT'

Jess let herself into the house, nervous at the silence enveloping her. She'd not been back in a few days but it was Marianne's funeral tomorrow and she needed to find something suitable to wear. She stopped in the living room first, checking to make sure nothing had been disturbed. It looked exactly as she had left it, and the kitchen was too... Wherever Ben had gone the night she was stalking him, it wasn't here. Jess picked up the knife from the floor and shoved it in the kitchen junk drawer where it joined the melee of batteries, screwdrivers, string, takeaway menus and superglue. She put the note in the recycling.

Upstairs, she leafed through her wardrobe. Her outfit had to be carefully curated: something that didn't scream jilted wife, or psycho killer, or sad, lonely spinster. Rifling through her old show clothes, she found a black, pleated skirt and long-sleeved, silk shirt. It was feminine, nice enough to look like she'd tried, but not so nice that people would think she was using the funeral as a PR opportunity. But a bit warm for the time of year... scraping back the hangers to hunt deeper behind the doors, she came across a cap sleeve top in which she wouldn't sweat too much.

She gave a snort. Who was she kidding? She was going to be a sweaty mess no matter what she wore. The thought of seeing Ben and Naomi was sending her stress levels off the charts, and she knew that it would be a huge effort to not say or do anything to ruin her friend's funeral.

She still didn't feel like she had enough evidence to prove Naomi was Marianne's killer. Yes, it was an awful thing Naomi was doing, and there was clearly no love lost between the two women according to Rosie, but did it really cost Marianne her life? Jake Lemmon was obviously quite famous by Gen Z standards; he wasn't Mick bloody Jagger, but from his reels and stories, he seemed like a fairly nice bloke. An affair with the pregnant wife of a copper was scandalous but not particularly career limiting. Murder seemed like a complicated way to keep Marianne quiet, given they were evidently planning to tell Ben sooner rather than later anyway. The state she was in, throwing her a couple of hundred quid and a bottle of vodka would have probably done the trick.

Jess chided herself for that last thought. Marianne wouldn't be bought; she might not be a copper anymore, but it would go against her integrity, and she knew Marianne would give up the booze and pills long before she'd sacrifice that. Picking up her phone, she searched for Jake on Instagram again. His official account was filled with images of guitars, a few 'candid' shots of him rehearsing or walking a dog and the occasional teaser pose from his bed, topless and looking slightly weather beaten. One such image had been posted the day after Marianne died, with a caption:

<<A lazy breakfast in bed this morning after an amazing gig last night! A special 24 hrs with a special person. #breakfast #hotellife #singer #pinklemmonade #ontour #london #paddington #whatgoesontour #secretlover #groupie #babyblue>>

Jess zoomed in on the photo. In the top corner, by Jake's shoulder, strands of dark, straight hair rested on his naked shoulder and a woman's manicured hand rested gently on his chest. A pale blue French manicure. *Baby blue.* Jess threw her phone down in frustration. Naomi and Jake had been together the night of Marianne's death, and there was no way they could have killed her. When she'd worked in television, she'd been called for at least two hours before her show, to get into makeup and mics and do the pre-production meeting. A rock star on a tour, no matter how small, would have hours of sound checks and rehearsal time on stage before they went live, which ruled him out; and the photo in bed the next day meant there was no chance he or Naomi had gone back the next morning to clean up. Jess sighed. They might be truly awful people, but neither Naomi nor Jake were killers. She was back to square one.

Back at Della's, Jess did up the zip of her skirt and slipped on a pair of black pumps. It was ten thirty and she had to be at the church in three hours. She'd allowed half an hour for traffic and parking, but she needed to leave shortly to be on time. She had a stop to make on the way.

A quick bit of mascara later and she left Della's, calling goodbye as she shut the front door. Getting in the car, she turned the key, only to find it wouldn't start.

'Shit.' She tried again several times before smacking the steering wheel so heavily it stung her hands. Frustrated and tearful, she got out and stalked back to the house. She hoped Della was feeling generous.

'What's up?' Della appeared at the top of the stairs, her hair wrapped in a towel. 'Are you okay?'

'My car broke down.'

Della whipped off the towel. 'Give me ten minutes, I'll drive you. I'll call Bill, get him to sort your car while we're gone.'

'What about your fish sales?'

'They can wait. This is important. Anyway, I want to go.'

'Who wants to go to a funeral? You didn't even know Marianne.'

'No, but I know you. You may have lost a friend, Jess, but don't forget you gained one too.'

Jess smiled. 'Thanks, Della.' She paused. 'Oh, and we need to make a stop at Penny Hill Lane. I promised Rosie I'd take her to the funeral.'

They hammered up the M1 at a top speed of 63 miles per hour, Della keeping her chatter to a minimum, for once. She'd dressed for the occasion: a form-fitting, black sundress that dipped deep into her cleavage and a pair of stilettos to match. Jess smiled. Marianne would have loved Della. She suspected she might have taken longer to warm to Darcy. But the four of them could have developed into a good team.

The thought made Jess catch her breath.

'Penny for them,' Rosie said.

'Huh?'

'Penny for your thoughts.'

'Oh... I was thinking about Maz, that's all,' Jess said. 'I think she and Della would have got on famously.'

Della grinned. 'She sounded like she was a lot of fun.'

'She was a lot of everything,' Jess replied.

'Did the police find any leads yet?' Rosie asked. 'I haven't heard from DCI Dickson at all, but I'm certain you've seen him more recently than I have.'

Jess gritted her teeth and remembered Ben's words about old busybodies.

'She must have put away some right nasty characters,' Rosie continued.

Jess nodded. 'She used to keep all the newspaper articles from her cases, the ones that were convicted.'

Rosie looked impressed.

'It was over ten years ago she was working on those sorts of cases. Most of them are either still banged up or dead and buried.'

'Bet she made a fair few enemies, though.'

'Yeah. But if any of them are suspects, the police will find them,' Jess said.

Rosie hurrumphed. 'I'm not sure the police could find their way out of a paper bag.'

'You might want to keep that opinion to yourself today,' Della said. 'I reckon this funeral will be crawling with plod.'

They drove in companionable silence until the crematorium was in sight.

'We're here,' Della announced. 'Why don't I drop you and Rosie off at the front so she doesn't have so far to walk, and I can find somewhere to park?'

'The side would be better,' Jess said. 'I don't want to draw attention.' She gave Della a meaningful look and then turned to Rosie. 'Is that okay with you?'

'I think I can manage a few extra steps, Jessica. And if I keel over from the extra effort, I'm in the right place.'

Jess climbed out of the truck and smoothed her skirt down before making her way with Rosie to the crematorium entrance.

Whatever she said about her mobility, it was slow going with the older woman, and it gave Jess plenty of time to look around at the people who'd come to say their goodbyes.

The sun beat down on her head. It was an unreasonably warm day for a funeral, which she couldn't help but associate with the grey, cold days of winter. She was glad she'd gone with the cap sleeve; the men were all sweating in their suits while the women were less encumbered by their outfits.

Della had been right: the place was full of police. There were a lot of familiar faces from Marianne and Ben's old days at the Met, but none who would want to be seen fraternising, on today of all days. It was better to keep her distance and avoid talking to anyone. Jess wondered if Graham Dickson would bother to show up. As if reading her mind, he suddenly appeared beside her.

'Didn't expect to see you here,' he said.

'Ditto.'

'They say perpetrators always return to the scene of the crime,' Graham looked around, smiling, while he spoke to her in threatening tones. He met her eye. 'And quite often, to the funeral as well.'

'People who care about the deceased also go to funerals,' Jess bit back. 'Although I'm not sure that's why you're here.'

Graham gave her a menacing look and melted into the crowd.

'Friend of yours?'

Jess turned to Rosie, feeling her heart beating noisily. 'Why don't you grab a seat. I'm going to wait for Della.'

'Please yourself,' Rosie shrugged. 'I'll be up the front if anyone wants me.'

She was immediately lost to the throng of people waiting in the shaded portico, and having lost sight of her, Jess turned and scanned the crowd. Ben, looking handsome as ever, stood in a sharp cut suit, it only serving to exaggerate his well-toned physique. Naomi came into view next to him. She, too, was in black, creating a perfectly pregnant silhouette against the green of the remembrance garden behind her. Jess turned away from them both, hoping they hadn't spotted her. She didn't need another scene; today was about Marianne. She walked quickly beyond the crematorium grounds and back out onto the street, to wait for Della. If she didn't hurry up, they'd miss the service.

The hearse pulled past and into the turning bay. Jess watched it go by with Marianne's coffin inside, bereft of flowers save a single, simple arrangement on the top. Della came from the opposite direction, making Jess jump as she tapped her on the shoulder. 'Where's Rosie? I could have met you in there, you know.'

'She's inside already.'

'I think we need to go in now too,' Della said, nodding towards the door. The men were already gathering around the hearse in preparation. 'You ready?'

'I just need a moment.'

Della backed away, giving a sympathetic smile. Jess watched as the coffin was pulled from the hearse and turned to follow Della inside. A throbbing, throaty noise made her stop and she looked back to see that a motorbike had pulled up, its heavy-set rider turning stiffly to face the coffin. Jess peered at the rider as his visor pulled open and gasped. It was the man from Marianne's cottage, the day she'd gone to see Rosie. It couldn't be a coincidence. She locked eyes with him, and in an instant, he pushed his visor down again.

'Excuse me! No, wait—'

The rider pulled away quickly, the roar of the bike disturbing the low murmurings of the pall bearers as they hoisted the coffin into place on their shoulders. A lump appeared in Jess's throat. Had she been looking in all the wrong places? Was he the key to all this?

From inside the crematorium, the organ began to play, and she made her way quickly to her seat next to Della, just in time for the procession to begin. Marianne's coffin moved past them at a slow, awkward pace. Ben's eyes were fixed dead ahead as he led the rest of the pallbearers – who she saw now, were all part of Marianne's old squad, paying their very last respects. Jess bowed her head, tears rolling down her face. She gripped Della's hand tightly and focused on the small space in front of her as she said her final goodbyes.

'WHAT THE HELL WERE YOU DOING IN MY FLAT, JESSICA?'

The wake was held at the Hughes's family home, and it was with some trepidation that Jess walked through the front door. It was one thing sitting in the back of the crematorium where she could hide from everyone, but another thing entirely to be in Mr and Mrs Hughes's front room clutching a plate of stale cucumber sandwiches.

Jess took the wine offered from a tastefully decorated table in the living room and gulped at it, looking around for someone to talk to and wishing she'd gone with Della to park the truck a few streets away where it wouldn't draw attention. She could see Rosie sat on a sofa looking very at home with a crowd of elderly relatives, but she wasn't about to go over there and deal with the inevitable gossiping. The crowd was still fairly thin – Jess suspected Marianne's old crew would have stopped at the pub on their way to the house. Perhaps Ben would be among them, and she hoped he was. That way, she could take her leave before he saw her there—

Someone cleared their throat behind her, and she turned, her eyes widening. 'Naomi.'

'You came.' The statement hovered somewhere between surprise and disgust.

'Just paying my respects.' First Graham, then Naomi. Why was she justifying her presence to these people? Jess blinked slowly and tried to relax her jaw.

Naomi nodded and stroked her belly, her baby blue French manicure dancing across the bump.

'Lots of familiar faces today,' Jess continued, trying to make small talk.

'No one that wants to talk to you, it would seem.' Naomi countered.

Jess counted to ten in her head. She absolutely *had* to stick to small talk. Now was not the time or the place—

'Hello, Jess.' Ben's voice startled her. It was smooth and soft – nothing like the angry snapping she'd suffered the last time they met. She turned to look at him, and involuntarily, instinctively, reached out and gave him a hug. He didn't return it, but he didn't bristle in her embrace either; Jess was buried in his chest too deeply to be able to see Naomi's reaction, but she imagined it was slightly pricklier.

She pulled away.

'I didn't think you'd be here,' he said.

Naomi snorted. Jess opened her mouth to say something, then changed her mind and turned back to Ben. 'Perhaps I shouldn't have come,' she said, quietly.

Ben threw a dark glance at Naomi. Was it her imagination or was something wrong between the two of them? They didn't seem quite as... together. Ben had been so angry with her at his house and then at the station, but today, it felt like some of that anger was aimed squarely in Naomi's direction. Did Ben know? Or suspect? She opened her mouth to say something more, then closed it again. She had sworn to herself she wouldn't bring up the investigation today – or the affair.

Naomi moved to stand between the two of them. 'Ben, we need to circulate.'

'In a minute, Nomes.' His eyes lit up. 'No way.'

A woman (middle-aged, middle class, mildly over-excited given it was a funeral) approached them. She looked vaguely familiar, although Jess couldn't place her.

'Ben?'

'Barbara! How are you?'

She air-kissed him three times. 'Gosh, it's been years! I hate that we're meeting again like this. At another funeral. Seems they're the only reunions we have these days.'

Ben gave a small, sad smile. 'You're right about that.' He indicated towards Naomi. 'I don't think you've met my fiancée.'

Barbara looked at Naomi and her baby bump. 'Looks like double congratulations are in order.'

'Thank you.' Naomi and Ben both spoke in unison, although it didn't sound like either of them meant it.

Barbara looked at Jess. 'And of course, I know who you are.'

'You do?' Jess said, frowning. She didn't remember this woman at all. 'I'm sorry, Maz never—'

'Barbara Edwards,' the woman said. 'The old DCS's secretary. I was at your wedding.' She gave a broad smile, which wasn't returned by anyone. 'Of course, I was blonde back then,' she said, patting her grey bob.

'Of course,' Jess said, giving a nod. Naomi scowled.

'Anyway, seems like divorcing DI Morgan here didn't do you any harm!' Barbara continued, oblivious to Naomi's snarl. 'A TV star and looking so good too. Good for you. Your name was mud around the Met for years, you know – they called you Yoko. Because you split up the band.'

'No, I didn't know that.' She gave a sideways glance across the room to where a bunch of the old team were now standing. 'How nice of them.'

Ben looked distinctly uncomfortable.

Barbara chuckled. 'You doing that private detective show sent them all batty. You were very good though; I was a huge fan.' She looked at Ben and Naomi. 'This woman, what a nose she has for secrets! Quite remarkable!'

Naomi shifted uneasily. 'Ben, I think I need to find a seat,' she said. 'Rest my legs.'

'Growing a human's hard work, isn't it?' Barbara put her hand on Ben's arm to stop him. 'Before you go, will you take a photo of me and Jess? We can use your phone, it's probably got a better camera than mine,' she said to Jess, indicating she should give it up to Ben. 'You can AirDrop me after. My grandson taught me how to do it.'

Jess handed over her phone to Ben, who took it with a small grin. Naomi simmered next to him while Ben set up the shot. 'Okay, say cheese!'

They stood together, smiling while Ben took the shot. Jess held her hand out to take the phone.

'Oooo... what about one with Ben too,' Barbara said, beckoning him. 'Naomi, would you mind?'

'I can take it,' Jess said, not wishing to make things more uncomfortable than they already were. 'You can have one with Ben and Naomi.'

'Nonsense!' Barbara said. 'You two can be in a photo together, can't you? Just like old times. Naomi, would you mind?'

Naomi looked like she very much did but snatched the phone from Ben anyway to snap the photo. Just as Barbara was gathering them together for the shot, Della appeared beside Jess, looking distressed.

'What's wrong?'

Della muttered into her ear. 'We have to leave,' she murmured, her eyes fixed on the archway that led from the living room into the dining room where the buffet sat waiting. 'Rosie just told half the funeral party that we travelled up here in a frozen fish truck, causing much hilarity from anyone who'd listen. We're the talk of the funeral. If Ben hears and puts two and two together – if he remembers me or the truck—'

Jess nodded and smiled at Ben, Barbara and Naomi.

'I'm afraid we have to go. Could I have my phone, Barbara?'

'Hang on, let me AirDrop them to myself.' Barbara scrolled through Jess's photo images. 'Oops, too far.' She peered closer at the phone. 'Naomi, is that you? Gosh I didn't realise you two were such good friends, there's about ten, twelve shots of you on here. Looking lovely, I might say. Where is this? A hotel? It looks very posh.'

A cold dread came over Jess. 'Barbara, if I could—'

Ben grabbed the phone. 'Let me see those.'

'Ben, wait—'

'What the—?' Ben swiped at her phone, and Jess tried to grab it from his hands.

'Nothing. It's nothing.'

He carried on swiping, his jaw falling open. 'This is my flat. When were you in my flat? WHAT THE HELL WERE YOU DOING IN MY FLAT, JESSICA?'

Barbara gasped. The rest of the room went very quiet. Jess could see Graham Dickson in the background, mid-hors d'oeuvres, looking interested.

'Ben, I can explain—'

'Too damn right you can!' Ben exploded.

'Ben,' Barbara said. 'Remember where we are.'

Jess looked around. Some people were making their way quietly out of the room. Others stayed, surreptitiously drawing closer to the drama to get a good look.

'Ben, let's go somewhere a bit quieter—'

'Oh, I'm sure whatever you have to say, it would be better to have witnesses,' Ben growled.

'It really wouldn't, Ben.'

'Just tell him what he wants to hear, will you?' Naomi spat. 'Anyone can see you're making a complete fool of yourself, and right in the middle of a funeral as well, for god's sake.'

Jess felt herself getting angry.

'Jess,' Della urged. 'Let's go.'

Jess shrugged her off. 'Not yet, Della. If Naomi thinks I'm making a fool of myself, maybe she'd like to explain how she's been doing the same to her fiancé.'

'What are you talking about?' Ben asked.

'Yes, what *are* you talking about?' Naomi added.

Paralysed with emotion, knowing if she said anything, it was going to cause irreparable damage, Jess couldn't answer. But Della, gently taking the phone from Ben's hand, scrolled down on the screen, and then held it up to Ben to see. 'This is me and Jake Lemmon.'

The colour drained out of Naomi's face. 'Ben, these women are clearly deranged. I—'

'Who's Jake Lemmon?'

'He's a musician. A YouTube sensation,' Della said. 'This was taken at a hotel in Paddington. And this—' she swiped again another couple of times. '—is Naomi, checking into the same hotel ten minutes earlier. To the same room.'

Ben stared at them all, incredulous.

'I don't know what they're talking about, Ben. I—'

'Quiet,' Ben said, cold fury etched over his face. He looked at Della. 'Tell me.'

'We were on another job, actually. It was quite the coincidence,' Della said, grinning with pride, before checking herself and straightening her mouth. 'Naomi and Jake checked into the same suite. Room 701. And—' she flicked through Jess's phone, to the images of the bank statements and the screen grab of Jake's Insta post '—it would appear it's not the first time.'

A hush had descended on the whole room now. Mary and Doug Hughes were standing, bewildered, by the buffet. Jess looked across to them and mouthed an apology which they returned with daggered, dark stares. This was not how she'd wanted this to go.

'Ben, maybe we should take this outside.'

He ignored her, his eyes blazing at Naomi. 'Is this true?'

'Of course not! I would never—'

Ben turned to Jess. 'Is this true?'

She nodded slowly, hating herself. Ben deflated as the truth sank in.

'When we saw them at the hotel, we'd already... that is...' Now she was getting herself into hot water. But she had to tell the truth. It was the only way out of this mess. She took a deep breath. 'I thought you might have killed Maz,' she said, in a quiet voice. 'You were the last person to see her. And you'd had that argument, about Naomi—'

'I told her that,' Rosie said from across the room, munching on a sausage roll. 'I heard you both, the morning she was killed.

266

Marianne was trying to tell you that slut you're marrying was cheating on you.'

The room gasped collectively, and Jess looked at the old woman who looked like she was weirdly enjoying all this. Bloody busybody.

Naomi blanched. 'How dare you! I – Ben, I swear it's not what it looks like—'

Ben looked dangerously from Naomi to Jess. 'Tell. Me. Everything.'

Jess swallowed. 'I was in your flat. I thought you might have something to do with Marianne's murder.' She didn't dare look at Graham Dickson. 'I overheard you talking on the phone, about searching my flat... Naomi went out just after you.'

Ben frowned. 'I didn't... you know what, it doesn't matter. What happened next?'

'Next... I fell asleep.' Jess heard a few titters from the crowd that had gathered and did her best to ignore them. 'But then Naomi came home, and I hid; that was when I overheard her talking on the phone. To a man. It sounded like they were more than just friends, like she'd... spent the night with him.' She shifted awkwardly. 'I traced a spa receipt on her credit card bill to a hotel in Paddington, and there she was with the same guy.'

He turned to Naomi, incredulous. 'Is this true?'

'It's complicated—'

'IS THIS TRUE?' His voice was filled with rage.

Naomi paused, then nodded. Several of the older women sitting with Rosie tutted and Naomi placed a hand protectively over her belly. The action caught Ben's attention, and he stared. 'How long, Naomi? How long's this been going on?'

'Ben, I swear, I was going to say something before the baby came—'

'How long?'

'Long enough.' Naomi paused. 'Since 2007, if we're being accurate.'

Another gasp went up from the crowd. Jess closed her eyes.

'We fell in love when we were teenagers. We were together for years, but then we split up for a bit, he did the whole music thing, started a band... I wanted a career, a steady life, no surprises. I came to London, to make a fresh start. But then we got back in touch... Ben, I didn't want to hurt you. Things were going really well with us, and I was very fond of you. I didn't realise I was pregnant. Not right away. I wanted to give us a chance... I honestly thought it was yours. It was only after I went for the first scan and the doctor told me I was a bit more pregnant than I thought, that I did the maths and realised it was Jake's.'

Her words hung in the air and Jess watched Ben crumple, as though he'd taken a punch to the gut. He sat down heavily on a dining chair. Jess tried to push the tears away. She knew, oh god, she knew how badly this would be hurting him.

'I didn't know if Jake would stick around once he found out about the baby; I didn't know if he'd want to be a dad... and you were so happy about it. I couldn't tell you the truth... I knew it would break your heart. But, once he'd got his head around it, Jake told me he wanted to be a part of his baby's life. He wanted us to be a family....' she tailed off and looked around the room. 'Would you all mind leaving us alone? This is a private conversation.'

'Stay,' growled Ben. 'I want everyone to hear what you've done.' He paused. 'So what, you were going to carry on banging your baby-daddy until my son – *his* son – came out clutching a guitar and I guessed the truth?'

'I don't know what I was going to do. I didn't want to hurt you.' Naomi began to cry. 'We had plans to tell you soon, move back up north and start a new life away from London. Then Marianne died, and—'

'She knew. I thought it was jealousy, the booze talking—' Ben's fists curled. 'The day before she died she called me, asked me to come over and so I did. You were right.' He glanced at Jess, then redirected his glare back to Naomi. 'She tried to tell me, said you couldn't be trusted, but I wouldn't listen.' His voice took on a bitter, low resonance. 'She told me she'd seen you. With someone else, at a private club she'd been doing a job at. But I yelled at her, told her she was wrong; told her she should keep her drunk nose out of my business.' He shook his head. 'You made me think I was going to be a father, raise a family. You knew what that meant to me, after – after... And then my friend gets a knife in her heart the day after I've defended you, and instead of being there for me, you ship off to some sordid hotel room while I'm out at work?' His face cleared with understanding. 'You were with him the night she died, weren't you? It's why you weren't answering your phone—'

'Ben, please understand, we're in love—'

'You've made me look a fool,' Ben spat. 'My whole life, I can count on one hand the people who I could trust, who I let into my life. You were one of those people. I've been trained to spot liars, but you blindsided me. Because I thought no one could be that manipulative, no one would lie about a *baby*.' His eyes filled. 'How dare you. How dare you come here and stand with me and hold my hand and mourn my friend.'

'I'm so sorry.'

'I don't think sorry begins to cover it.'

'I'm – I'm sorry,' she repeated pathetically, looking around the room. She was met with nothing but stony faces and tutting from the grannies on the sofa.

'You should leave,' Ben said. 'Now.'

'Ben, please—' Naomi looked up at him with pleading eyes. 'I've got no way of getting home—'

'Give your boyfriend a call. He can send a limo. And don't bother coming back to the flat. I'll pack up your stuff and send it on.' He threw a cold look.

Naomi opened her mouth and closed it again. She walked away, the crowd parting like the Red Sea for her all the way to the door.

Ben quickly followed without so much as a goodbye and the wake wrapped up not long after. Too much damage had been done; and although Mary and Doug Hughes had remained polite, they clearly wanted everyone to leave, to mourn their daughter in peace.

Della drove them home at top velocity, the truck protesting all the way. No one said much; Della was concentrating hard on the road, Rosie was lost in thought gazing out of the window, and Jess was busy trying to process everything that had happened. When Della pulled up to the end of Penny Hill Lane, Jess turned to Rosie.

'Here you go. Home safe and sound.'

'Thank you for the ride, Della. It was nice to meet you.'

'Quite the day, in the end,' Della commented.

Rosie nodded. 'Quite the day.'

Jess helped Rosie out of the truck and made sure she had her house keys.

'Thank you for the lift.' Rosie said.'

'Sorry it was so traumatic,' Jess replied.

Rosie waved a hand. 'I've attended worse funerals. It's not so bad when you don't have strong feelings about the deceased one way or the other.'

Jess frowned. 'I thought you liked Marianne?'

'Shows you how much you know about me,' Rosie said. The old lady shut the door and let herself in. Jess waved her goodbye, watching her walk up the street to her cottage. She was right, Jess realised. She didn't know her at all.

'DON'T YOU HAVE ANY FRIENDS YOUR OWN AGE?'

'I only saw you yesterday. Don't you have any friends your own age?'

'Hello, Rosie. Can I come in?'

The old woman held the door wider, reluctantly. 'You can make the tea.'

Jess came in and shut the door, hiding her yawn behind her hand. She had slept heavily, falling into the single bed at Della's almost as soon as she got through the door. To her annoyance, though, the sun woke her early; her curtains left open from the night before. It had only taken a few moments before the events of the previous day had come swimming back into focus and she'd been wide awake, brain humming about what to do next. Bill had fixed her car just like Della had promised he would and the obvious thing had been to talk to Rosie; and so here she was, back at Penny Hill Lane, hoping the old lady could give her the answers she needed.

It was surprisingly bright and fresh inside the cottage, with a modern monochrome palette. Black and white tiles lined the floor and a pale damask wallpaper stretched up the stair walls and through the hallway. Complementary black and white photographs were pinned neatly on the walls: wedding days from various decades, children grinning, men leaning on vintage cars while women in miniskirts and bouffant hair stood by their sides. A large format photo of what must have been Rosie on her wedding day took centre stage, with her moustachioed husband standing proudly next to her. Jess sat on the stairs to take off her shoes and took in the rest of the hallway. The furniture was black ash, but substantial, not cheap looking. A pair of white china vases sat on the top of the console table along with a mother-of-pearl black and white letter tray. On the wall by the door, little bronze dog tails stuck out, a coat and scarf hooked over one while the rest were left empty for guests. From what Jess could see, the whole place was meticulously clean.

'Bit different from what you were expecting, dear?' Rosie was already halfway down the short corridor to the kitchen.

'It's very smart. Did you do it yourself?'

'When my husband died, I decided to shake things up a bit,' she said. 'I did a lot of reading, bought magazines. I always like to research a project thoroughly before I start. Then, once I had a plan, I went out and bought what I needed and took my time until it was done. I'm patient that way.'

Jess gave her a smile. 'I think you did a great job.'

'Thank you.'

Jess followed her into the kitchen. A bright space that looked as though it had been extended at the back to create a little dining nook for two. The skylight let in the glorious afternoon sun and the bifold doors were pulled open to let the air in.

'It's very lovely, Rosie. You have a good eye.'

'Thank you. My husband always had very set views on what a home should look like, even when he wasn't here to see it.'

'Was he away a lot?'

Rosie turned to pull a couple of white china mugs from a cabinet. 'We had the same furniture since we got married. When he died, I gave the lot away to charity. My sons were annoyed I didn't sell it, and even more annoyed when I started spending what they consider to be their inheritance on this place.'

'I can make the tea,' Jess said. 'Why don't you take a seat.'

Rosie did as she was told and carried on with her story. 'Anyway, they said I should save my money, or start giving some of it to them, if I had it going spare. But I wanted to make it look nice.'

A smart, grey tea caddy sat in the corner of the worktop and Jess took a couple of bags and dropped them into the mugs. Rosie gave a tut.

'There's a teapot right in front of you.'

'Sorry.' Jess took the china teapot from where it sat on the counter and opened the lid. There were teabags already in there, used and soggy; she looked around for the bin.

'Under the sink,' Rosie sighed. 'Honestly, would have been quicker to do it myself.'

Teapot emptied and rinsed out, Jess looked around for any obvious sign of a kettle.

'It's the hot water tap on the side of the sink. You press the button and it gives you boiling water,' Rosie said, indicating the small gadget. 'Saves counter space.'

While Jess made the tea, Rosie retrieved a couple of plates from a cupboard and set about slicing up some fruit cake from the fridge. Jess watched her steady hands carving and wondered how old she was. The photos in the hallway would indicate she was maybe in her late sixties, early seventies, but she was still sharp as a tack and didn't seem to have any problems physically. Maybe she got married young.

'Seventy-one,' Rosie said.

Jess started. 'How did you know what I was—'

Rosie tapped her temple. 'Been around long enough to know what people are thinking when they're gawking at me. Not much else people want to know about you once you get past sixty anyway. Just how old you are, how much money you have and whether you're going to have a purse full of coupons at the checkout.'

'That's not true.'

Rosie shrugged. 'Give it time, dear. What are you – fifty-five?'

'Fifty-one.' Jess tried not to sound too indignant.

'Well, be prepared. The change doesn't just happen to your ovaries.' Rosie took a bit of cake. 'You might be lucky. You don't have children, or grandchildren, for people to put you in that box. And you've been on the television. People pay attention to that sort of thing. It makes you matter more; god knows why.' She chewed on her cake. 'I tried to enter a game show, one of those daytime quiz things, after my husband died. Just for something to do, to make my mark on the world. But they wouldn't have me.'

The conversation was making Jess sad. She bit into her cake. It was delicious. 'Did you make this?'

Rosie laughed. 'I bought it from Tesco. But it's sweet of you to think I can bake. Another stereotype: the cake baking granny. I don't subscribe to stereotypes. Unless it suits me to be one, of course.'

'Like you were with the police.' Jess gave her a sly smile to indicate she was joking, but Rosie didn't return it.

'I don't trust the police.'

'You should, you know. They aren't all bad. Most of them are good people.'

'They don't seem to like *you* all that much.'

'They've got their reasons.' She sipped her tea. 'You trusted Marianne though, and she was the police.'

'Ex-police. And I never said I trusted her. *She* gave *me* a key, not the other way round.'

'Did she have friends?' Jess asked. 'I mean, do you think she was lonely?'

Rosie's mouth clammed shut as she chewed on her cake and kept Jess waiting until she'd swallowed. 'Never had a lot of visitors,' she eventually replied. 'Your ex. Another man used to come sometimes, maybe it was a boyfriend. She never really spoke about him.'

Sensing now was a good opportunity, Jess slid the photo of the mystery motorbike man towards her across the table. 'Is this the man you're talking about?'

'He looks a bit of a brute,' Rosie said, picking up the picture. 'It could be him. Hard to tell from this photo; he's got a helmet on.'

'He's very large. Six foot three, maybe more. And big. Broad. Well built. Not fat.'

'I can see that.' She peered at the photo again, deep in thought.

'Have you seen him at the house, Rosie?' Jess persisted. 'He had a motorbike. You'd probably have heard him before you saw him.'

Rosie handed back the photo. 'They both had bikes. But your ex had the decency to park on the street around the corner. This one used to roll right up to the door.'

Jess felt a rush of adrenaline. 'Did he visit the day of her murder? Or maybe the night before?'

Rosie narrowed her eyes. 'Are you suggesting I've been withholding information again? Only my memory isn't what it used to be and it's hard to keep track of all the comings and goings.'

Jess held up her hands in surrender. 'No judgement here. I'm grateful for anything you can remember to help me solve the puzzle. I just want to find out who killed Maz.'

Rosie breathed out heavily. 'It was the night before when he came over, I think. Monday. I didn't say anything about it because I knew she was still alive the next day, when your ex came and they had that argument.' She frowned. 'It could have even been the night before that, to be honest. It's difficult to remember the days...'

'What did you see?' Jess tried to stay patient. The timeline was so important. But regardless, she wanted to know what motorbike man had been doing there.

'He came over, maybe ten or eleven o'clock. I'm guessing it was the man you're talking about, anyway. I didn't actually see them, but the noise of the motorbike woke me up. You're not supposed to ride down this street. It's pedestrian.'

'Did you hear them talking at all?'

Rosie shook her head. 'I didn't hear anything. I heard the motorbike, the door and then maybe an hour later, I heard him drive off. It was late. I was in bed, trying to sleep.'

'Are you sure? It's important. If there's anything—'

Rosie got up and carried the plates to the sink. 'You know, Marianne could never take no for an answer either. You two might not have spoken in years but you definitely share that trait.'

Jess took the hint. She polished off her tea and stood up.

'Thanks, Rosie. You've been very helpful.'

'Have I?' Rosie looked surprised. 'I didn't mean to be.'

She made her way to the front door, the old lady following behind. Jess turned to say goodbye, gesturing to the photos on the walls. 'Are these your family?'

'My sons,' Rosie said, nodding towards a picture of two boys. 'In their forties now, of course. They visit me from time to time.'

Jess pointed to the wedding photo. 'Is that you?'

Rosie nodded. 'Best photo we have of us together.'

Jess's phone pinged and she glanced quickly at the message. 'I have to make a call. Thanks for the tea. I'll try not to bother you again.'

'That would be nice.' Rosie gave her a half-smile and shut the door.

Darcy was sitting in Della's kitchen when she got back.

'We did some research,' she said, smugly. 'We got the number plate of the motorbike from the crematorium's security cameras and ran it through the system.'

Jess raised her eyebrows in surprise. 'You did?'

Della nodded. 'The bloke's name is Robert McEvoy. He's a chef from Barnsley. Moved to London about seven years ago. The bike's registered to a Fulham address, and Robert – or Bobby, as his company website referred to him – is the joint owner of a small restaurant in the area. He's single, no kids, lives on his own.'

'A chef from Yorkshire? How the hell would he know Maz?'

'That's the interesting bit.' Darcy said, tapping at her phone. 'I'm sending you a local news report I found online, from thirteen years ago. Prior to his new life as a restaurateur, Bobby McEvoy was banged up for five years.'

'He's an ex-con?' Jess tried to control her excitement.

'Got done for possession of cocaine with intent to supply.'

Jess did the maths. Thirteen years ago would have been the heyday for Marianne and Ben. She didn't know much about what they did or where they were, but she knew they were working with the drugs squad and a lot of their jobs were in the north. If Marianne had been the one to get Bobby arrested... if he'd spotted her in London, found out who she really was... It all made sense, suddenly. She checked the time. It was still early, and she had nowhere else to be. If she hurried, she could be at Bobby's house in an hour.

'Get together what you need for a surveillance job tomorrow,' she said. 'I need to go out.'

'Are you going to find Bobby McEvoy? Can we come?'

'No,' Jess said. 'I need to do this one on my own.'

The street where Bobby McEvoy had registered his motorbike was a typical one for the area, made up of rows of identical terraced houses, most of them carved into flats and each resident paying through the nose for the privilege of living in five hundred square feet of real estate in Zone 2. He must be a pretty decent cook to afford anything around here. Or he had made a *lot* of money from drugs.

Google maps had said it would only take her half an hour but it hadn't calculated the pre-lunchtime rush across the river. By the time she got to Bobby's street she was hot and fed up with stop-start traffic and crazy cyclists cutting her up and giving her a heart attack every time they brushed by her wing mirrors. Edging by Bobby's and parking her car further up the street she adjusted her sunglasses and got out to stretch her legs and take a look around. She hoped the sunglasses would be enough to keep Bobby – and anyone else, for that matter – from recognising her. Luckily she'd not made a huge effort this morning; it was no wonder Rosie had put her nearly five years older than she was. Without a scrap of makeup, hair barely brushed, and some elasticated joggers and an old scraggy T-shirt she'd pulled on first thing, she had a veil of middle-age invisibility that would most likely deter anyone from giving her a second glance.

The motorbike was parked outside Bobby's address. Its presence meant Della and Darcy's research checked out. The bad news was that it meant Bobby was home, meaning a quick unofficial look around wasn't on the cards. Not that Jess would ever do that again, given the trouble she'd got herself into last time.

She paid for an hour on the parking app and began a slow amble towards the house. It was on the opposite side of the road and she held her phone to her ear and pretended to be on a call to cover the fact that she was taking a video. She couldn't stop to stare in the windows, but she hoped she might capture something useful this way.

A young dog inside a nearby house scared her witless as she approached. It yapped and jumped at Jess, nose and paws pressed against the bay window, until a ball flew into the back of its head from deeper inside. It yelped, leapt down from its sentry post and went chasing after the guilty party. Jess could hear the owner's deep voice shouting at it to 'stop being a wanker.' She shook her head. Loads of people had got dogs during lockdown and were sorely regretting it a few years on. Jess knew of several people – clients – for whom a stipulation of the divorce was that the other party *take* the dog with them. Jess had thought about getting a dog in recent years. Damon had suggested it; something to come home to, in lieu of someone with two legs and no tail. Granted, a dog would never provide much in the way of scintillating conversation or a surprise candlelit dinner for two, but it might raise the alarm if she had a medical emergency or bite an unwelcome intruder on the arse if one came calling. It had been especially tempting after the death threat arrived. But she knew it would be unfair on both her and the animal. She didn't want to be tied down to a pet who needed caring for. She didn't have the inclination to walk for miles in the pouring rain with compostable bags full of dog shit lodged in her coat pocket. Nor did she believe that a dog would really make up for the lack of a significant other in her life. In any case, she considered herself more of a cat person.

Bobby McEvoy didn't have a dog, mercifully. She slowed to a virtual stop as she walked by his ground floor flat, capturing what she hoped would be useful footage. The end of the road, she noted, led to Parsons Green. She turned around when she got there, heading back towards her car and glancing at her watch before settling down in the driver's seat to wait for signs of movement from Bobby McEvoy's house.

'YOU CAN GO IN, YOU KNOW.
THEY DON'T BITE'

Forty minutes later she was rewarded.

Bobby came out of the house and locked the front door. Jess waited for him to saddle the bike, but instead he turned right and walked towards her end of the street. She held her breath as he came closer, but he passed by on the other side of the street, oblivious to her. She waited a minute, watching him in the rear-view mirror as he turned right at the end, and then got out of the car. He was headed to the high street. Jess had a decision to make: follow him, or help herself to his flat. She decided to follow Bobby. If he was clever, there wouldn't be much to find in his house anyway, and if he wasn't, then she'd find another time to get inside.

She followed him along the road and paused a moment, browsing a newsstand, as he made his way into the tube station. It was heaving with commuters, and Jess struggled to close the distance between them as Bobby McEvoy made his way down the stairs. He didn't stop for anyone; several people on the stairs and along the platform tutted quietly as he muscled past them, although no one dared to make any more of a fuss than that. Jess pursued him as nonchalantly as she could but tried to keep the gap from widening. She heard the train pull into the station and accelerated down the remaining stairs to jump on board. Bobby was a carriage ahead; she made her way to the end of hers and sat down on an end seat, keeping him in her eyeline. She pushed her sunglasses back onto her face and felt beads of sweat running down her cleavage. She wished she'd worn something cooler. And maybe brought a mask too. The tube was disgusting at the best of times, but in the midday heat of a midsummer day with the stale breath of a hundred thousand people flying at you in thirty-degree heat, it was particularly revolting.

They pulled into Putney Bridge and Jess watched Bobby stand steady by the doors. She stood up too, mirroring him, and waited for him to step off before doing the same. She was nervous now, terrified he'd stop and turn on her, figure out who she was and what she wanted and shove her onto the tracks. But he kept going, and so did she, until they were back on the street and she could get some distance between them again. She assumed they were near the end of the journey but Bobby began jogging towards the bus that was waiting at the stop outside the station. Jess followed him as fast as she dared to. She couldn't afford to lose him now. She made it just as the doors were closing and stood panting near the front, well away from Bobby McEvoy so as not to draw attention to herself. A couple of stops later, he hopped off the bus. She helped a woman with her buggy, then got off as well.

On the street, Bobby McEvoy strode along in a sure-footed way that told Jess that wherever they were going, he'd been there many times before. Jess, conversely, hadn't ever been to this part of town. It was a sort of no-man's land that wasn't quite Putney or Barnes, with streets dotted here and there and a vast expanse of common land stretching ahead of them. It was very exposed, which made Jess feel better in one way. But when Bobby suddenly took a turn towards the wooded area beyond, she was a little less confident.

He had a bag with him; a sports bag that looked heavy. She'd seen it on the tube and wondered what was in it. Was he still dealing? Was that how he was making enough money to live in Fulham and run a restaurant? Maybe it was cash. Or a tarpaulin and rope to wrap her up and bury her in... she stopped walking, letting him pull further into the distance. What on earth was she doing, following a convicted criminal and potential murderer into a remote area of Putney Common? She should have told Della and Darcy to stay close, so she had back-up, or at the very least, someone who knew where she was... pulling her phone out, she messaged Della and Darcy on their newly-formed WhatsApp group.

'I'm in pursuit of Bobby,' she typed. 'I'm on Putney Common. Near a church. I'll check in again in five minutes. Call me if you don't hear from me. Call the police if I don't answer.'

She tucked her phone into her trouser pocket and looked up. Searching the tree-lined area in front of her she tried to locate Bobby. She panicked, not catching sight of him anywhere. Surely, she hadn't lost him at the crucial moment? Squinting into the sun, she tried to spot movement – and saw with some relief that he'd corrected his course a little and was heading straight for the church. Sure that was where he was going now – there was literally nothing else but scrubland for hundreds of metres either side, Jess took a circuitous route around the common to approach the building from the north side, where he wouldn't be able to see her coming.

A second man (rucksack, baseball cap, unseasonably warm jacket) was ahead of her, also clearly headed in the same direction. She was nearly at the church now: an old, reverent beast of a building with imposing stained glass and a tall, stern looking spire. Jess paused again, afraid of what she was walking towards. Was it a drug deal? A money exchange? She felt a chill, suddenly, even in the hot midday sun. Marianne had been stabbed to death. Even if Bobby McEvoy hadn't been caught by Marianne, he could have met someone on the inside who offered him money to find and kill her. It wouldn't have been hard; chefs have plenty of access to knives. And they're trained to clean up after themselves too.

Jess hid herself behind a tree as the man with the rucksack went in through the ramped side entrance and then followed, being careful to open and close the door with the utmost care. She found herself in a little vestibule with a couple of chairs and the toilets to the right of a door. Neither Bobby McEvoy, nor the man with the rucksack, were anywhere to be seen. She crept towards the door which creaked gently as she pushed it open, to reveal a beautiful, vaulted nave filled with stained glass and intricate wood carvings. It was cool too, offering Jess some respite from the heat of the day. She did a quick scan. She had a pretty good view, with only a few lines of sight compromised. She stood still, ears pricked, waiting to hear a movement, but there was no sign of life; indeed, it was unusually quiet, even for a church. Where had the two men gone? Not that she had any idea what might happen if she found them; or worse, if they found her first. Fear pumped through her and she tried to ignore the unseasonable chattering of her teeth and shaking in her legs. Maybe she should have messaged Ben, rather than Della and Darcy.

She didn't know what to do. Hiding in a church wasn't as easy as Dan Brown thrillers would have you believe and this one in particular seemed to lack any kind of pillar or font to stand behind. The pews were not benches that could be scuttled between or slid along, but rather rows of chairs, some of which interlaced together, all of which bunched and moved in irregular rows like the Very Hungry Caterpillar.

Voices were coming from a room at the far end of the nave. Jess moved forward until she found her way to the south transept. The voices were louder now, and she darted behind the pulpit to see if she could hear what they were saying.

She heard Bobby speaking, his gravelly Yorkshire tones sounding rich and powerful as his voice resonated through the church. At first, she couldn't catch what he was saying, the echo making it hard to pick anything up. She edged slightly closer to hear properly.

'—didn't need to kill her. She was harmless—'

Another voice. 'She was loaded.'

A third. 'Do they think it was drugs related? Will they trace her back here?'

They were definitely talking about Marianne. Jess got her phone out. She needed to record this, send it to Ben—

'Excuse me. What are you doing?'

The voice came from behind her and Jess turned slowly and froze. A woman (mid thirties, ratty hair, dark circles under her eyes) eyed her suspiciously.

'Can I help you?'

'Erm...'

'You can't have that in here,' she nodded at the phone. 'You'll get us all in trouble.'

It was a funny turn of phrase for someone to have at a drugs deal. The woman took Jess's phone out of her hands and swiftly shut it down, before handing it back.

'There you go. You won't need it in there anyway.' She nodded towards the room where the voices were coming from.

She didn't look like the sort Jess imagined would be guarding a meeting like this. She looked more like a vicar's wife, or—

'Have you come for the meeting?' The woman gestured towards the doorway. 'You can go in, you know. They don't bite.'

Jess looked at her doubtfully. 'I'm not sure about that.'

'First time, is it?' The woman said, sympathetically. 'Don't worry. They'll look after you. It's all about taking steps – and you've taken the first one, by turning up.'

Jess nodded, a horrible realisation coming over her. This wasn't a drugs deal at all. It was an AA meeting.

'Come on,' the woman said, linking arms with Jess and forcing her towards the open door. 'We can go in together.' She gave a toothy smile.

Utterly humiliated at where her own stupid assumptions had led her, Jess had no choice but to go with the woman. A group of men and women were sat inside the room, in a circle. They looked up as the two women entered.

'Found a straggler.'

A woman (grey curls, dark skin, generous eyes) sat as part of the circle, but the rest of the chairs angled towards her slightly and Jess assumed she was the group facilitator.

'What's your name, dear? Just your first name.'

'Jess,' she said, forgetting, in her embarrassment, to give a fake name.

'Hi Jess,' the group chorused.

'Is this your first time?'

She nodded.

'There's no pressure to share your story, but when you're ready to speak, we're here to listen.'

'Thanks.' There was something comforting about this small, carpeted and rather airless room, or maybe it was the woman talking to her, that made her feel nurtured and safe. She'd almost forgotten why she was there, until she felt the heavy stare of Bobby McEvoy land on her. Recognition dawned on his face. He knew who she was; which meant she had to get out of there, and fast. Jess shrank away from the circle and ran blindly from the room.

'Wait, come back!' Bobby McEvoy's voice vibrated through the room and several others followed suit, but she had already begun pushing her way through the gauntlet of kamikaze chairs in the church outside. She glanced round to see Bobby McEvoy was closing in on her, followed by a number of others, who were all pushing past one another to get out of the room and watch the showdown between them.

'Jess, please, come back.'

'Leave me alone!' She yelled, her voice shaking. 'I know what you did to Marianne.' The oversized Yorkshireman had nearly caught up with her, and she picked up one of the chairs and threw it at him as hard as she could. The crowd of onlookers gasped.

'Ouch,' Bobby said. 'What the hell was that for?'

'You killed her,' she blurted. 'You drugged her and you killed her. You did time because of her and you wanted vengeance and you killed her.'

'What? No.' He shook his head emphatically and moved a couple of the chairs aside. 'You've got it all wrong.'

Panicking, Jess shoved a row of chairs forward to block his way. 'She was in Yorkshire, you were arrested—' She backed up and tripped, losing her balance and falling to the floor, banging her elbow on the way down. Ignoring the pain, she tried to lever herself up. Bobby had closed the gap between them in two giant strides and was practically on top of her now. Admitting defeat, Jess closed her eyes and put her hands up. 'Please, don't hurt me.'

No one was more surprised than she was when he held out his hand to help her up. 'That's the last thing I'd do,' he said.

'SHE WOULD HAVE DONE ANYTHING FOR EITHER OF YOU'

The meeting had been thoroughly disrupted; the vicar's wife, who'd persuaded her inside in the first place, told everyone in a rather disapproving voice to help themselves to tea and biscuits. Avoiding her stern gaze, Jess apologised to the group for the rude interruption to their meeting. When she'd made her way around everyone, Bobby found a quiet corner for them to talk.

'We met in London,' Bobby said. 'At a meeting. I had done time and had been out of prison for a few years. I'd got clean while I was in there and learned to cook; I'd come down south to get away from all the bad influences in my life. Things were going well for me.'

'She didn't arrest you then? For the drugs?'

He shook his head. 'I ended up as her sponsor. Back then, I didn't even know she was police. She only told me when she spoke about you and Ben. Marianne talked about you a lot,' Bobby continued. 'You were a huge regret in her life. As her sponsor, I encouraged her to try and make amends, but she was too ashamed of what she did to contact you. She said she didn't deserve your forgiveness.'

Jess breathed heavily and tried not to cry, firstly from the relief of not being attacked or killed, and secondly because finally, here was someone she could talk to, who absolutely understood the complexities of her relationship with Marianne, and who she could mourn alongside, like she'd hoped to do with Ben.

'You didn't stay for the funeral,' she said.

'They're a bit of a trigger for me,' Bobby replied, smiling. 'Know thyself, and all that. But I said my own goodbye.'

'At the cottage,' Jess said.

Bobby nodded. 'I came to see you, before that, at your house; I was on my way home from work and it was late. I wanted to talk to you, but I didn't know what to say, so I rode off. And then I saw you at the cottage, coming out from next door.'

'You could have said hello, when I called out to you.'

'The old lady never liked me or Marianne. I didn't want her calling the police and reporting me for loitering or anything.'

Jess frowned. 'She can be a little brusque, but I think she means well.'

'Better safe than sorry, when you've already got a record.'

They sat in silence for a while.

'I should have got in touch with her sooner,' Jess said, cupping her tea in her hands. 'I could have saved her a lot of pain.'

Bobby shook his head. 'She had plenty of demons to excise,' he said. 'It wasn't up to you to do that for her. She would have come to you, when she was ready.' He put down his empty mug. 'She lived with a lot of regret. She was trying to make it up to you in other ways, to avoid the confrontation, but I said to her it would eat her up, if she didn't speak to you.'

'What other ways?' Jess said. She wondered if Marianne had tried to poison Ben against Naomi for her benefit. It was an odd way to say you were sorry, but in Marianne's addled state, maybe it made sense.

Bobby shook his head. 'I'm not sure I should say. She told me in confidence, and I don't know if she ever meant for anyone to know—'

'Please,' Jess said. 'You are my last solid lead, and it turns out you're the best thing to have ever happened to her, so, if you know anything that might help—'

'She was trying to find out who sent your death threat.' Bobby pursed his lips. 'She'd got it into her mind that if she could find out who did it, and *rescue* you, that you'd forgive her for what she did.'

Jess was taken aback and tears sprung into her eyes. 'I didn't have any idea...'

'I don't know how far she got,' Bobby said. 'When I went to see her, the night before she died, she'd been drinking. She wasn't in a good way, it's the worst I've seen her for a long time, to be honest. She was upset about some woman called Naomi; she wasn't making much sense.'

'Ben's fiancée,' Jess explained. 'She'd been cheating on him.'

295

'I'm sorry if I've scared you,' Bobby said, 'I wish I could tell you more.'

'It's okay,' Jess said. 'You've been hugely helpful, really.' She wanted badly to talk to Ben. He would know what to do; she didn't trust Graham Dickson, and Ben would at least listen to her. But the funeral; the way things were left... it was even less likely now that he'd return her calls.

Bobby spoke again, the soft Yorkshire tones soothing her panic a little. 'She loved Ben – and you – fiercely, you know. She would have done anything for either of you.'

Jess nodded, feeling the lump in her throat again. Bobby jerked his head towards the vicar's wife, who was looking pointedly at the clock. Everyone else had left.

'I think that's our cue to go.'

They stood up, Bobby towering over her. Jess looked into his eyes. They were rather beautiful, if sad; that haunted look that people get when they've seen too much. Jess gave a small, encouraging smile.

'Did she say anything else? Maz, I mean.'

'Nothing coherent. Something about a photograph and the past coming to find her... To be honest, Jess, she was pretty far gone. It's why I was there. She'd called me in a state, and I was trying to get her to sober up, come to a meeting. She was rambling about a lot of things that didn't mean much to me. In the end I fed her some coffee, put her to bed and left.' He bowed his head. 'I can't believe that was the last time I saw her.'

'You weren't to know,' Jess replied. 'None of us were.' She felt herself go pink with embarrassment. 'I'm sorry I accused you of killing her in front of your meeting.'

'At least it's all anonymous,' Bobby smiled. 'Although I'm sure throwing a chair at me will have given them all something to dine out on for the next six months.'

They laughed, diffusing the tension a little, and walked towards the door of the church.

'Seriously, Jess, is there anything I can do to help?' Bobby said. His voice softened again, and he smiled shyly at her. 'Any friend of Marianne's is a friend of mine.'

'Actually, there is one thing. She handed him her car keys. 'You could move my car when you get home, so I don't get a ticket. It's parked on your street, near number 99. I'll be back to get it tomorrow.'

He laughed. 'You followed me all the way from Fulham?'

She nodded sheepishly. 'Sorry.'

He put the keys in his pocket. 'Tell you what, how about I drive it back for you? Give me your address, I'll drop it over.' He looked at her. 'I saw our friend at her lowest, at her worst, the past few years. But when she was sober, I got to know a little bit of the Marianne from before too. That Marianne would be intensely happy to know we'd met, and that I'd made amends for her as best I could today.'

Jess smiled. 'She wasn't the only one who needed to make amends. And I'm going to make sure I do my best for her too.'

It was time to go home. She couldn't stay at Della's forever, and her meeting with Bobby had made her realise that she couldn't avoid the inevitable; she had to deal with whatever was facing her.

She grabbed a taxi, not wanting to wait around for buses and trains. When she got in, she gazed in the hallway mirror and was mildly embarrassed to see the state she had been in, talking to Bobby McEvoy. The after-effects of walking in the brilliant sunshine across barren Putney Common had made themselves apparent, her face now assuming the pinkish-purple glow of sunburn that tightened on her cheeks and forehead. Her hair was clumped on the top of her head, and she had sweat patches under her arms. It wasn't the best look to storm an AA meeting, but then nothing about that had been conventional. She headed upstairs for a shower. She needed time to think, to process the day and try to unravel the clues that Marianne had left behind.

She walked into the living room and stopped, dead. A man was sat in one of her easy chairs, bound in sticky tape by the arms and legs. His mouth was covered over too, his eyes were wide in alarm. He had a huge bruise blossoming on his cheek.

'*Dev?*'

'SHE'S A FUCKING LUNATIC'

'Mmm-mmm-mmm!' His muffled, panicked voice brought her back to reality. She ripped off the mouth tape and he gasped; his breath heavy with sobs.

'She's crazy. She's a fucking lunatic,' he panted.

Jess felt dread creep over her. 'Who did this to you, Dev?'

'That tall, blonde woman who works for you.'

'*Darcy?*' Jess went cold, her head spinning with possibilities. Could she be... *the killer?* She'd professed to be an avid fan of the show, who'd known about the book, and the agency, and the death threat and who *knew where she lived...* Jess barely knew her, she'd never met the kids, or seen her ex-husband... Darcy, who had a temper, who punched people for being married to two different women, who hated adulterers, who she'd let in her home...

Before she could untie him, a voice floated in from the garden.

'Jess, is that you?' A voice called from the back garden.

'She's here?' Jess felt like her heart leapt out of her mouth along with the words.

Dev nodded. 'Said she was having a cuppa before you went out for her birthday.'

'Jess!' Darcy appeared with a mug in one hand and the letter opener in the other. Her maxi dress swirled out around her and her hair looked freshly blow dried. She looked at Dev. 'Why did you take off his mouth tape?'

'Why did you put it on?' Jess said, taking a step back. 'How did you get in my house? And what the hell are you doing with that knife?'

'It's not a knife, it's a letter opener, silly,' Darcy said. 'I found it in the drawer. Useful things, letter openers. Not something everyone has these days, either. Rather an old-fashioned—'

There was a cheery rap on the front door.

'Oooo... that will be Della. Wait there, I'll get it.' Darcy set the letter opener down on the desk and made her way to the front door.

Dev looked at Jess. 'See? I told you. She's crazy.'

Jess dived for the letter opener and stuck it in her back pocket just as Della walked into the living room, a garish looking package in her hand. She looked resplendent in a strappy sundress that clung to every lump and bump in a surprisingly seductive manner; her hair was freshly bleached and she gave off a heady mix of garlic, coconut shampoo and CK One. 'Alright, boss? You're not coming out looking like—' she stopped short when she saw Dev. 'What the fuck?'

Dev whimpered. 'Please... can someone get me out of this chair?'

'Not a chance in hell,' Darcy said.

'You're one of those bastards from next door who fed booze to my girl,' Della said, unable to tear her gaze away from the tape strapping his arms to the chair.

'I caught this man posting another death threat through your door,' Darcy said, coming back into the living room and perching on the arm of the sofa. 'You're welcome.'

'You did what?' Jess was halfway between confused and terrified. She reached into her pocket and gripped the knife.

Dev looked panicked. 'I was only coming over to let you know that—'

'You said he'd been lurking about,' Darcy said. 'Della went off to do her fish rounds but I decided to pop over here after you left to follow Bobby. I thought I'd get some case notes ready for tomorrow and get together the surveillance kit like you asked.'

'But how—'

'Under a flowerpot is a lame place to stash your spare key.' Darcy said, shaking her pretty hair from side to side. 'Anyway, I was in here, working – I invoiced Nina Foster, by the way – and I heard the letter box and I knew it wasn't the postman – he'd already been in the morning. I punched him good and hard for you, Jess. Like I said, you're welcome.'

'I was leaving you a note,' Dev said to Jess, his voice deranged. 'I was putting it through the door when she opened it. She took one look at me and went crazy. She knocked me out, and when I came to, I was like this.'

'She's got one helluva right hook, I'll give her that,' Della said.

'Where's the note?' Jess said.

Darcy pointed at the desk. 'In that envelope. It's why I had the letter opener,' she frowned. 'Where's it gone? I swear I put it on the desk just now.'

Jess breathed a sigh of relief. Darcy wasn't a killer; she was just over-zealous. She pulled the letter opener from her pocket, confident now that Darcy wasn't intending to use it on Dev (or, frankly, her) and placed it on the table, picking up the already opened envelope. She remembered all the times Dev had been outside her house, chatting with the press, picking up the package with the knife in it. Could it be—?

'I've got a confession to make,' he said, suddenly.

Jess looked up at him, turning the envelope over in her hands. Della stood, looking menacing in her spaghetti strap sundress.

'I opened that package,' Dev said. 'The one that was left at our house. I saw what was inside.' He nodded at the blade on the table. 'You shouldn't be anywhere near that, by the way. Your DNA will be all over it now.'

'What the hell were you doing opening my mail?'

'I know I shouldn't have, but you're in a lot of trouble. The walls aren't exactly... I can hear you on the phone, I've spoken to the press outside.'

'It's really none of your business. As I said before, we aren't friends.'

'Tristan said to drop you a note. He said you're a decent person who's been dealt a bad hand. He might think differently when he finds out what's happened to me this afternoon, of course.' He nodded towards his hands, fingers splayed out. 'Please, could you cut me free, one of you? My fingers are starting to go numb.

Jess pulled the note out of the envelope.

Jess,

Stop ignoring me. You're in trouble. I can help.

On the flip side was his name – Dev Devanga – and an office phone number. Jess groaned and put her head in her hands.

'I'm a lawyer. I tried to tell Darcy I wanted to help you,' Dev said, 'but she wouldn't listen. She had a red mist come over her and—'

'Oh yeah,' Della said. 'We've seen that version of Darce and it isn't pretty.'

'You're a lawyer?' Jess said.

He nodded. Dev spoke quickly, his eyes still glued to the knife. 'I was coming – Tristan said it was the neighbourly thing to do – to offer to go with you to the station next time you were taken there. To represent you.'

Darcy's eyes widened. 'Oh my god,' she said.

'I was hoping there wouldn't be a next time,' Jess said to Dev. 'Although I can see now why there might be. Hold still.' She picked up the knife and began cutting through the bindings and freed his hands. Della handed Dev his phone.

'Please don't call the police,' Darcy said, her eyes filling with tears. 'I am so sorry. I swear, it was an innocent mistake. I've got two children, I can't go to prison, they'd have to live with their father and he's a cheating, lying son of a—'

'I'm not going to call the police,' Dev said. 'Even though I bloody well should. You're in enough trouble. Your prints are all over a murder weapon.' He looked at the knife Jess was using to saw through the tape holding his legs in place. 'Assuming that's what I think it is.'

'What?' Darcy paled. 'That's... that's the knife Marianne was stabbed with?'

'I don't know for sure,' Jess said. 'But it was in that package Tristan brought over.'

'But it was in your kitchen drawer,' Darcy said, slightly horrified now. 'Who keeps evidence of a murder in their kitchen drawer?'

'I didn't know what else to do with it,' Jess said, miserably.

'Throw it in the river? Bury it in the garden?'

'Ignore your crazy friend,' Dev said, glaring at Darcy. 'You need to take it to the police. Right away. Explain it was sent to you in the package and let them rule out your DNA.'

'They won't do that,' Jess said, cutting through the last of the tape. 'I'm being framed. If I wander into a police station clutching the murder weapon, Graham Dickson will arrest me on the spot. And to be honest, I wouldn't blame him.'

'You should go to Ben,' Darcy said. 'We know he isn't the person trying to frame you. Maybe this will help him prove who is.'

'You shouldn't speak anymore,' Dev said, rubbing at his wrists. He pointed at Darcy. 'You – she shouldn't be allowed – you should fire her, *right now.*' He could barely spit the words out in order, he was so angry.

'Hang on a minute,' Della said. 'She made a mistake. She was just trying to protect her friend.'

Jess looked at Dev apologetically. 'She's right,' she said, a hint of pride in her voice. 'Darcy was looking out for me. Things have been a bit scary lately.'

Dev gave a curt shrug, but his voice had softened slightly when he next spoke. 'It still doesn't give her the right—'

Jess laid her hand on Dev's arm and gestured to the chair, and to Darcy, 'I am so very sorry about all this.'

'Not as sorry as I am,' Darcy said, stepping forward. 'Dev, I owe you a huge apology. I'll pay for any medical bills.'

'For what?' Dev said.

'Your face...' She realised she'd landed herself in it and looked at Jess, eyes wide with panic.

'Thanks for your offer to come to the police with me,' Jess interrupted, trying to change the subject. 'It was kind.'

'You're welcome,' Dev said, gruffly, touching his cheekbone and wincing. 'Are you going to go?'

Jess shook her head. 'Not yet. I'm taking Darcy's advice and I'm going to visit my ex-husband first and get the help I should have asked for when this all started.'

Dev looked at the women and sighed. 'Tristan will have my head on a platter...'

'Why?'

'Because, despite my better judgement, I'm going to take you on as a client.'

'You still want to help me?' Jess asked, astounded. 'But I don't... I can't pay you.'

'Nonsense,' Della said. 'We can offer a retainer. Do you and Tristan like fish?'

'YOU SHOULD GET YOUR LOCKS CHANGED'

Ben opened the door to her. In the few days since they'd seen each other, he had the beginnings of a beard, grey hairs poking their way through the darker ones and giving him a rather scruffier look than she was used to seeing. His eyes were hollow, with dark bags underneath. Jess stepped forward to hug him but checked herself at the last moment. She wasn't sure either of them were ready for that.

Ben gestured her inside. 'Do you want a cuppa? You'll have to wash up your own mug and I'm not sure there's much milk.'

Jess moved into the living room and looked around at the mess. She went through to the kitchen and started lifting plates out of the sink so she could run the water.

'Let's get this done first.'

'Jess, you don't have to, I was only joking—'

'I want to.'

Ben began clearing plates up from the living room while Jess filled the kettle and put it on to boil, before running a sink full of hot, soapy water. She quietly washed then rinsed the plates, cups and bowls as Ben piled them up beside her, loading what she could into the already-full dishwasher and putting the rest in the sink. When they were halfway through, she stopped and added teabags and hot water into a couple of clean mugs.

'Where do you keep your sugar?'

'Usual place,' Ben said.

She found the bowl in the cupboard above the kettle, put a spoonful in each of their mugs, stirred and handed him one of them. He took it gratefully.

'Take a break,' Jess said. 'I'll finish up here.' She continued the washing up, slowly making headway with the mess in the kitchen before going into the bedroom to collect the glasses, mugs and plates she knew were there too. She smiled at Ben on the way back through, and he half-returned it as she passed. Then, as though he had thought better of it, he set his tea down.

'Okay, enough avoiding the question. Sit down with me and let's talk.'

Her heart gave a lurch. 'I've nearly finished, let me just—'

'Jess,' he said, gently taking the pile of crockery from her. 'Let's talk.'

They sat on the sofa, mugs of tea steaming on the now-clear coffee table.

'First thing's first: what the hell were you thinking, letting yourself in here like that?'

Jess flushed. 'I thought you killed Maz. Only for a little bit. Like, a fleeting moment. You had a key to her house; you had an argument; you were the last person to see her—'

Ben shook his head. 'The second last person. The last person was her killer, remember.'

Jess looked over at the draining board full of clean crockery. 'How have you been living like this, Ben? You used to be so fastidious—'

'Stop changing the subject.'

She swallowed. 'Things didn't add up. And Naomi had been so rude when I'd called by—'

Ben flinched at the sound of her name.

'It felt very personal. And then Rosie told me about your argument with Maz, that she'd overheard you talking about Naomi, and I got to wondering if *she* might be the suspect instead, you know, because she was jealous or something.'

'Jealous?'

'I thought you and Maz might be...'

'God, no, Jess. I would never have—'

'It's not like you haven't been unfaithful before.' It was a low blow and Jess tried not to meet Ben's eye. 'Everyone said it was a crime of passion, and the killer was most likely known to the victim. It made sense.'

'And when she called the reporters, no doubt,' Ben said.

'When she did *what*?'

Ben looked awkward. 'I called her from Marianne's house that night, when I found out she'd been killed. Told her I'd seen you there,' he said. 'She told me the next day that she'd tipped off the press. I was livid; you know how I feel about that sort of attention. Maybe it's my fault for not wanting to talk about it, but Naomi doesn't know a lot about my under-cover days, and she doesn't really understand why I want to keep a low profile after all these years. She agreed to leave things alone, but she was furious I'd taken your side. Then when you came here and stormed into the flat, I knew she'd go back to the papers again out of spite. She leaked your relationship with Maz to them too. I'm sorry they've been harassing you. I trusted her.' He shook his head. 'I was stupid. She was using both of us to keep the press off her own back.'

'No,' she said gently. 'You loved her.'

He cleared his throat. 'How did you find out about her and Jake? Did you—' he looked around. 'They weren't here, were they?'

She shook her head. 'I told you what happened. The flat was empty when I got here.'

And you had a good look around and then fell asleep.' Despite himself, Ben snorted with laughter.

'It wasn't funny, Ben. I thought I was going to get killed. I thought she'd see the phone and..... I'm not very proud of myself,' she finished in a small voice.

'I haven't needed to use that phone in years. It had loads of messages on it, though, when I opened it up today. Naomi must have helped herself to it and been using it for her sordid little hookups with *Jake*.' He spat the name like venom.

'Sorry.'

Ben held out his hand. 'Key.'

'Huh?'

'I assume you kept it when we split up.'

She fished the key out of her back pocket and handed it to him. 'You should get your locks changed.'

'First thing tomorrow,' he replied. 'Don't want any other psycho ex-wives letting themselves in.'

'How many do you have?'

'Ha ha.'

'Sorry,' she said with a coy smile. 'Anyway, besides the massive apology I owe you, I came to tell you, I think I have a lead.'

'You do? When the police have nothing?'

'I think they're looking in all the wrong places. Or more to the point, I think Graham Dickson is deliberately leading them there.'

She told him about the fingerprints that couldn't be hers, and of her suspicions that she was being framed. She told him about Bobby McEvoy, seeing him at the cottage and then following him to the church, and about Marianne trying to solve her death threat mystery.

'You're an idiot,' he said, when she'd finished. 'You could have got yourself killed. What if Bobby McEvoy hadn't been a nice guy after all?'

She straightened up, indignant. 'I'm not a total amateur, Ben.'

He raised an eyebrow. 'But you're not trained, either. This could have landed you in serious trouble. It's not a bloody Agatha Christie novel, it's a murder investigation.'

Jess was irritated by his tone. 'I know that. And it's why I'm coming to you now. I've reached the part where I need some help.' She pulled out a freezer bag containing the letter opener and the death threats from her bag and placed them gently on the table. Ben picked them up between his finger and thumb, turning the bag around so he could see it from all angles.

'What's this?' Ben said. 'Tell me I'm not looking at—'

'I don't know. It was sent to me, in a package with one of the notes. My lawyer told me to bring them to you. Well, not you exactly, but... It's probably useless now though, Darcy used it yesterday and it's got my prints all over it from cutting him free—'

'I beg your pardon?'

She shook her head. 'Doesn't matter. A little misunderstanding on Darcy's part. The point is, I can't turn it in as evidence. Graham Dickson will arrest me on the spot.'

'What makes you think I won't?'

'You know I didn't do it.' She pointed at the knife. 'I thought, maybe there's more evidence on the knife that would prove that: DNA or whatever.'

'If there is, it will be trace amounts,' he said, turning over the plastic freezer bag in his hands. 'But it has to go to forensics, Jess. I can't do anything with it here.'

'I don't know why Graham Dickson is so hellbent to pin this on me,' she said, 'but if you take this to him before we find evidence that someone else did it, he'll find a way to get me banged up. Those prints of mine that they found at the scene? They couldn't have been there. I wore gloves.'

He looked up, sharply. 'What were you wearing gloves for?'

She cleared her throat. 'I may have taken a look around, for myself, before you arrived.'

'Jesus Christ!' Ben shook his head. 'You're lucky that's all they've got on you.'

She decided not to mention the videos on her phone, and for a while, a silence enveloped them until Ben spoke again, more quietly this time.

'She'd been struggling so much, the past few years. She was unhappy, she'd lost the job she loved and she was on her own... and you know, Maz was never good on her own. Always needed someone around even if they didn't last very long.' He dropped the bag on the coffee table and put his head in his hands. 'I told her she needed to get her shit together and stop meddling in my life to make herself feel better about hers. I can't believe I left it like that. I can't believe she's gone and I don't get to say sorry.'

'That makes two of us.'

'I knew she'd been drinking when she called me.' He sunk his head even further. 'That's what she did. She'd get herself in a state and then call me and ask me to come over... she told me she was in love with me.'

'I don't need to know—'

'I didn't say it back, Jess. I mean, I loved her like family, but I suppose I was never *in* love with her, not like with you—' he stopped abruptly. 'But I did love her. In spite of everything, I loved her.'

He began to cry. In all the years she'd known him, Jess had never seen Ben cry before. She sat still, not knowing what to do and then, taking a deep breath, she closed the space between them and put her arm around him. He leaned into her, clung to her, his raw sobs muffled by her stomach. The early evening sunshine gave a soft glow to everything in the room, the light catching the greys in his hair as he wept.

Finally, he released her and wiped his eyes.

'Shit, sorry Jess. What with Maz, then Naomi and the baby, it's all been a bit much, you know?'

'It's fine.' She paused. 'And I'm sorry about the baby. Really, I am. One of us deserved to be happy.'

'But it should have been you.'

She hesitated. She could keep her secret; it had been that way for ten years already. But she needed to unburden herself, to let him know.

'It nearly was, you know.'

Ben looked at her. 'What do you mean?'

'I was pregnant. But it didn't work out.'

'Who's was it?'

She frowned.

'Sorry. It's none of my business. That was a stupid question to ask.'

'It was yours, Ben. I didn't tell you, and then by the time I could, we'd split up. And then I lost it anyway, so it didn't matter.'

Tears welled up in his eyes again. 'How long?'

'Six weeks.'

'Shit.' He looked down.

Jess felt awful. 'I shouldn't have said anything.'

'No, no... I can't believe you went through all of that on your own. I'm so, so sorry.'

'It's okay.'

Ben shook his head. 'I was a dick.'

Jess laughed. 'Yes, you were.'

'I suppose you could call this karma.' He sipped his tea and grimaced. 'Ugh, it's gone cold. And you made it too strong. You always make it too strong.'

'Sorry, force of habit.' She looked at his mug, suddenly reminded of something. 'That morning at Marianne's, the last time you saw her, did you have a cup of tea?'

Ben nodded. 'I never finished it, though. We'd already started arguing by then, and then I left.'

Jess hesitated. 'I need to go back to the cottage.'

'Why?'

'Something Maz said to Bobby, about the past being where the answers are. My death threats... Maz was trying to solve a mystery. It can't be a coincidence. What if she did, and there's evidence inside her cottage that's the key to the whole thing, that the police didn't find or think was relevant?'

'It's still classed as a crime scene.'

'Lucky for us you're a senior police officer with a key.'

Ben shook his head. 'I could lose my job.'

'I know.' She looked him straight in the eye. 'But it's Maz. We both owe it to her to find out what happened.'

Ben got up and poured away his tea. 'For the record, it's a terrible idea.'

'Is that a yes?'

He nodded, raising an eyebrow. 'I suppose it is.'

Jess gave him a hug and a peck on the cheek. Suddenly self-conscious, she took a step away. 'We'll go tonight. I'll meet you there after dark, say ten?' She looked at the knife and the notes on the table. 'What will you do with those?'

'I'll hang onto it all for now, see what we can find at Marianne's that might have been missed, or glossed over. What you said about Dickson worries me.'

'Do you think he's involved?'

'I don't know,' Ben admitted. 'Graham Dickson would have to con a lot of people for them to miss anything at that crime scene.'

'I guess I made it a bit easier for him,' Jess said.

'You did. But Marianne was a good copper too. She'll have left something, somewhere, that tells her story.'

'I hope so.' Jess smiled and looked around. 'Things look much better here already.'

Ben looked at the kitchen, which was now a mountain of draining crockery. 'Thanks... for being here. And for helping to clear up.'

'I barely scratched the surface. Of anything, really.'

'Still... I appreciate it.'

'See you later.'

'IT WAS PROBABLY A MOUSE'

They met at ten, on the side street by the level crossing.

'Rosie is more vigilant than she lets on,' whispered Jess, as they walked down Penny Hill Lane. 'Not that she's hiding things from the police deliberately,' she added hastily.

'Do you think she saw the killer?'

'I don't think so. She swears no one came to the house after you, until I found Maz's body.'

Ben frowned. 'It does seem convenient that she only volunteers information if you happen to be looking for it at the time, though.'

'Everything she's told me has been checked out, so I have to trust she's reliable. In her own way.'

They reached Marianne's front door and Ben checked behind them for passers-by before quickly slipping the key in the lock and opening up. Ducking under the police tape, they went into the house and waited until the door was shut before turning on a torch.

'We need to make sure no one sees the lights from outside,' Ben said. He looked towards the living room uncertainly.

Jess indicated to the kitchen. She didn't want to go in the living room any more than he did. 'Let's base ourselves in the back of the house. There's a solid wood door between the kitchen and the hallway and only a tiny window by the back door. We can pull the blinds down and put the light on and no one will notice we're there.'

'No,' Ben said. 'Torches only. It's not worth the risk of someone noticing. But we'll pull the blinds and curtains anyway. It'll lessen the chances of anyone seeing any movement inside.'

They moved into the kitchen and began looking around.

'It's so bloody neat in here,' Ben commented. 'Tidier than it ever was when I visited. Did forensics load the dishwasher before they left?'

'It was like it when I arrived on the scene. I thought it was odd at the time too.'

'Whoever did this needs to come to my house.'

'I don't think you mean that.'

They stood in silence for a moment, before Ben looked back towards the hall. 'There's nothing here. I'll take a look upstairs and bring back anything I find. You keep an eye out for any signs we've been spotted.' He slipped out of the kitchen quickly to avoid the light leaking into the hallway. Jess heard his footsteps moving up the stairs and then across the creaky ceiling.

'We won't let you down this time, Maz,' she murmured. 'I promise.'

Ben reappeared a few minutes later. 'Nothing,' he said.

Jess looked at her hands, despondent. 'Did you try the spare room?'

He nodded. 'There's nothing there. Or if there was, it's gone.'

A thought occurred to Jess. 'What about the loft? Did the police go up there?'

'It wasn't in the report. Is it even boarded out?'

Jess shrugged. 'I dunno. But we should see if there's anything up there. It's the only place we didn't look.'

They moved upstairs. There was still enough light coming in from outside for them not to need their torches. When they reached the landing, Jess located the loft hatch while Ben searched around for the pole to unlock it.

'Here you go,' he said, finding it behind the door of the spare room. He pushed up the hatch and it clicked up and then down, opening to reveal an inbuilt ladder. He pulled the ladder down with the hook section of the pole, and Jess tried not to cringe at the grinding, clicking and crashing of the mechanism rolling into place.

The ladder made contact with the ground and Ben gestured to her.

'Ladies first.'

Jess went up, poking her head into the large loft beyond and waving her torch around to get the lay of the land. Boxes were stacked up, looking well ordered, with a clear pathway laid out that led to the unlit depths beyond. Much as she didn't relish the idea of spending the evening in a spider and mouse-infested crawl space that was at least ten degrees hotter than the sun, it was the perfect place for them to work uninhibited. No windows and no doors; no one would ever know they were here.

'It's fine,' she whispered. 'Come up.'

Ben followed her up and, when he was at the top, pulled up the ladder and closed the hatch. Instantly, the room felt more claustrophobic than before. The ceiling threatened to crowd her at every turn and Jess could already feel the prickling of a sweat coming on.

'Okay,' Ben said, throwing the light on and moving across the boarded area to where there were several boxes stacked. 'Let's see what we've got.'

They rifled through the boxes, unearthing memories of Marianne from before even Jess knew her: photo albums and family heirlooms, favourite toys and an old mac computer from the nineties. Moving further into the loft, they grazed past Christmas decorations and camping equipment, vacuum-packed clothes, ski boots and dozens of stale smelling paperbacks. Jess tried not to think about Marianne's poor parents coming to clean all this up. She resolved to offer to do it for them, when the investigation was done and the house released. It was the least she could do.

They were nearly at the far end of the loft when Ben yelped with excitement.

'What did you find?'

'A workstation.' Ben moved a couple of boxes out of the way to reveal a small area that Marianne had obviously been using as a makeshift office; a box was pulled up to a wooden tea crate and a notebook and pen were placed on one side. He flicked through the notebook and put it down; he looked disappointed.

'It's nothing. Just a few notes about mystery shopping.'

'Why would she come up here to do that?'

'Hang on... there might be...' Ben shifted the makeshift desk crate and Jess heard something dislodge.

'Wait. Something just fell.'

'It was probably a mouse.'

'No, it wasn't.' She went over to the crate and shone her torch between it and the boxes behind. Reaching in with two fingers, she prised a makeshift display board fashioned out of flattened cardboard from the small gap. Pinned to it was a copy of Jess's first death threat, along with a couple of newspaper cuttings.

Ben moved around the crate. 'Let me see that.'

She propped the board up on the wooden crate. As she did, a piece of card that had been pinned in place, came loose and fluttered to the floor. Jess picked it up; the note with its thick black writing made her shiver.

I SHOULD HAVE KILLED YOU
THE FIRST TIME WE MET

'Ben,' she said, her voice shaking. 'She had one too.'

Ben took the note from Jess and read it, his face falling. 'Shit.' He looked back to the board and startled, pulled away the masking tape that held one of the articles in place. '*Shit*'.

'What?' Jess grabbed the cutting. A photo of a familiar-looking man stared out from between the lines of copy. Jess felt herself go weak as she stared at the image of the man, his heavyset features making a mockery of his small handlebar moustache. 'I know this guy. I've seen him before.'

Ben stared at her, his complexion pale. 'We both have.'

TEDDY JONES GETS TWENTY YEARS IN COURTROOM SHOWDOWN

Report by Jessica Sinclair

Teddy Jones was sentenced to twenty years at Her Majesty's pleasure today after a complex and dramatic court case that produced long-awaited evidence of sexual assault, attempted rape, prostitution and human trafficking. His brothers, Joe and Billy Jones, were well-known in the area and had previously been charged and imprisoned for their own grisly roles in the Midlands-based crime ring. ☐

BROTHERS GRIM

Joe and Billy Jones were arrested last year after a raid on a flat in Birmingham uncovered seventeen women and girls, some as young as fifteen years old, being trafficked from eastern Europe for prostitution. Joe Jones was convicted of additional drugs related charges while Billy's charges included aggravated assault and grievous bodily harm. Although police had been working the case using undercover officers to keep tabs on the girls and build up evidence against all three brothers, they had failed to find enough to convict older brother Teddy. Sources say Teddy was less outgoing and more guarded than his brothers, using his wife and family to shield him and mask his role as the lynchpin of operations, and making his crimes almost impossible to trace. No doubt he will be feeling betrayed today by his brothers, who offered to give evidence against him in a tell-all deal with this newspaper, along with an anonymous witness statement that confirmed to the jury that he was indeed guilty of the heinous accusations against him. Head of Serious Crime, Philip Watson, is quoted as saying 'It took a lot of sacrifice and diligence on the part of our officers, but eventually, we got him. He was an evil piece of work. He deserves every single one of the twenty years.'

'CAREFUL YOU DON'T GO THROUGH THE FLOOR'

She stabbed her finger at the photo. 'I covered this story years ago, when I was still working for the paper. Maz must have kept it – she used to do that when I had a big story.' She looked at the date. 'Twelve years ago.'

'I remember.' Ben stared at the photo, lost in a memory.

'The other two brothers were found guilty and got banged up, but Teddy got off.'

'We didn't have the evidence to put him away.'

'But you did.' She returned her gaze to Ben. 'I got it for you. I got the brothers to confess he was part of it all, that he'd raped those poor women they were selling on the streets to – how did they put it? – *road test* them.' She felt an old anger rise in her. 'You tried to stop me from running this story. Told me I should leave it alone.'

'Teddy Jones was a dangerous man. You were poking your nose into places it shouldn't have been. You were putting people's lives in danger—'

'The story was *huge*. Career changing huge.'

Ben snorted. 'You got that right.'

'What's that supposed to mean?'

'You weren't the only one whose life changed when you decided to visit the Jones brothers and get their confessions.'

'Is this jealousy, because I did what you couldn't, and got them to talk?'

'We were on that job!' Ben exploded. 'Maz was attacked. The evidence we got, the attempted rape victim who finally put him away? That was *her*.'

Jess sat down heavily on the nearest box. 'I didn't know.'

'I know you didn't.' He stood over her, intense and taught, the muscles in his jaw clenching. 'You didn't know any of it.'

'So tell me.'

He sighed. 'I was working undercover as a courier for Teddy's brothers, making a few deliveries here and there, drugs mostly, but sometimes passports, money and so on. Then Teddy Jones asked me to shift the girls from one place to another: a promotion, of sorts. I did it a few times before I mentioned my girlfriend had a flat he could use, for the girls to stay in.'

'Marianne.'

Ben nodded. 'After his brothers were arrested and charged, Teddy was spooked. He was convinced someone on the inside was out to get him. He was looking for the snake in the grass. We nearly had enough on him by that time, we were so close but you kept bloody interfering...' Ben looked away.

'It was my fault. I left early, I needed to be back for our appointment with the doctor... Maz said she'd be fine, she was headed out too. The girls in the flat had been moved, and it was empty; I left her locking up.' His voice caught. 'Teddy was in the car park, waiting for her... had her pinned down with a knife to her throat before she managed to reach her bag and zap him.' He breathed heavily. 'I wasn't there to protect her. She went through so much,' Ben said quietly. 'It was lucky she was carrying that taser, or it would have been a lot worse.'

Jess swallowed. She understood now, that day the burner phone had gone off and sent Ben running, it had been Marianne calling. He'd had no choice but to leave her and go.

Tears sprang to her eyes. 'I'm so sorry, Ben. I didn't... I was obsessed with the story, I didn't stop to think it might be your case.' She corrected herself. 'No. That's not true. I didn't want to think about the *possibility* of it being your case.' She hung her head. 'If I made things more complicated, or caused that man to do something to Maz—'

'No one was to blame. She knew the risks, it was part of the job.'

'The victim was never named in open court.' Wounded, Jess shook her head. 'You should have told me.'

'I don't know why you never thought it was her. All the clues were right in front of you.'

'I never thought of her as a victim of anything, I suppose.' Jess began to cry. 'Poor Maz. She was so brave. She didn't deserve this.'

Ben looked down at her and then knelt to give her a hug. His arms encircled her body and he held on tightly, stroking her sweaty hair away from her tear-soaked face and making soothing sounds while she wept. She allowed herself to feel his body against hers and for the first time since she'd walked away from him all those years ago, she felt safe.

They stayed like that for a long time, until the tears had passed with a final shudder and sniff, and they pulled away from each other slowly, Ben standing and flexing his stiff legs. Jess looked at the photo again.

'He got sent down for a long time. Do you really think it could be him?'

'Who killed Marianne?' Ben shrugged. 'He'd have had to find her first. And he's probably still banged up. I can find that out easily enough – he'd be getting on a bit by now, though. Dead, even. He was in his fifties when he was arrested and jail time isn't easy at that age.'

'Maybe he paid someone he met on the inside, to do the job.'

'Maybe.' Ben was quiet. 'Or maybe it was someone on the outside.'

'Graham Dickson?'

Ben shook his head, conflicted. 'Dickson wasn't working on the case,' he said. 'He had nothing to do with it.'

'Okay,' Jess said. 'But if it's not him, who would it be?'

Ben shrugged. 'I don't know. His wife, maybe?'

'He had a wife?'

Ben nodded. 'I know. Unbelievable.'

'But even if he's had help on the outside, if Teddy Jones is the one who sent the notes to me and Maz, I still don't understand why she is dead and I'm—'

'Alive?'

'He was a rapist. He trafficked women and turned them into prostitutes. He had no idea of Maz's real identity, and he'd have had to work pretty hard from the inside of a prison to find out. But *I'm* the one who got his brothers to turn on him. *I'm* the one who printed their story, it was my name on the byline. I would have been easy prey.'

'Maybe the letter was a warning, a threat. You weren't the one who put them or him in prison, ultimately.'

Jess sucked her cheeks in. 'Why hasn't he come for you?'

'I always watch my back.'

'You just got taken in by a woman who's having someone else's baby. You may have lost your touch a little.'

'Ouch.'

'I'm only saying, maybe we both need to be careful.'

'It won't take long to get to the bottom of this.' He glanced at his watch. 'I can have someone haul Teddy Jones out of bed first thing to get the answers.' He stood and brushed himself down. 'In fact, I'm going to talk to him myself.'

'You won't be allowed within three hundred feet of him and you know it,' Jess said.

'I'll get the boss to sign off.'

'How will you do that, without telling him what we found and how we found it? Graham Dickson can't know, not until we know for sure whether he's clean.'

'All the more reason to bring it to his attention. I want to see the look on his face.'

'He can't know where you got the information.' Jess took out her phone and snapped a photo of the evidence on Marianne's desk, then sent it to Ben. 'Print this out,' she said. 'Get someone to deliver it to you at the station first thing and tell Graham it's a tip come from an anonymous source.'

Ben shook his head. 'You're getting too good at this.'

'I learned from the best.'

They tidied up the unwanted files back into the boxes and turned off the light. When they were done, she turned to face Ben.

'Thanks for doing this with me. It's been, not fun, exactly—' Jess felt herself sway a little; the heat was intense and they hadn't brought any water up with them. Ben caught her as she stumbled off balance.

'Careful you don't go through the floor.' He pulled her close and suddenly, they were too close; the mood had changed from before, when she was upset – Jess could feel the tension between them and broke away quickly. Reversing out of the loft and down the ladder, she made her way back across the landing while Ben dealt with the squeaks and shrieks of steel as he closed the ladder back into the hatch. Jess put her head into Marianne's room and looked out of the window, the moon's full white glow lighting up the neat front yards and the allotments beyond.

'Pretty magical time of night, isn't it?' Ben said, coming up behind her.

Jess nodded. She felt a crackling of energy between them and shifted away slightly. 'We should go. You have an early start in the morning.'

'How about one for the road first? I bet Maz has a bottle in the freezer.'

'I know she has.' She hesitated, looking into his eyes and trying to read them in the semi-darkness of the hallway. 'Okay. One.'

Their eyes were used to the dark now and they made their way down to the kitchen without needing torches. Without exchanging a word, Jess opened the freezer and got the vodka out. Ben searched the drawers and found a couple of tumblers.

'Cheers,' Ben said, pouring the vodka and holding his glass up.

'Cheers.' She drank quickly, the astringent taste of the alcohol taking her breath away.

'I think she'd have enjoyed seeing this,' Ben said, after a while. 'She hated that she'd got between us, after bringing us together in the first place.'

The moment had come, finally. It felt so pointless to ask, while they sat in their dead friend's kitchen drinking her cheap vodka, but she had to know.

'Why did you do it, Ben?'

'What?'

'I couldn't ask the question all those years ago, I didn't want to hear the answer. But I wondered, why her?'

Ben shook his head. 'It was... after Teddy... Maz had lost a lot of confidence, started drinking more – not like, obsessively, just big nights out and stuff. You and me, we weren't in a good place. The whole trying for a baby thing was stressful, we were fighting a lot; I wanted a break, wanted to be outside of that reality for a moment. I got drunk with her one night, when we were on our way home from a job. It just... happened. It was a massive mistake, it changed everything between us.'

'But you carried on.'

Ben hung his head. 'When you found me here with her, it was the last time. We'd agreed that we had to stop, that it could never happen again. I knew our marriage was already dead in the water, but I didn't want to hurt you even more, and Maz and I both knew the damage it would do to our careers if anyone found out. And the damage it was doing to our friendship.'

'So you didn't... after I left... you weren't together?'

'No. That shit you pulled with HR meant we didn't work together again either and we just... it was easier to let things drift apart. I stayed in CID, she went to uniform, and we just got on with life.'

'But didn't you try to help her? She was your friend; your partner, for god's sake.'

'I thought a desk job might be what the doctor ordered, after her ordeal with Teddy, and everything that happened with us. Something calm, dependable and safe. I ran into her a few times, at birthday parties mainly. She seemed okay.'

He downed his vodka and poured himself another one. 'I didn't hear from her for a few years, then one night I got this string of text messages, telling me all sorts about how she was sorry and that she loved me. That she was in love with me, and always had been.'

'Did you reply?'

He shook his head. 'I figured she was drunk, that, you know, she was looking for a reaction.' He paused. 'Then about three years ago I got a call from her, saying she wants to meet me. She sounded different – told me she'd got sober. That she needed to make amends. We met for coffee, and it was better. Like old times... no, not like old times. They were gone. But she was more like the Maz we used to know.'

Jess smiled. A memory of her friend, from when they'd first met, fell unbidden into her mind. A fresh faced, glorious girl who'd been everybody's favourite.

'I used to meet her once a month, maybe, for a coffee,' Ben continued. 'But in the past few months, the drinking started again. That's when I began coming over, to check on her. I didn't know what had triggered it. But she was in a dark place.'

'I'm sorry I wasn't there for her either.'

'You couldn't have saved her. She needed to do that for herself.'

'But she was.' Jess indicated the photo of Teddy. 'All this, it was for me. She was trying to make amends, and it got her killed.' Tears rolled down her face.

'To Marianne,' Ben said, and held up his glass. 'I miss her.'

'I miss her too.' Jess chinked Ben's glass and they both drank deeply. She set her glass down. 'You know, she had people around her who loved her. Bobby, and Rosie too.'

'Rosie?'

'The old lady next door. She looked out for her, even when you couldn't.'

'She was fine, for a long time.' Ben's voice filled with sadness again. 'And then she wasn't. When she called me on that Tuesday, told me to come over... when she told me about Naomi and Jake, I cracked. I shouted, told her she was a drunk and a liar.'

'You weren't to know it was the truth.'

'I could have listened, though. I could have stayed with her that night, looked after her and helped her to straighten out. If I'd done that, maybe she'd still be alive...'

'Ben, you couldn't have done anything. Teddy Jones had a plan. Even if it hadn't been that night, he would have got to her.' It was her turn to comfort him now. Jess moved her chair closer and gave him a hug, stroking his broad back and nuzzling into his neck. The candles flickered in and she felt his arms around her, holding on tightly. They stayed that way for a while, until he finally pulled apart from her.

'Jess...'

Ben reached out and caressed the side of her cheek. Their faces were inches away. His eyes bore into hers and suddenly she felt her heart pounding and her lips parting. She met his gaze and looked for some kind of sign to pull back, away from him, but there was none. Slowly they drew closer, until their lips met in a kiss.

The world stopped turning. All the pain of the past melted away, as his familiar kiss enveloped her. Memories of the thousand kisses they'd shared flowed unbidden into her mind: their first, their wedding day, the night they conceived their baby—

'Shit!' Jess pulled back.

'Oh god, I'm sorry.' Ben looked away. 'I'm sorry.'

Jess downed her vodka, wiped her mouth and looked at her ex-husband in the candlelight. He looked distraught at what had happened, although she had to admit she was less offended and more surprised. She laughed, to diffuse the tension. 'It's okay. It's been a long day.'

'A long month.' He rubbed his hands up and down his thighs. 'Still, that's no excuse.'

'It's okay.' Della's voice was ringing in her ears, warning her not to do anything stupid, but she wondered, if she leant into him, if he'd kiss her again...

This time neither of them pulled away. Swinging her up from the chair, he half carried, half pulled her out into the doorway, pushing himself hard against her until she could barely breathe. Without coming up for air, they crashed from kitchen to hallway and up the stairs to the spare bedroom, oblivious to anything but each other. A heady mix of vodka, grief and memories, Jess barely registered what was happening in any real sense. All she knew was that they wanted and needed each other. And that, for tonight, was enough.

Some hours later she woke, the light from outside finally disturbing her reverie. Her head felt groggy, and she had a dry mouth. That'll be the vodka, she chided herself. Some water would sort her out. Moving slightly, she came to with a start when she realised her arm was tied to the bed.

'Ben?' She sat up with some difficulty, onto her elbow, and got her bearings. Had Ben arrested her, as a joke? It wasn't funny. She pulled, hard, on the cable tie; it dug into her wrist and caused her to gasp in pain. 'Ben!'

There was no answer. Jess looked around for her phone, but it was nowhere to be seen. She began to panic as a cold realisation crept over her, and a terrified whimper escaped from her mouth. It had to be... but it couldn't be... he was supposed to be in prison...

'Ben! Are you there?' Ben had found Teddy... Or rather, Teddy had found Ben. He'd found both of them. Or maybe it wasn't Teddy after all... her mind flitted to Graham Dickson. Had Ben gone to him for the warrant? Surely Dickson would have opted for killing her rather than chaining her to a bed, though. Her mind raced. *It was a crime of passion. Someone she knew. The wife, maybe...* 'Ben!' She called out once more, her voice hoarse and shaking. Where was he? Lying unconscious, maybe, or dead at the foot of the stairs... she stifled a sob and called out again. 'Hello? Anyone? Please... let Ben go. Let me go. Whoever you are, you don't have to do this.'

She heard footsteps on the stairs and her heart thudded so hard it practically jumped across the room. 'Ben?'

To her surprise, Rosie appeared at the door. 'Ben went home a few hours ago, dear. Now you've just got me for company.'

'IT'S A BIT LATE FOR BEING COY'

She didn't panic, at first.

'Rosie?

The old lady smiled and nodded. 'Good night's sleep, dear?'

'Rosie, I have to get out of here. I need to tell the police—'

Rosie shook her head. 'No police. I told you not to trust them.'

Jess struggled to sit up, a new fear beginning to form in the pit of her stomach.

'I think we'll wait a bit before I cut you free. You and I need a little chat.'

Jess tried to breathe normally. 'Where's Ben?'

'I told you, he left a few hours ago.' Rosie looked her up and down and gave a sly smile. 'Seems like you enjoyed yourselves last night, though.'

Jess realised with a flush of shame that she was naked. Luckily the duvet was still covering most of her; she used her free hand to pull it up and over her breasts a little further.

'It's a bit late for being coy.'

Jess felt a needle of fear begin to push into her. The older woman seemed a little different to the Rosie she knew from before – colder; she was suddenly acutely aware that no one except Ben knew where she was. And he'd obviously realised what they'd done the night before was a massive mistake and scarpered as soon as he was able.

'He left you a note,' Rosie said, seeming to read her mind. She picked up a piece of paper from the bedside table. 'Dear Jess, I'm sorry about last night. I shouldn't have taken advantage of the situation. I didn't mean blah blah blah – oh for god's sake I can't read this mush.' She threw it at Jess, who scrambled at it with her left hand.

...I didn't mean for that to happen again between us. There's so many old wounds and I feel like we were beginning to heal some of them. I hope, whatever you are feeling, that you're not angry with me, and I'm sorry I'm not here to tell you that in person. I don't regret last night one bit. But I couldn't wake up next to you today. I hope you understand.

I'm going to find Teddy and talk to him. I've left the key on the table in the kitchen; please lock up after yourself and drop it by sometime. You know where I live...

B x

Jess let the paper fall to the floor.

'Rosie, how did you know we were here?'

'I missed you coming in last night, you must have been very quiet when you crept through the front door. But I'm a light sleeper and these walls are paper thin. I heard you, downstairs, then rattling about in the loft, and then, well... that ex-husband of yours seems to be a real hit with you ladies. It was almost like being in the room with you.' She gave a smile. 'Of course, now I *am* in the room with you.'

'How did you get in? You gave your key to the police.'

Rosie smiled and waggled a keyring with a full set of keys on it. 'That was a copy. I've got all the keys, a full set, right here. Back door, bathroom door, even the one for this room.' Her smile faded. 'You should be ashamed of yourselves, fornicating in a dead girl's house.'

Jess flushed again. 'It's not for you to judge.' She pulled on her right arm again, more certain than ever now that something was horribly off. This couldn't be just about her sleeping with Ben in Maz's house. Could it?

She swallowed. 'Rosie, you need to let me go. If you're concerned I came in here unlawfully, you've read Ben's note: you can call the police.'

Rosie blanched. 'You know how I feel about the police,' she said. 'Anyway, one word from lover boy and they'll let you go without any kind of proper investigation into what you've really done wrong.'

'I haven't done anything wrong!'

'You sound just like her.'

Jess felt her blood run cold.

'I mean, I could barely understand her, she'd drunk so much. She was adamant that she'd done nothing wrong either. Of course, *I* know differently. I knew what she was like: bewitching people, making them half-crazy with lust, then acting surprised when they tried to make a move. Some people call that a prick tease, you know.'

The older lady had a menacing, agitated tone to her voice. Jess cleared her throat. 'Rosie, please, let me go, we can talk, maybe go over to yours and get a cup of tea or something—'

'Oh, I've made you a cup of tea already.'

'You did?'

She nodded at the bedside table where an insipid looking drink sat next to the cutting of Teddy Jones' court case. Suddenly, Jess realised why he'd looked so familiar. It wasn't because she'd covered the story – it was, she realised with horror, because she'd seen him *on the wall of Rosie's hallway.*

'Teddy Jones was your husband.' She couldn't disguise the fright in her voice.

Rosie folded her arms and smiled. 'I knew a clever girl like you would get there eventually.'

'But your surname—' she realised she didn't even know Rosie's surname.

'You never asked me, did you. But in any case, it's not Jones. I changed it back to my maiden name after Edward was arrested.'

'But what are the chances of you ending up living next to Marianne?'

'What are the chances indeed. For years I had no idea that I'd ended up living next door to the bitch that put him away.' She grinned. 'It was you that clued me in.'

'Me?'

'I found her door open in the middle of the day, drunk as a skunk on the sofa, television blaring. Your god-awful show was on. She'd pointed at the screen and said to me, 'We were best friends once.' I made a strong pot of coffee, and she told me the whole story of your sorry little love triangle while she sobered up. Oh, the things I learned about you!' Rosie exclaimed. 'Once she started, she couldn't stop. I felt a bit sorry for you,' Rosie said. 'Even though you were silly to let one little affair ruin your marriage. You should have turned a blind eye; you'd still have him in your bed on the regular then.'

Jess tried not to blush.

'I looked you up. Saw you'd covered Edward's trial, and his brothers' too. Made money off my family's misfortune. Got Joe and Billy to rat out their brother. I decided I'd put the frighteners on you.'

'So you sent the death threat to the studio.'

Rosie nodded. 'Not my best work. I couldn't get the wording right. It was very difficult not to sound like a hoax.'

'But it was a hoax.'

Rosie looked at the cuffs binding Jess to the bed. 'Maybe at the time.'

'How did you find out about Marianne, though? She gave evidence anonymously in court.'

Rosie laughed. 'She was always inviting me over, using me as an excuse to crack a new bottle open then drinking it all by herself. She got drunk, completely drunk. Told me all sorts of things and never remembered.'

Jess tried to shuffle nearer the bedside table. 'Didn't she realise who you were? Didn't she spot Teddy – Edward – in the photographs on your wall?'

'Oh, I didn't ever invite her into my house.'

Jess remembered what Bobby had said, about Rosie not really liking either of them. How had she got all this so wrong? 'But Teddy was a criminal… a rapist.'

'He only behaved like any man would naturally when there's an attractive woman standing in front of him.'

'I'd hardly call holding a knife to someone's throat natural, Rosie.'

'She drove him to it!' Rosie snarled. 'She made him crazy! Then she zapped him with that thing and killed him.'

'But Teddy didn't die. He went to prison.'

'He *did* die. In prison. Had a weak heart, apparently – not that he knew about it until it was far too late. That zapper she decided to use made it worse. Only in prison, no one noticed, and no one cared. So, he had a massive heart attack and died, a few years into his sentence. They say it could have happened any time, but I know the truth. *She* did that: *she* made his heart weak.' She paused, looking at the mugshot again. 'He would have been out this year, on good behaviour. He would be coming home to me.'

Jess narrowed her eyes. 'You still loved him? After all he'd done, to you and to those other women?'

'He never did anything they weren't asking for,' Rosie said, getting up and walking over to the small fireplace opposite the bed. She bent down and fiddled with something near the floor by the fire. Jess heard the sound of rushing air, and then realised it wasn't air, it was gas.

'Rosie, what are you doing?'

She stood up and brushed dust from her clothes. 'Marianne could never forgive herself for what she did to you, but she did love your ex-husband. Told me she could never find another man to measure up. Now I think about it, you should be saying thank you to me for getting rid of her.'

'I'm not like you, Rosie. I'd forgiven Maz for what had happened. She suffered because of it, had to walk away from a job she loved. And it sounds like she was still punishing herself.'

'Tell me, Jessica, did it feel good to sleep with him, in her house?' Sarcasm dripped from her words. 'I saw him leave this morning, you know. I couldn't figure out who was here last night, at first; but then I realised it must be you, being nosy again. You just won't let sleeping dogs lie, so I thought I'd come over and tell you I saw you, scare you off. But when I found that photo of Edward in the kitchen, I knew you had to go too, before you figured out the connection and told someone.' She took the keys from her pocket and made her way to the door. 'I couldn't let you do that, you see.'

The room was beginning to fill with the smell of gas. 'Rosie, turn it off. Please.'

She laughed again. 'Sorry. I won't be doing that.' She nodded at the tea. 'But that's got a nice dose of diazepam in there, if you want to go to sleep quicker.'

'Did you drug her too?'

'I knew it was only a matter of time before she put herself into a coma, all the drink she was throwing down her neck. I just helped it along. Invited myself over on Tuesday afternoon – god, she was in the mood to drink, after that row with Ben. I added some crushed up pills to a cuppa and made her drink it – told her it was to try and sober up. Waited for her to fall asleep long enough for me to stab her through the heart.'

Jess thought of the knife sitting in the plastic bag along with her notes. 'It was your letter opener,' she said. 'A black and white handle, to match your hallway.'

Rosie nodded. 'No one even noticed it was missing, great coppers they all are, coming in for cups of tea, taking statement after statement from some old biddy and not even thinking she might be the one who'd done it.'

She was right. No one had even bothered with a background check, evidently; Rosie had been dismissed as a harmless busybody, no thought given to her as a suspect. Jess felt a huge sob rise in her throat, suddenly, and scanned the room again. The windows were shut tight, but maybe if she shouted loudly enough, before she lost consciousness—

'No one will hear you. Not much foot traffic until the next train and that won't be soon enough for you. I wish I'd thought of doing it this way before, you know. Much less messy. Maybe a bit riskier to come in and clean up afterwards, though. Can't bear a messy house, you see. It's why I came in and gave the place a quick once-over after she died. This time I'll have to remember to air the place properly before I put the lights on.'

Jess's heart sped up in panic. 'Rosie, please let me go. It's not too late. If you let me go, and confess, they'll take it easy on you.'

'It's kind of you to suggest it, but no. I think I'll nip back to my house, pack a bag, and get myself on a plane before anyone notices you're gone. Edward always wanted to retire somewhere sunny; maybe I'll go to Spain in his honour.'

'People know where I am. They'll find me.'

'Oh, I very much doubt that, my dear. No offense, but you don't seem like you have many friends. And we both know the one person who did know you were here, isn't coming back.'

She shut the door and Jess heard a key turn in the lock.

'Rosie! Rosie! Come back! Rosie!'

The gas filled the room.

'TELL ME I WASN'T NAKED'

Voices shouting. Bright sunshine. Fresh air.

Jess flicked her eyes open. She had a faint recollection of the door being kicked in, of being carried down the stairs. She'd been sick more than once and her chest hurt like she'd gone several rounds with Mike Tyson; but she was out, and alive, as far as she could tell. Strapped on top of a trolley, staring at the blue morning sky, she stared upwards, appreciating the cloudless view and thanking her lucky stars she wasn't up there looking downwards instead.

She breathed deeply, registering the plastic mask over her nose and mouth; the elastic felt tight against her cheeks and she could hear a gentle whoosh when she breathed. The concerned face of a stranger (fuzzy, hair, man's voice) lurched into view, blurry at first.

'Jess?'

She tried to lift her arm in response, but it felt like she had a hundred kilos of concrete strapped to them.

'Jess? Jess? Oh my god, she's awake!' Della's voice bellowed and Jess tried to focus on where it was coming from.

'Jess? God, you gave us a scare.' Darcy's face appeared above her and a comforting hand was placed on her shoulder.

'Ladies, please, give her some space.' The medic tried in vain to shift the women out of his way so he could check on her. 'Jessica. Can you hear me okay? How are you feeling?'

Jess struggled to make the words. 'Okay,' she said, her voice muffled through the mask. 'I'm okay.'

'Thank god we found you in time!' Della said.

She felt so weak. 'How?'

'We came to your house,' Darcy said. 'Bobby tried to drop off your car. I found him waiting at the door.'

'We knew you'd gone to see Ben yesterday,' Darcy continued. 'We took a chance and went to the station in case you'd been arrested. We found Ben, but you weren't there. It took a bit of persuading but he finally told us he'd left you at Marianne's house in the early hours of this morning.'

'Which we will *definitely* need details on when you're feeling up to it,' Della said, winking.

'Anyway,' Darcy glared at Della, 'Ben got a call from Inspector Dickhead while we were there. They'd run Teddy Jones through the system and come up with a link to Marianne's neighbour.'

'Rosie,' Jess said, attempting to sit up. The dizziness was overwhelming. 'She tried to kill me—'

'It's okay,' Darcy said. 'The police are looking for her right now. She won't get far.'

Della was visibly upset. 'I'm glad you're okay, boss. Paramedics said we were lucky to find you when we did. Another hour and you'd have been...'

Jess took the mask off for a second and breathed in the fresh air heavily. 'Thank you.'

Della patted her arm and Darcy wrung her hands. 'Seriously, we're so relieved. Ben came in to look for you, shouted there was gas and told us to start opening windows.' She looked sheepishly over at Marianne's cottage. 'I'll admit I got a little carried away and smashed up the bay window with the crowbar we had in the truck.'

Jess turned her head slowly and looked across the grass at the carnage. Glass and remnants of the white window shutters were all over the front garden. Upstairs, Marianne's bedroom curtains flapped about in the breeze.

'Ben tore the kitchen apart looking for a sharp knife to cut the cable ties on your wrists,' Della said. 'He took the stairs three at a time on the way back up. Carried you down like you were Lois Lane. Not that you looked all that much like Lois Lane, I've got to say. More like ET.'

Jess's stomach lurched and she looked down at the blanket covering her. It had dinosaurs all over it and definitely didn't look like it belonged to the NHS. 'Tell me I wasn't naked.'

'Starkers,' Della said, laughing. 'Don't worry though. We got the sheet from our emergency bedding in the truck before the ambulance arrived.'

Jess cringed. 'Oh god.'

'Funnily enough, none of us were focused on your birthday suit at the time,' Darcy said. 'We were more worried about you getting to your next birthday.'

'Nothing Superman hadn't seen a few hours earlier anyway,' Della smirked.

'Della!' Darcy gave her a look. 'Leave it alone.'

The medic appeared back in her vision. 'We need to get you to hospital, Jessica. You've been exposed to a high dose of carbon monoxide, and you'll need oxygen until the levels in your system are down to a normal level.'

'Is she going to be okay?'

The medic nodded at Darcy. 'She didn't lose consciousness completely and seems cognisant, so it's what we'd call a moderate exposure. It's still serious and there can be some longer-term effects to watch out for, but the doctors will be able to tell you more. Right now she needs rest.'

'Gives you a bit of time to sort out what you're going to say to them anyway,' Della said, nodding her head towards the crowd gathering at the end of the street, well beyond the cordoned off area. 'Bloody press. Someone must have leaked the story.'

'For the love of...' Jess closed her eyes. 'Can you deal with them?'

Dev appeared, with Tristan at his side. 'We came as soon as Darcy called us,' he said. 'I'll issue a statement on your behalf.'

'We'll distract them,' Della said.

'Tell them she'll answer all their questions once she's discharged from our care,' said a second medic (dark skin, neatly trimmed beard, glasses), who'd been packing up their bags and getting the ambulance ready for departure. He turned to Della. 'You can follow us to the hospital if you like. Do you have a car?'

Della visibly grew an inch and flicked her hair in a most uncharacteristically flirtatious manner. She nodded at the fish truck parked up on the curb next to the ambulance. 'That's mine.'

The medic raised his eyebrows. 'Nice wheels,' he said.

'Thanks.'

The medic gave her a smile and then turned his attention back to his partner. 'Let's load her up.'

'Wait! Where's Ben?'

'I'm here.' Ben jogged across the grass. 'I'm right here. Thank god you're okay.' He held Jess's hand and squeezed tightly.

'Thank you, Ben. You saved my life.'

'Yeah, well, I wish maybe I hadn't been in quite such a hurry to get out of it, then you wouldn't have been in this situation.'

'Rosie did pass along your note. With great delight, I hasten to add.'

Ben's face turned serious. 'I am so, so sorry.'

She held his hand. 'You weren't to know. I should have put two and two together when I saw that photo.'

'So should I. When Graham told me Teddy was Rosie's husband—'

'Graham?'

'He's not bent, Jess. He had the wool pulled over his eyes too.'

'What about the fingerprints?'

'Turns out Rosie's got a contact of her own on the force,' Dev said.

'Probably more than one,' Ben grimaced. 'We're going to have to root them out. The son of Teddy's second cousin was one of the uniforms on the scene that night. He took your fingerprints and planted the evidence and helped Rosie post the death threats to your house. We raided his flat half an hour ago, found your fingerprints in a file and a swab with your DNA on it.'

Uniform Two's face swam into Jess's memory. 'He was in my house,' she said, weakly. 'I let him in, he searched my bag—'

'Excuse me, but I really do have to get this woman to hospital now.' The medic came over.

Ben nodded and stroked her hair. 'I got the all clear from the fire brigade to go back inside to get your phone.' He cleared his throat. 'And your clothes.' He placed a neatly folded pile of belongings on her blanketed feet and handed her the phone. 'Here you go. Will you be okay with Della and Darcy? I'm going to stick around here for a while until the incident team turn up. I'll come and check up on you later.'

'And we'll be next door, when you get home, if you need us,' Tristan said.

She nodded, feeling tired again. Her head was swimming. 'Ben... did you catch Rosie yet? She said she was heading to an airport.'

He shook his head. 'We've not found her yet, but it's only a matter of time. She might have stayed under the radar up until this point but there's no way she'll be able to leave the country without us finding her first.'

'Let me know when you do.'

He leaned in and kissed her forehead. 'I'm glad you're okay. Della and Darcy did a great job, raising the alarm when they did. And Bobby, too.'

Bobby stood shyly behind them all. 'Hi, Jess, I brought your car back.'

Jess smiled at Bobby, seeing the concern on his face and suddenly wanting, more than anything else, not to be wrapped in a dinosaur blanket. 'Thanks Bobby.' She paused and looked round at her friends. 'Thank you all. Lucky someone missed me. A few months ago, no one would've noticed I was gone.'

The medics carried her into the waiting ambulance. She lifted up her head and saw Dev and Tristan heading towards the press pack where Della and Darcy were proudly explaining their part in everything. Ben was standing by the cottage, directing police and fire like he was born into the job. Bobby stood to one side, watching her fondly. She raised her hand and he made a 'I'll call you' sign. She gave him the thumbs up.

The medic swung the doors closed on the ambulance and she laid down and closed her eyes, relishing the safety.

'You alright, Jessica?' said the medic.

She shook her head. 'Not yet. But I will be.'

'Let me put that phone in your bag,' the medic said. 'You can take a look at it once you're feeling better.'

She let him slip the phone out of her hands.

'That is a big old number of missed calls you've got,' he chuckled. 'There's someone called Damon who is very keen to talk to you.'

'Oh, for god's sake, hit redial,' Jess said.

The phone rang once before Damon picked up.

'Jess! You're alive!'

'Barely,' she croaked.

'I thought – I thought you—'

'This is the medic speaking. Jess's going to be fine,' the medic said. 'She just needs *rest*.' He emphasised the last word and rolled his eyes.

'I'm not going to even mention the book, I promise,' Damon said. 'But Jess, you should know, the publishers are going to *die* when they hear what's happened—'

'I'll speak to you later, Damon,' Jess shook her head, laughing, and burst into a coughing fit.

The medic placed an oxygen mask back over her mouth. 'She'll call you back tomorrow,' he said, and with that, Jess was blissfully relieved of her phone, and of Damon. For now, at least. She smiled to herself. Damon was right – it was going to make a hell of a final chapter.

Forty-eight hours later she was discharged, with strict instructions to call her GP if she experienced any further nausea, dizziness or confusion. Della and Darcy listened diligently to all the instructions the nurse was giving them, nodding in unison like two toy dogs in a car rear window.

They wheeled her out into the sunshine.

'You're gonna be fine, boss.'

'The doctor said you need plenty of rest, though.'

'Dev and Tristan are on call any time you need them,' Darcy said. 'But don't worry; we'll take care of the business. We've already lined ourselves up another job this week.'

'Which job?'

'Elaine Taylor. She's a frequent flyer, from what she tells us?'

'She was on the show, one of our first guests,' Jess said. 'Paid out an extortionate amount for multiple investigations of adultery over the past ten years by her husband Carl, who it turned out was quite partial to a prostitute or two. Or three. Sometimes all at once.'

'Why on earth doesn't she leave him?'

'The money, I expect,' Jess said. 'She can't seem to walk away. She hires a P.I., confronts him with the photos, he buys her something nice like a Cartier bracelet or a Tesla, and she forgives him. He promises never to do it again and she agrees to stay. She says it's a love affair, of sorts.'

'I suppose some people can forgive more easily than others,' Darcy said.

'I wouldn't say she forgave him,' Jess replied. 'In fact, I definitely suspect Elaine signed a prenup she wished she hadn't. But she makes the best of the situation she's chosen for herself, I suppose.'

'Still, I wonder if it's worth it,' Darcy mused. 'It wouldn't be, for me. I'd rather walk away from financial security and be happy, than be dripping in diamonds and fast cars and fritter my life away in a loveless relationship.'

Jess looked around the car park.

'Where's the truck?'

'It's been drawing a little too much attention, so I asked Ben to come and pick us up. Didn't think you'd mind.' Della winked. 'You never did tell us what happened.'

'I think it's pretty obvious, Della,' Darcy said.

'Yeah, but is it going to happen again, is what I really want to know?'

Jess looked at the man getting out of the car, who she'd loved and lost and loved again. 'I'm not sure.'

Ben dropped Della and Darcy off first.

'We'll come by later. We've got to get to north London and see a man about a prostitute,' Della said.

'Sounds good to me,' Jess replied. 'I'll see you later.'

She waved them goodbye. Ben put the car in gear and they drove off. It was the first time they'd been alone since the night at Marianne's house and the atmosphere felt charged, suddenly.

'I'm going to take a break for a while,' she said, interrupting the silence. 'Rent a cottage in the country, get my book written.'

Ben looked surprised. 'Didn't take you for the country sort.'

'I need a change of scenery. After everything that's happened – not just with Rosie but the past year – I need to look after myself a bit better. Take some time out.'

'What about the business?'

'Oh I think Della and Darcy have got that in hand,' Jess said. 'Which is just as well. Damon wants me to write another book, a different one, about Rosie. Reckons diving into the mind of a woman hell bent on avenging her human trafficking rapist of a husband would make for a fascinating story.'

'What do you think?'

'I think I'll wait a while until she's firmly under lock and key.'

'Her trial date will be set soon. It shouldn't take long.'

They pulled up outside Jess's house. 'Here we are. Home safe and sound. And no reporters waiting either.'

'They've got what they wanted. I offered to give a press conference tomorrow, provided they leave me alone.'

'Jess, are you sure that's wise—'

'Don't worry. I won't mention you at all. Graham is doing most of the talking.'

He helped her out of the car and walked her to the front door. They stood, for a moment.

'Jess, I—'

She interrupted, not wanting him to say anything more. 'You were right, in your letter. What happened between us was closure, of sorts. It wasn't a sign that we should get back together. You're coming out of a relationship that I'm assuming has completely messed you up. We're both still coming to terms with losing Marianne – and what she meant to us, and what we meant to her. And... being honest with myself, I need to be with someone who I can trust, one hundred per cent. I wish it was you, Ben; but it isn't. It can't be.'

Ben hung his head. 'So this is goodbye, then?'

She nodded. 'I may not have been able to make things good between Maz and me before she was killed, but I'm glad something good came out of her death. Knowing that you and I are... that we have closure, finally, and that things are okay between us... it's made me very happy.'

'You'll always have a place in my heart. I hope you know that.'

She kissed him gently and opened her door. 'Bye, Ben. Thank you for saving my life.'

She closed the door and let the familiar sights and smells of her home wash over her, before moving into the kitchen and putting the kettle on. She had a lot to do before she could leave, but a cuppa was essential after days of stewed hospital tea. She opened the fridge to see if there was any milk worth saving in there; there was a fresh bottle, along with a shelf full of goodies: apples, satsumas, cheese, salami, and finally, a salmon fillet wrapped in a criss-cross pastry with a note on the top. She grabbed the note and smiled as she unfolded it to see Della's childlike handwriting inside.

Dear Jess,

Here's a little care package from me and Darce. We know you're thinking of going away for a while and we wanted you to know that if you do, Sinclair Investigations will be in good hands. We're so grateful you gave us a chance when we both needed it. Now it's our turn. Enjoy the en croute. You need to cook it at 180 for thirty minutes. Dx □

At the bottom of the note were two stick figures next to a crude drawing of a truck. 'Darcy' was tall, with great squiggles of hair cascading down. 'Della' had boobs drawn in and heels on the bottom of her short little stick legs. On the side of the truck was written 'Sinclair Investigations' and underneath it, written in tiny lettering, 'the original, and the best'.

Jess smiled and laid the note on the table. She put the oven on, then went upstairs to pack.

ACKNOWLEDGEMENTS

"Wahoo! I did my first murder!" – Faye Brann, 2022.

Yep... 2022. While the story was relatively fast in its inception, the subsequent journey was not, and there were times when I wondered if I'd ever get this book baby into the hands of readers. This year, when I finally decided to move forward with self-publication instead of pursuing a traditional book deal, it was exciting, but nerve-wracking, and I clearly had no idea what I was letting myself in for. It has been a real eye-opener, to learn how to run a publishing business – every single aspect, from design and production to distribution, sales and marketing – alongside writing the actual book. Let me put it another way: anyone who thinks being self-published is somehow 'less than' has clearly never done it!

Self-publishing is a complete misnomer, of course; no one does it by themselves and there are several other wonderful people who I genuinely could not have done this without. Firstly, my agent, Davinia Andrew-Lynch, who has encouraged me every step of the way, to make a success of this sometimes-impossible career. Thank you for your ongoing support and dedication, and for helping me develop *Kiss Marry Murder* into the book it is today. To Deana, my editor, I cannot believe it's been 10 years since we graduated but I'm so happy we are still talking about writing projects and now working together too! Thank you so much for your words of wisdom and encouragement, I hope I can pay it forward soon. And to Lucy, for her diligent proofreading, thank you. I really appreciate your hard work to help make sure the end product was as good as it could possibly be.

Before sending a book out into the world, there are usually a few unsung heroes who suffer the early drafts for no other reason than they are very kind people (and/or completely mad). To Jason, Estelle and Pippa, thanks for putting up with what turned out to be a very 'beta' version of the final story. I hope that you've enjoyed revisiting it in its finished form! And a big thank you to my mum, Cheryl, who read my final manuscript not once, but twice, to make sure she wasn't imagining she enjoyed it the first time round! Thank you for your honesty, and for always being on my side. I love you.

A huge shout out to Helen Lederer, for giving me a platform and for continuing to champion the witty women writers of this world. Helen, what you do with Comedy Women in Print is so vital – not just the prize, but the community you've built from it. Writing would be a hugely lonely business for me otherwise, and much less fun! Additionally, my 'CWIPsters' and fellow authors Nina and Kathleen, thank you for your unswerving support and inspirational conversation – especially to Nina, for tweaking the book title to such perfection over an onion bhaji during one of our cheeky lunchtime curries. Who knew Dishoom would provide the backdrop for such highbrow literary conversation?

Last but by no means least, the two wonderful men in my life. My husband Steve, thank you for believing I could do it all over again. As the cool, calm and collected half of our partnership, your good sense and steadfast support is so appreciated, as is your ongoing tolerance of my crazy. And to my son Nathan, who is more understanding and proud of my creative endeavours than I could have wished for. The feeling is mutual, you amazing human. Keep creating, keep being you. xxx

Finally, to all the extended family, friends and readers who kept me going, asking me incessantly when my next book would be out and forcing me to get focused about what I wanted the answer to be... It's HERE! So, if you enjoyed it, do me a solid and leave a review and then share it with everyone you know... and thank you for having me back in your lives. It's a privilege and a joy to continue to write for you.

Peace, love and chocolate Hobnobs,

Faye x

Keep up to date with news of my future publications!
Visit www.fayebrann.com and hit 'SUBSCRIBE'.

TINKER, TAILOR, SCHOOLMUM, SPY□
Winner of the 2020 Comedy Women in Print Prize

'Naturally funny... page turning, smart and sassy' - Helen Lederer, comedian, author and founder of the CWIP Prize

'I just loved this book... put on a smile on my face' - Libby Page, *The Lido*

'Fresh and different... and skilfully written' - Yomi Adekoke, *Slay in Your Lane*

Available in e-book, audiobook and paperback
Published by HarperCollins, 2021

Discover more at www.fayebrann.com